THE STORM

AN OMEGA THRILLER

BLAKE BANNER

ISBN-13: 978-1-63696-335-8

ISBN-10: 1-63696-335-8

Cover design by: Damonza

Printed in the United States of America

www.righthouse.com

www.instagram.com/righthousebooks

www.facebook.com/righthousebooks

twitter.com/righthousebooks

THE OMEGA SERIES

Dawn of the Hunter (Book 1)
Double Edged Blade (Book 2)
The Storm (Book 3)
The Hand of War (Book 4)
A Harvest of Blood (Book 5)
To Rule in Hell (Book 6)
Kill: One (Book 7)
Powder Burn (Book 8)
Kill: Two (Book 9)
Unleashed (Book 10)
The Omicron Kill (Book 11)
9mm Justice (Book 12)
Kill: Four (Book 13)
Death In Freedom (Book 14)
Endgame (Book 15)

ONE

HURRICANE SARAH WAS HEADING FOR NEW Orleans. It was the only interesting thing the news had told me since early October; since my meeting with Omega in Washington, since that last cryptic message from Marni, asking why the hell I hadn't followed her from Tucson to Washington[1]. Since then, for almost two months, she'd fallen off the radar. There had been no clue, no message, no contact at all about where she was or what she was doing. I'd promised my father on his deathbed that I would look after her and protect her from Omega, but so far she had made that almost impossible.

And then there was the hurricane.

It was the largest and most violent in recorded history—almost a thousand miles in diameter—with winds reaching 230 MPH, surging in off the Atlantic and headed for New Orleans. And it was out of season, striking in late

---

1. See *Double-Edged Blade*

November, which was practically unheard of. Hurricane season was August and September.

Omega's purpose was to exploit climate change and overpopulation, in order to consolidate their global, political power. Marni's self-imposed mission was to expose Omega and bring them down. That was why she had murdered my father, that was why the Biosphere Projects had drawn her to Tucson. So maybe, just maybe, hurricane Sarah might draw her to New Orleans. It was a long shot, but it was the only shot I had right then.

So I'd called Kenny, the butler I had inherited from my father, and had him send the Zombie 222, my converted '68 Mustang, down from Weston to DC, with a kit bag in the trunk. It was sixteen hours to the Big Easy, following the I-81 and then the I-59 from Chattanooga. I wasn't sure what I was going to do when I got there. I had a few ideas—contact the Coastal Protection and Restoration Authority (CPRA), check out the university's Climatology and Earth Sciences departments, see if she had been in touch with them or any of their professors. That was the sort of direction my mind was taking. But that was before I reached Laurel, Mississipi. At Laurel, everything changed.

I had stopped at the Exxon service station at exit thirty-five, just south of the town. It was eight AM and I'd sat by the window with a large coffee and a couple of donuts. The sun had been up for an hour and a half, but outside, the sky was heavy with dark gray clouds, and the tall pines across the road were bowing and tossing in a wind that wanted to get rough.

Whoever had been at that table before me had come from Louisiana. There was a copy of the *Baton Rouge Advo-*

cate on the table. So after I'd got bored of watching the bowing pines and the random drops of desultory rain splat on the window, I pulled over the paper and turned to the front page. And that was when everything changed.

It changed because I was staring at the face of my friend and comrade in arms, Bat Hays.

I was nineteen when my parents divorced and, to get away from my father, whom I hated with a passion, I had joined the British SAS. For ten years, that had been my life. I had left, a couple of years back, aged thirty, with the rank of captain and a handful of friends who were more than brothers; men who would give their lives for me, and I for them. Bat Hays was one. Now he was staring at me from the front page of the *Advocate* with his hands cuffed behind his back.

His black, obstinate, proud face stared at the crowd as he was led by cops to a patrol car. Nobody would see the fear he felt. Nobody but me. This guy who had faced death a hundred times and laughed at it with his Cockney humor, would be completely lost and helpless in the jaws of the relentless system of the law.

The headline said:

MAN ARRESTED IN SARAH CARMICHAEL MURDER

I read on. "Bartholomew Hays, 30, originally from London, England, was arrested yesterday and charged with the murder of Sarah Carmichael, of Burgundy, in the parish of West Feliciana. Mrs. Carmichael was found shot to death in her bed by her husband, real estate magnate Charles Carmichael, on the night of Friday, 3rd November, shortly before midnight.

"The Killer fled after he was disturbed by Carmichael on

his return from dining at a restaurant. Shots were exchanged but the killer escaped through a window into the woods..."

I stepped out into the drizzle, under the lowering sky, and climbed into the Zombie. I hit the ignition and the powerful, dual electric engines kicked in. There was no roar, no thunder, no sound at all. This machine delivers eight hundred bhp, one thousand eight-hundred foot-pounds of torque straight to the back wheels, and will go 0-60 in just over one and a half seconds. But she is totally silent.

I lit a Camel, pulled quietly out of the lot, and took the 84 west as far as Natchez. It was one hundred and thirty miles, and I did it in just over an hour. At Natchez, I took Route 61 south, through Burgundy and Hardwood, to St Francisville, where the Parish Jail was. All the way, the sky loomed, darkening and lead-heavy over the green woodlands, and the wind tossed and twisted the trees.

I found the Clerk of Court, an elegant 18th century red brick building with a pretty dome, on Prosperity Street. I was directed to the bail office, paid Hayes' three thousand five-hundred bail in cash, and headed back up Myrtle Hill Drive to the parish jail. It wasn't hard to find, though it didn't look much like a jail. It looked more like a golf club, set among green lawns and attractive, modern buildings. I figured it was part of the enlightened movement to ensure that criminals did not feel like social outcasts. I could think of several cheaper ways of achieving the same end, but then, I'm a social outcast.

I left the Zombie out front. The tropical, humid heat made it feel like late August or September, and in the time it took to cross the parking lot, I already had damp patches on my shirt. I pushed through the big glass doors into what looked like a hotel reception and told the guy on the desk who I was and why I was there. He made the call and twenty minutes later Bat, six foot two of solid muscle with an army kit bag over his shoulder, was brought out. He stopped dead in his tracks when he saw me.

"What the fuck...?"

"Hello Bat, what have you been up to?"

"What the fuck...? How the fuckin'...? Where the... *Fuck...!*"

I smiled and slapped him on the shoulder. If he'd been a fellow American, we would have embraced, but Brits don't do that. We grinned and shook hands and that was enough. It was good to see a friend.

"I see your vocabulary hasn't improved."

He laughed. "Am I glad to see you, sir! Everyone 'round here's gone stark fucking bonkers. How did you know...?"

"Come on, I'll explain in the car."

We stepped outside. The humidity had turned into a warm drizzle that dried as soon as it landed. We crossed to the car, climbed in, and slammed the doors, closing out the ominous presence of the weather. I fired up the engines and, as we pulled away, I asked him, "You got a pad?"

"Yeah, mate. I got a nice little place on Congress Street. Up in Burgundy. Nice fuckin' ride! Why don't it make no noise, though?"

I raised an eyebrow at him as we slipped silently onto Route 61 and headed north toward the small town of Burgundy. I tossed him my pack of Camels and handed him my Zippo. He took them both gratefully and as he lit up, I said, "You have some explaining to do, pal."

He inhaled deep and blew smoke at the ceiling, then lay back and closed his eyes.

"You ain't fuckin' joking, Captain. But I need somebody to explain it to me first."

"I know the answer, Bat, but I have to ask, you understand that, right?"

He nodded.

"Did you kill her?"

"You know me, Cap. I couldn't. Not a woman. Besides, I'm done with all that."

"All what?"

"Violence, killin'. Done it. Done it with the best. Got the fuckin' T-shirt. Don't want it no more. I want to do something else with me life. Know what I mean?"

"I know what you mean. Why didn't you call me?"

He looked reproachful. "Where? You fuckin' disappeared, didn't you?—sir! Nobody knew where you'd gone. Sarge said you'd gone to Wyoming, but nobody was sure. He didn't know where in fuckin' Wyoming. Wyoming's a big fuckin' place. It's like a country!"

"Bradley? The Kiwi?"

He grinned. "Yeah, old fucker. He's still with the Regiment. He'll never quit. They won't let him." He was quiet for a bit, thinking. "How'd you know I was here?"

"I didn't. I was headed for New Orleans. I saw your picture in the paper. You're famous."

"Infamous, more like."

"Who was Sarah Carmichael?"

"Wife of the local big wig. Got a reputation for being some kind of angel, concerned about the environment, helped the poor, good works. You know the kind of thing.

Hubby's a land developer. Got a big mansion in the woods outside Burgundy."

"You knew her?"

He shrugged and I knew he was going to lie to me. "She came into the club a few times."

"Club?"

"I work as a bouncer at a local club, sir..."

"We're not in the Regiment anymore, Bat. Call me Lacklan."

"I'll try. Anyway, I work as a bouncer at the Blue Lagoon, in Burgundy. They have live jazz. I play the trumpet sometimes..."

"Yeah, I remember. You were good. So...?"

"She'd come in some nights, have a drink, listen to the music."

"With her husband?"

"Sometimes."

"But not always?"

He sighed, noisily. "Yeah. Not always."

"So you talk to her?"

"Look, Cap, I know what you're drivin' at. But she was just an independent woman, who liked jazz, and would go out sometimes of an evening, sometimes in company, sometimes alone. People talk. Especially in a small, religious community like this. But she was sophisticated, intelligent. She liked the music and sometimes she'd come alone. And she'd always leave alone. No big deal."

I nodded. "OK, Bat. I'm going to get you an attorney. We'll get you off these charges."

"I can't afford it, sir."

"I can. We'll think of a way for you to pay me back. The money isn't a problem. Saving your ass is."

He nodded. "Thanks."

I gave it a moment, and as we approached Burgundy, I said, "You don't have to tell me everything, at least not yet. But when your attorney gets here, you'll have to tell *him* everything, in detail, warts and all. You understand me? Because if you don't, whatever lies you tell, will trip you up and bite you in the ass down the line. And after that, I'll beat seven bails of shit out of you." I looked him in the eye. His eyes were hard and stubborn. "They still have the death penalty here, you know that, right?"

"Yeah, I know."

"And a black Brit killing a white American woman? That's not good. Be smart. Not for me, for you."

"Gotcha."

Burgundy was one of the old towns. The streets in the outskirts were broad and leafy. The houses were Creole, one and two story clapboard, painted in many colors, red, white, blue, mauve, and green—often on a single house. There were broad gardens and a superabundance of trees. Downtown the streets were narrower, and the houses were interspersed with larger, stone buildings with wrought iron balconies and tall green and blue shutters in the French style. As we moved through the town, the bright colors, the buildings, and the narrow streets with their carnival flavor of mardi gras were strangely at odds with the dull weight of the clouds and the damp, claustrophobic heat.

I found Congress Street and he pointed me to a bright green, one-story house with a gable roof. "That's us, sir."

"You got a hotel near here?"

He frowned. "You can stay with me, Cap."

I pulled up outside his door and shook my head. "As far as Carmichael, local law enforcement, the courts, and Burgundy are concerned, I am just your commanding officer. I'm concerned for you and, above all, for the reputation of the Regiment. Drop your kit bag, we'll find a hotel, have some lunch, and then you tell me what happened."

He nodded. "Yeah, got it."

I watched him go inside through the windshield. He was one of the most dangerous men I had ever met, but right then, he looked oddly vulnerable. I looked up at the blackening sky. Under that sky, the whole world looked vulnerable.

TWO

The Hotel Soniat was a couple of streets away on Chartres Avenue. It was an old, colonial building constructed around a central patio with a fountain in the middle, four orange trees and galleried landings on the second and third floors, where the rooms were. A guy on reception with a pencil moustache, a film of sweat on his forehead, and heavy glasses told me his name was Luis and the dining room was open. We followed his directions through an arch and into a second patio, where the walls were covered in jasmine and there were geraniums growing out of artfully broken pots.

The place was empty and a bored-looking waiter greeted us with ill-concealed surprise. He showed us to a table under a creaking, hundred-year-old ceiling fan. They had air conditioning, but with an empty hotel and an equally empty restaurant, they were not about to turn it on.

"The storm is coming," he said. "They never come this far inland, but the media..." He shrugged, like the name said it all. "The town is almost deserted. We're all hoping it will turn north and blow itself out over the Atlantic, but it ain't looking good. Some people are evacuating already."

We ordered a couple of martinis and a couple of steaks and he went away to get them. I watched Bat while he studied the dining room in minute detail. Suddenly, he said, "That storm's something, ain't it? They say it's the biggest in recorded history."

I gave him a moment. He continued his minute study of the walls. Finally, I sighed loudly.

"Quit stalling, Bat. What happened?"

He puffed out his cheeks and blew, balled his fists on the tablecloth and stared down at them.

"I don't know, sir, Lacklan, mate." He looked at me with wide eyes and shrugged. "Cross my fuckin' heart and hope to die."

"What? You don't trust me?"

"Don't talk stupid. Sir. Of course I trust you. I'm just..." He spread his hands. "One minute I was workin' at the club, minding me own business, and the next minute, Detective fuckin' Jackson of the Burgundy fuckin' Police Department is arresting me for the murder of Sarah..." He hesitated fractionally and added, "Carmichael."

I watched at him for a moment, trying to read his face. Meanwhile, he studied his hands and sucked his teeth.

"You know what, Bat? I'm getting mad. I have serious business to attend to in New Orleans. I came here, like you would have come for me, like any of us would. But now I'm here and you're stonewalling me. I should tell you to go fuck yourself, and leave."

He frowned a small frown and flattened out his hands,

like looking at the back of them might give him a different perspective. After a moment, he said, "It was Friday, 10th of November, a week after she was killed. Detective Jackson come 'round to my gaff, hammering on the door, wanting to talk to me. I let him in and offered him a cup of tea, like you do, and he starts askin' me questions about Sarah Carmichael. Did I know her? Where from? How well did I know her? Did I know her husband? All that kind of stuff. Had I seen her hangin' out with anyone? Anyone comin' on to her or getting aggressive with her?

"I told him what I told you. I worked at the club. She come in sometimes to listen to the music. I knew her to say hello, never saw nothing special, no more than that. He asks if he can take my prints. I had nothing to hide so I says yeah, and he takes my prints with a mobile scanner. After that, he buggers off, and I thought that was the last of it. To be honest, Cap, I thought it was just routine stuff. I'd expected it after I heard she'd been murdered.

"But couple of days ago he turns up again..." He gave his head a little shake. "I couldn't believe it. He says he's arresting me for her murder. I says, 'On what grounds?' He says, 'On the grounds we got your fuckin' prints on the murder weapon!'"

Our drinks arrived and after the waiter had gone, we drank to old friends. He smacked his lips and sighed, then went on.

"Like I said, I couldn't fuckin' believe it, sir." He shook his head at the table top. "It's got to be a mistake. I told them that in the interrogation, 'There's got to be a mistake,' but Jackson says, 'No, mate. These modern scanners don't make fuckin' mistakes, do they? They are one hundred percent accurate.' So I'm fuckin' screwed. And what I want to know is, how my fuckin' prints got on the murder weapon. It don't make no sense."

"That's what I'm wondering."

"Yeah, well, well you might, sir, but it gets better, because not only are my prints on the fuckin' weapon, they are at the scene an' all, in the bedroom and in the livin' room. And I ain't never been to that house."

"Have you got a theory?"

He sat back in his chair with a face that said he had, but he didn't want to tell me about it because I wouldn't believe him. "It's far-fetched, but it's the only thing I can think of. You probably won't believe me. I wouldn't."

"Try me."

He picked up his glass and swirled it around for a bit, examining the ice and the olive as he did so.

"First week of October. Must've been the Wednesday, 'cause I was playin' in the band that night. Bloke come in. Flash git, sharp suit, oiled hair all shiny. Nasty piece of work, you could tell. Really white teeth, kind of blindin', always smilin', smooth, too smooth. Know what I mean? Black guy, must've been six three or four, taller than me. Anyway, he comes in and while I'm playin', I can see him having a natter with Harry, the barman. And I can see Harry lookin' at me and tellin' him something. You know, like he's tellin' him something about me."

He paused to sip his drink.

"I never tell nobody about the Regiment. But Harry helped me out couple of years ago when I was in trouble, we become mates, so I told him once. Never told nobody else. But now Harry's gone and told this sleazy geezer. So when

I've finished me set, I go to the bar to get a beer and this bloke comes up."

"The tall guy who'd been talking to Harry?"

"Yeah. Says his name is Ivory. On account of his teeth, I suppose."

The waiter brought out our steaks, set them in front of us and wished us a healthy appetite in French, and withdrew. We ate in silence for a bit, then Bat went on.

"Anyhow, so I'm having me beer at the bar and Ivory comes over and introduces himself. He was so fuckin' tall an' thin, with these shifty fuckin' eyes, it was like talkin' to a fuckin' snake. He says he's recruiting for a job, the pay is superb and am I interested? So I tell him, that depends on what the job is, don't it? And *he* says, he can't tell me. His boss would have to tell me." He spread his hands to accompany his ironic smile. "Well, I know straight away it's something dodgy, right? And I tell him I ain't interested. Then he tells me how much it pays."

He stopped and cut into his steak.

I said, "How much?"

"Twenty grand for a day's work."

"It was a hit."

"I don't know."

"That kind of fee? It was a hit."

"Probably."

"What did you do?"

"I asked him if it was a hit. He told me again that I'd have to discuss it with his employer." He made a 'whatcha gonna do?' face. "I ain't flush, know what I mean? I could use a bit of the old spondulix. So I think, no harm in talkin', and I tell the bloke, OK, take me to your leader."

He paused, stuffed a chunk of meat in his mouth, and talked around it while he ate.

"That's when it got a bit weird."

"Weird how?"

"He makes a call on his mobile—his cell phone. Then he tells me to follow him. We go outside. It's late, 'bout two AM, and we're standin' on the pavement, fuckin' sidewalk as you call it, and he gives me a fag. We're lightin' up and this big fuckin' black Lincoln comes 'round the corner from Main Street and pulls up in front of us. Two big fellas get out, in suits. One of 'em's black, the other looks Swedish, know what I mean? Blond, big 'tash. And the blond one says, 'We gotta put a bag over your head.'"

He burst out laughing and I smiled at the thought of anyone trying to put a bag over Bat Hays' head.

"You can imagine, right? After fuckin' Iraq and Afghanistan, *and* fuckin' Palestine. So I says, 'No thanks, mate. Forget it.' So Ivory is really apologetic and says it's just to protect the identity of his employer, and the fee is to make up for the inconvenience. And also, they will pay me an extra two grand, in cash, that night to compensate me. My hands will be free at all times.

"So I'm thinking, twenty grand—and I could *really* use twenty grand right now. So I agree. We got in the car. They put a bag over my head and we drove. I tried to keep track. Towns here are all on a fuckin' grid system, ain't they? So I'm doing the old 'Right, right, left, straight for two minutes...' But they're cute to me so they're goin' all 'round the fuckin' shop to put me off, and I lost track. We ended up outside the town. When we got out of the car, it was very quiet, very still. The ground was rough, gritty, like old tarmacadam that's crumbling, and there was an echo, like there was tall buildings nearby. We went through a door and my guess is that it was a warehouse or a hangar. It had that kind of echo to it, like a vaulted ceiling in a church. You know the kind of thing."

I nodded. "Yeah."

"So we crossed a concrete floor and you could tell by the sound that it was a big, empty space indoors, and they sit me on a wooden box. There's a wooden table in front of me. There's some muttering, and then this muffled voice says, 'Mr. Hays, forgive all the cloak and dagger stuff, but I'm afraid it is necessary.' He talks a bit posh, at least, posh for a Yank. You know what I mean, don't you?" I said I did and he continued. "So he says, 'I am going to remove your hood, but before I do, I'd like to give you a small test. I hope you don't mind. I think the fee warrants it.' So I tell him I don't mind. I hear a couple of clunks on the table and he tells me there are two pistols there, and he would like to know if I can identify them..."

"Shit. And you did..."

"Thinkin' back, it was stupid. But hindsight makes us all smarter than we really are, dunnit? I suppose I was thinkin' of the money, and I had no idea then what was going to go down later, did I?" He shrugged. "It's no excuse, I know. I picked up both guns, handled them, felt them all over. One was a Colt revolver, 38. The other was a Colt 45 automatic." He took a deep breath. "She was shot with a .38. Must have been the same one."

"You told the cops about this?"

"Yeah, but obviously they don't believe me. Who would? I wouldn't."

"It's elaborate."

"Yeah. Careful planning—and well in advance."

"At least three guys involved."

"Yeah, the guy who spoke could have been Ivory or one of the other two. The voice was muffled."

"So what happened next?"

"They removed the hood. It was very dark. There was a table in front of me but the two pistols were gone. Other side of the table there was a bloke. I couldn't make out any details. It was just a shadow. There was nobody else there. And the same voice what had spoken earlier says, 'We have a contract to offer the right person, and we understand you have experience in special operations.' I says, 'What kind of contract?' He says, 'It's a hit. You'll be given the details if you accept. It pays twenty thousand dollars.' So I tell him, 'Thanks, but no thanks. I was a soldier, I ain't no assassin.' They put the hood back on and we were done there.

"I thought there might be some trouble. They might want to get rid of the witness, but there weren't. Now I know why. They took me back to the car and delivered me home, with two grand stuffed in my pocket. I had a bad feeling at first, but nothing come of it, so I forgot about it. Till now."

The waiter cleared away the plates and I ordered two Irish whiskeys. We waited in silence for him to deliver them. When he'd gone, I took a swig and let it settle, warm in my belly.

"You fucked up pretty bad."

"Don't I know it?"

"OK, so here is what we are going to do. I'm going to get the best criminal attorney in Baton Rouge. I'm going to have him come over and we'll have a conference with him. Meantime, I'm going to talk to Carmichael and Jackson. Maybe we can make them see sense."

"You don't believe I done it, do you, Captain?"

"I know you didn't."

He smiled. "How come?"

He knew the answer, but he wanted to hear it. "If you'd done it, they'd never have caught you."

He stared at me for a long moment, then raised his glass to me. "Cheers, sir. I appreciate it."

THREE

I phoned the Advocate while we were sitting over our whiskeys and spoke to their crime and legal editor. He gave me the name of Louisiana's leading criminal advocate, David Hirschfield. "This guy," he'd said, "leaves no closet unrifled and no nose un-bloodied. He's a monster, a scary man."

He sounded like my kind of guy. I called his office and got his secretary.

"I'm afraid Mr. Hirschfield has a full caseload at the moment. It is quite out of the question."

"I will double his fee."

There was a small, patronizing laugh. "Believe me, Mr. Walker, money is not the issue. Mr. Hirschfield has some very powerful clients and he can't simply palm them off to a junior."

"Can I talk to him in person?"

"Mr. Walker, as I have said to you, he is *far-too-busy*."

She punctuated the words in order to drive them home.

I could feel the anger rising inside me. "No. You don't understand. I am going to employ Hirschfield. There are no two ways about this."

"*Mr.* Walker! I have already *told* you that it is out of the question! Now kindly..."

I thought about it for a full second, then took a decision I knew in time I would regret. But I figured I'd regret it when the time came. I interrupted her.

"I want you to listen very carefully to me," I said. "Mr. Hirschfield was recommended to me by a friend at the Pentagon..." She gave a splutter that told me what she thought of that. I continued regardless. "I am going to give you a phone number to call so that you can confirm that, and I will pay whatever Mr. Hirschfield cares to charge. But I need *him*, and I need him *now.* I will give you half an hour, and then I expect him to call me back in person. Is that understood?"

She had gone very quiet. I gave her Ben's number. Bat was staring at me like he was wondering what was in the whiskey. I hung up and called Ben's number. It rang once.

"Lacklan. I am surprised to hear from you. What's up?"

"I know I am going to regret this, Ben, but I need a favor."

"Name it. I promise you will not regret it."

I told him about Hirschfield and he went real quiet.

"What do you need a criminal attorney for, Lacklan?"

"I don't want you involved in this."

"I'm already involved. It's too late for that. Is it for you? What have you done?"

"No. It's a colleague. I've got it covered. I just need Hirschfield on board."

"A colleague? From the SAS?"

I sighed. I could sense him making signs at somebody.

"Tell me what it's about."

"I told you, I don't want you involved. Hirschfield's secretary is going to call you..."

"No, she's not. I'm going to call Hirschfield. He'll take care of your case. But there is a simpler way of doing this. I'll call the DA and have them drop the case."

"No. Just talk to Hirschfield, then stay the hell out of it."

"Fine. You understand you do not owe me personally, you owe Omega."

"I understand that."

"You won't regret it. Expect his call."

I hung up.

Bat was staring into his glass. "I remember you said your dad was a big shot."

"My dad is dead. It's best you don't know about this."

He held my eye. "I don't want you owing favors on my behalf, sir."

"Lacklan. We're friends. It's done. Forget it." I smiled. "Now you owe me."

I didn't have to wait half an hour. Five minutes later, my cell rang.

"Mr. Walker?"

"Speaking."

"You have some powerful friends."

"Mr. Hirschfield?"

"Call me David and I'll call you Lacklan. You promised to double my fee and you shall. I shall probably be in trouble with the Mob because of this." He laughed loudly. "But it pays to keep our friends in Washington happy. Now, tell me how I can help you."

"I need you to win an unwinnable case."

"That's what I do."

I gave him a rough outline. "I need you here in Burgundy by tomorrow."

He was silent a moment. "The Carmichael case, is it? I'll be there tonight. You are aware there is a storm coming, aren't you?" He sighed noisily. "But, Mr. Walker, from what you've told me so far, I can't make any guarantees as to the outcome."

"You do your best. I'll do the rest."

He shrugged with his voice. "Fair enough. Tell me where you're staying. I'll book a room."

I told him and hung up, watching Bat across the table.

"What do you know about Carmichael?"

"Not a lot. Filthy rich. Deals in real estate. People say he doted on his wife. They were married for about five years. He was a lot older than her."

"Office in town?"

He hesitated. "I think he works from home."

I raised an eyebrow at him. "She tell you that?"

"She might have mentioned something."

"How close did you get to her, Bat?"

"Look, leave it out, will ya?"

I stood. "OK, I'm going to talk to Carmichael. Try to stay out of trouble, at least till I get back."

"I'll do me best."

In the lobby, Luis was watching a small TV behind his desk. I caught a glimpse of a brightly colored weather map with a giant white spiral in the middle. It looked as though Sarah was making landfall on the Bahamas.

One Sarah was dead, but the other, it seemed, was very much alive. I drove, under a low and dangerous sky, through empty streets out of town and onto Route 61. Then I headed south, toward Hardwood and St. Francisville, for a quarter of a mile.

The gate to his property was set back from the road. I slipped through it and moved down the long driveway, through rich green lawns and an abundance of river birches, red oaks, and southern pines. They looked oddly luminous in the gloom, against the watercolor sky.

His house was a large, colonial mansion in the Georgian style, with stone Grecian columns and a gabled portico. Two broad steps led up from the gravel drive to the door. I parked, climbed the steps and rang the bell. The door was opened after a minute by a pretty maid in a uniform. I told her who I was and said I needed to see Charles Carmichael.

She went away, came back a minute later, and led me across a vaulted hall with a checkerboard floor to double walnut doors. She knocked, poked her head in and said, "Mr. Walker to see you, sir." Then she stood back to let me in.

His library-cum-office was what you'd expect, having seen the façade of his house, and his hall. It was the deep south at its most elegant. The walls were lined with dark wood panels and shelves loaded with heavy tomes. The rugs looked Persian and there was a nest of Chesterfields set around a cold fireplace.

When I went in, he was standing by a heavy oak desk to the left of the door. He was in his late fifties, with graying, well cut hair and a suit of the same color. He had his arms crossed and he did not look happy. He didn't waste time.

"Who are you?"

"Former Captain Lacklan Walker, I was Bartholomew Hays' commanding officer in the British Army."

"You're an American."

"My mother is English."

"What do you want?"

"I'd like to talk to you about what happened."

"Why?"

I sighed. "Mr. Carmichael, I am not here as an enemy. I have reason to believe that Hays did not kill your wife. If I am right and he is convicted, your wife's killer will go unpunished."

He scowled at me. "What you mean is that you want to protect the honor of your regiment."

I studied him a moment, his posture, the set of his jaw. "Are you a military man, Mr. Carmichael?"

"Yes. Marine Corps."

"Then I won't waste your time and mine by lying to you. Of course I care about the reputation of my regiment. And of course I care about a soldier who served under me with honor and courage. But not to the exclusion of all else. If he did this, then he must be punished. But if he did not..."

"He did it. His prints are in her bedroom and in my drawing room. His prints are on the gun, God damn it!"

"I have reason..."

His face flushed and he took a step toward me. "How dare you! Reason? What possible reason? You come into my house, wanting to enlist my help to protect the man who *murdered* my wife!"

I stood my ground.

"What reason? Putting it bluntly sir, if Hays had done it, his prints wouldn't be all over your house, or on the weapon. They wouldn't have the weapon, and they wouldn't have him in custody."

"Get out of my house before I call the sheriff and have you thrown in jail!"

"On what charge?"

"Trespass—and complicity in murder!"

I held his eye for a beat. "I'm going to let that pass because I can see the pain you're in, Carmichael. But the man who killed your wife is walking free, and if Hays goes down for it, your wife's killer will have got away with murder. Think about it."

His voice was cold and steady and his eyes were hard. He repeated, "Get out."

I nodded and left.

Outside, back under the heavy cloud, I paused by my car to light up a Camel and think about what I would do next. It had to be Detective Jackson, but judging by Carmichael's reaction, I didn't expect him to be very receptive.

The cop shop was at the other end of town, on Bordeaux Street. It was a small, modern building with a big parking lot and a big radio antenna. There were four patrol vehicles and a couple of unmarked cars. You got the impression they were normally busy, but did most of their work on the streets, where they didn't have to record it. Right now, it was quiet. I guessed the slow, steady exodus continued, and the people who were here were staying indoors.

I parked by the entrance and went inside. There was a bored-looking sergeant at the desk, watching the news.

Hurricane-force gales were battering the Bahamas and there was footage of palm trees bent almost horizontal as the spray from giant waves drowned them. He glanced at me and made a question with his face, while he kept one eye on the news.

"I need to talk to Detective Jackson, about the Bartholomew Hays case."

He sighed like I was being unnecessarily demanding and made a call on the internal phone, then continued watching the news like I wasn't there. A minute later, Detective Jackson stepped out in shirt sleeves with a loosened tie. He was a big man, not tall but big, with balding black hair turning to gray at the temples, and thick stubble where he was either growing a beard or he'd forgotten to shave. His eyes were dark and suspicious and examined me a moment before he spoke.

"You have information about Bartholomew Hays?"

I nodded. "Yeah. Can we talk somewhere?"

He held the door for me and led me through to his office. It was small and functional. "Take a seat."

He sat behind his desk and I sat across from him. "My name is Lacklan Walker, I was Hayes' superior officer in his regiment in the U.K. I know him as well as anybody. He served on a number of operations with me. I am pretty sure he did not commit this murder."

His only reaction was to blink, once. "You been to see Mr. Carmichael, right?"

"He called you?"

"Yeah, he said you might try to come and see me. I was expecting you. I am going to say the same thing to you as he did. Hays' prints are at the scene and they are on the weapon. You are wasting your time and, more important, you are wasting *my* time."

"You don't even want to hear what I have to say?"

He gave a small, humorless laugh. "What can you say, man? Can you explain to me how his prints appeared in the Carmichaels' bedroom?"

I shook my head. "No."

"Can you tell me how they appeared downstairs in the living room, where he has supposedly never been?"

"No, I can't."

He leaned forward and pointed at me. "Can you explain how his prints got on the murder weapon?"

"Maybe."

He shook his head. "Uh-uh, no you can't. There is no maybe. Either you can or you can't. And you—can't. And if you can't explain those three things, you are wasting my time."

"Bartholomew Hays did not kill Sarah Carmichael."

"Can you prove that?"

"Not yet."

He narrowed his eyes at me. "What do you mean, not yet?"

"I plan to find out who killed her." I smiled and gave my head a small shake. "Bat Hays is one of the most skilled assassins you are ever likely to meet, Detective. I know because I have seen him work. I know he didn't kill Sarah Carmichael *because* his prints are at the scene."

"That is bullshit."

I shrugged. "Suit yourself."

I stood and he pointed up at me. "Stay out of my way, Walker, or I'll run you in for obstruction of justice."

I put my most patronizing smile on the right side of my face. "Save it for somebody who might believe you, Jackson. You just stumbled into a bigger league."

I went out and looked up at the sky. It was early afternoon, but it was as dark as evening. A gust of wind whipped my hair and howled through the pines across the road, making them bend and creak. Sarah was going to be trouble. Sarah was going to cause havoc.

FOUR

HIRSCHFIELD CHECKED INTO THE SONIAT THAT evening at eight. He had the desk call me down after he'd settled in to his room and we met in the cocktail bar.

The cocktail bar was all dim blues and greens, and for some reason, they had a large fishing net on the wall behind the bar. Hirschfield was sitting on his own at a table behind a fern and beckoned to me as I came in. He stood as I approached. He was a big, bombastic, well-dressed man anywhere between forty-five and sixty-five. He had very black hair, huge hairy hands and huge feet, and gold rings on most of his fingers. He had big eyes that read you while you talked, with the same attention and concentration other people use to read books.

I held out my hand. "Mr. Hirschfield, it was good of you to come so soon."

"David, please. And I'll call you Lacklan. Sit down. What will you drink?"

He was waving with his left hand at the barman and pointing to an armchair with his right. I said, "Irish, no ice."

He bellowed, "Santos! A Bushmills here, no ice! You got that? No ice!"

We sat and he said, "Let *me* talk. I want you to understand something. If it were not for your big shot friends in D.C., I would not touch this case with a sterilized bargepole. I read the papers on the way down. You don't stand a chance in hell. I hope you understand that. I wanted to talk to you before Hays came. I don't know if he did it, and frankly, I don't care. Most of the clients I represent did what they were accused of doing, whatever it was. That's my niche. It's why I am the best and it is why I am a very rich man. I wasn't joking when I said I had upset the Mob to be here with you. That's why you'll pay double. But unless you've got something special up your sleeve, my advice to you is, plead guilty. I want you to understand that, right from the start, because I don't want your powerful friends knocking on my door telling me they are disappointed. I'm telling you straight, from the start, as it stands, this case cannot be won."

The waiter brought over my drink and set it down on a turquoise mat with a dish of peanuts. When he'd gone, Hirschfield said, "Shoot."

I nodded and took a moment to think. "First, it's important you understand that Hays is not guilty. He did not kill this woman. He is not going to plead guilty, because he didn't do it."

He held up one of his big hairy hands.

"That may be the truth, Lacklan, but to me it is a matter of indifference. Truth is a concept for philosophers to play with. What we deal in, is *facts*. And right now it is a fact that

Hayes was at the scene of the murder, and it is a fact that he held the murder weapon."

"I understand that. Now I want to move on and I need you to listen to me. You're going to get the prosecution's file and we are going to go over it with a fine-toothed comb for inconsistencies. They have to be there because he was not at the scene and, though he did hold the gun, he did not shoot Sarah Carmichael with it. How are we going to find inconsistencies? Because I am going to take everybody in this parish apart, from Detective Jackson and Charles Carmichael to the janitor at the local primary school, and I am going to find who did kill her. I am going to get enough facts for you to create, at the very least, a reasonable doubt. The plea is not guilty. Period."

He spread his hands and shrugged. "You pay the piper, you call the tune. Let's get Hays here and talk to him."

I ordered him a Scotch and he arrived ten minutes later. I made the introductions and Bat told his story for the second time while Hirschfield remained absolutely silent, and seemed to read him like he was reading a document. When he'd finished, Hirschfield slumped back in his chair, made a temple out of his fingers and studied it with an expression of deep disappointment, like he'd been hoping for a solid gold Hindu monument and he'd got a Calvinist chapel instead. After a moment, he bellowed at Santos and made a stirring motion with his finger, which meant 'bring another round.'

"So, am I to understand that you were both in some special elite unit in the United Kingdom?"

Bat nodded. "The SAS. It's a regiment. Best in the world."

"Naturally." He turned to me. "And you were his superior officer. You did operations together." I nodded. "See, that's good, brothers in arms, code of honor, the jury are going to like that. The whole British thing on the other hand..." He blew out through large lips, "That could go either way." Then he shook his head. "The story, my friend, I have to tell you, without more than your say so, the story is a crock of horse shit. If you could at least bring in some Muslim terrorists seeking revenge, well, then we could challenge the jury, make sure they are all Jewish and Christian, and perhaps play on the whole jihadist, fundamentalist thing. But I need more, much more. So far, you have given me next to nothing to work with. A simple story. What you have given me is a simple story. And a simple story is not enough."

"I'm going to find the guy who took him to the meeting. If I can, I'll get the guy with the moustache too."

"That would be something. What about the revolver? My office has already requested the prosecution file and we are going to be all over that like VD. But tell me about the revolver, a .38, right? Who found that, and where?"

Bat shrugged. "I dunno, mate. All I know is, they found the murder weapon, ballistics is a match, and my prints are on it. Only way that could have happened is if it's the gun that the feller asked me to identify. Like it was a test."

He grunted. Then he gestured at me with both hands. "This is your department. Who wants this woman dead? Who benefits from her death?"

I looked at Bat.

He sighed. "Look, I barely knew her. I saw her a few times at the club, but all I know is she was popular. People liked her. She was involved in charity, helped people, got very involved in environmental issues, and that's a big deal 'round here since Katrina."

Hirschfield nodded and pouted. "You're not kidding. But it's not much to go on."

Santos arrived with a tray of drinks and peanuts. He deposited them and left. Hirschfield took a pull, savored it, and heaved a big sigh.

"All right, gentlemen, it won't be easy, but we'll give it our best shot. Here is my reading of the situation, and what needs to be done. I will get the prosecution file tomorrow or I shall want to know why. I will go over it with, as you say, a fine-toothed comb. I shall apprise you, Lacklan, of every weakness I find, and you will do what you can to pick holes in it. I shall not inquire into your methods, but I will say this. This is not the U.K. Illegally obtained evidence is *not* admissible, however probative it may be. If you obtain evidence illegally, cover your damn tracks!" He took another pull and went on. "Things that spring to mind off the top of my head, find this man who lured Bat to that meeting, find his associates, find the warehouse if you can. Meanwhile, let us look at the timing of the murder, at what time the call was made, where was Bat at that time? What was he doing? Let us also, above all, look into Sarah Carmichael's life. Who might have wanted her dead? Who might have benefited from her death? If she went to jazz clubs without her husband, with whom did she go? What is this woman's story? Why did she end up murdered in the prime of her life? I need..." He paused and eyed us both. "I need a *compelling* story to tell the jury, and it is your job to find me that compelling story!"

We moved to the dining room. Again we had it to

ourselves, with Ella, Billie, and the divine Sarah Vaughn to keep us company. We ate and drank too much, and Bat and I said little, but laughed a lot. It was not hard to see why David Hirschfield was as successful as he was. His vast personality, his booming voice, and his needle-sharp mind were captivating. He had a hundred stories to tell, and you believed every one of them, because he told them with huge authority.

But for all his power and authority, later, as I let myself into my room, knowing that Bat was walking home through the dark, empty streets, with the black sky lowering over his head, I knew that what we needed for the jury, and for Bat and me, was not a story, however compelling. What we needed was the truth.

MORNING CAME with a mild hangover that a cold shower, a pot of coffee, and some scrambled eggs on rye in the dining room turned into a mild headache. The news said that Hurricane Sarah had veered south and was battering the coast of Cuba. There was some hope that it might blow itself out in the Gulf. I took my coffee outside and looked up at the sky. The sky didn't seem to agree with the experts on the TV. The sky looked like it was preparing itself to eat Burgundy alive.

It was while I was lighting a cigarette that the big, black Lincoln rolled up and the driver climbed out and looked at me with amused eyes.

"You Cap'n Walker?"

"I was. Now I'm just plain Walker."

"Mr. Carmichael sends his compliments, wondered if you'd care to breakfast with him this mornin'."

I drained my coffee and left the cup on the windowsill. "Reckon I would, at that," I said.

He came 'round, touched his cap, and opened the back door for me.

"James, at your service, Sir."

I smiled. "Were you in the army, James?"

"Marine corps, Cap'n. An' if you'll excuse me sayin' so, Sir. Once you been a cap'n in special ops, you *always* a cap'n in special ops. You earned somethin' nobody can ever take away from you, Cap'n."

I nodded my thanks and climbed in the back. When we'd pulled away and were headed east on Congress Street toward Rampart and Dauhpine, I asked him, "What rank did you leave with, James?"

He smiled in the mirror. "Just corporal. Never saw no active duty. I was invalided out on account of I broke my leg during an exercise. S'why Mr. Carmichael give me the job."

"I remember, he said he was in the Marines."

He glanced at me in the rear-view again as we turned onto Dauphine and headed for Route 61. "Gunny," he said simply.

I nodded. A Gunnery Sergeant. A tough man. "Good employer?"

"Couldn't wish for better. Do right by him, he'll do right by you. Good man."

"I came to see him yesterday."

"I know that."

"He kicked me out."

He gave an amused wheeze. "I know that too."

"Any idea why the change of heart?"

"I have some idea, but it's best he tell you hisself. But I *can* tell you he's a good man. He's tough, but he's fair an' just."

We went the rest of the way in silence and ten minutes later, we pulled up in front of the gabled portico and the Grecian stone pillars.

The door was opened by the same pretty maid who'd let me in the day before. She smiled.

"Good morning, Captain Walker, Mr. Carmichael is expecting you."

She led me across the checkerboard floor to a breakfast room at the back of the house. It was bright, with French windows that gave onto a well-kept lawn bordered by mature oaks and river birches. He stood as I entered, smiled ruefully for a moment, and approached me with an outstretched hand.

"Captain Walker, I hope you will accept my apology for my behavior yesterday. I was out of line. An officer's desire to protect the reputation of his regiment, and his men, is something to be commended, not condemned."

I took his hand. "No need to apologize, Mr. Carmichael. I could have been more sensitive in my approach."

"Water under the bridge." He gestured me toward the table, set with a white linen cloth. "Will you join me for breakfast, Captain?"

I sat. "I am no longer a captain, Mr. Carmichael. Lacklan, Walker, or if you insist, Mr. Walker will do."

"Very well, Lacklan, then please call me Charles."

The pretty maid reentered with two plates loaded with

bacon, eggs, fried mushrooms, tomatoes, and devilled kidneys. She set them before us and poured coffee. He thanked her and she withdrew.

"I hope you acquired a taste for the English breakfast while you were over there. I think it is one of their greatest achievements."

I sipped my coffee and watched him eat a moment. As I cut into the bacon, I asked him, "Charles, forgive me for being blunt, but why the change of heart?"

He dabbed his mouth with a crisp, white napkin and regarded me with direct, unwavering eyes.

"A number of reasons, Lacklan. Once my anger had subsided, I decided to look you up. Many of your files are sealed, naturally. But I have connections and I got access to some of them. Not all, but enough to know that you are a man of exceptional integrity." He paused, sipped his coffee, and smacked his lips. "You omitted to mention that your regiment was the SAS. To make Captain in the Special Air Service is no mean feat. It takes a very special kind of man." He nodded, as though agreeing with himself in some internal dialogue. "I myself was in the Marines."

"Gunnery Sergeant."

He smiled. "James has been talking, I see. He's a good man."

"He says the same of you."

He looked grave. "Loyalty is a big deal for me, Lacklan. To my country, to the Corps, to my family, to my friends..."

"To the clan."

He nodded and met my eye. "Yes, to the clan. So it seemed to me that I owed you at the very least a fair hearing."

"I am very grateful to you for that."

"So..." He gestured to me with an open hand. "Please, tell me what you have to say, and I guarantee that at the very least, I will listen with an open mind."

FIVE

I HELPED MYSELF TO MORE COFFEE, STARED AT IT IN the cup for a bit, and then sipped it.

"Charles, just because of who he is, Bat Hays is one of the most effective, professional killers you are ever likely to meet. I know because I have seen him do it. Do you mind if I smoke?"

"Be my guest. I'll join you."

We lit up. I took a drag and started talking again.

"There were four of us. We tend to operate in units of four. There was myself, Hays, and two others. We were in the jungle, I can't tell you where. We'd taken up a position by the river, waiting for two boats. We had intel that they would be loaded with drugs, which were to be exchanged for weapons. Our task was to sink the boats and kill the men onboard. No prisoners. No survivors.

"We waited twenty-four hours. On the second afternoon, we heard the boats approaching. They were big, slow launches. We saw them coming from two hundred yards away. We were armed with a grenade launcher, an AW 50 cal. And C8 Carbines. They were sitting ducks. They had no idea we were there. They didn't stand a chance."

He was frowning, wondering where I was going with the story. I tapped ash and looked him in the eye.

"As the boats entered the killing field, the guys were waiting on the instruction to open fire. That was when we saw that as well as men and drugs, the boats were also loaded with women and children. There must have been at least twenty women of all ages, and a dozen kids. For a second, we froze. There had been no hint of this in the intelligence we had received. Not one of us there was going to open fire, but it was Bat Hays who put it into words. He turned to me and he said, 'You can fuckin' court martial me if you like, but the day the British Army makes war on women an' children is the day I become a fuckin' Frenchman!'"

He tried to smile at my cockney accent, but it faded at the implication of my words. Before he could answer, I went on.

"He was serious. He could have faced court martial, or worse. But he would not have opened fire on a woman or a child, unless his life or that of his comrades were in direct peril. That is not something I can take to court, and it's not something I expect you to take at face value, on my say so. But it does give you the measure of the man."

He studied me for a moment. "I assume there is more than that. The way a man behaves on the battlefield can be very different to how behaves in his private life. We both know that."

I nodded. "Sure. I just wanted you to know what kind of man we are dealing with. Now, here is how I know, beyond any doubt, that Bat Hays did not commit this murder. I have, personally, seen Hays execute a dozen kills in non-combat situations. Like any man trained by the Regiment, he is as good as it gets. It is inconceivable that he would have carried out the kill in such a sloppy, unprofessional way."

I saw his cheeks color and his eyes shine. I knew my phrasing was brutal, but I had to make him see the truth of what I was saying.

"Even if his personality could have changed so much for him to do this, it is impossible that he would have left prints at the scene. It is impossible that he would have left his prints on the weapon. And, Charles, if Bat had taken a shot at you, he would not have missed. Whoever broke into your house that night and killed your wife, there is no way it was Bat Hays. I may not have proved it to you yet, but I know it for a fact."

Carmichael's moment of anger had passed and he was staring into his coffee cup, listening to what I was saying. Now he crushed out his cigarette and sighed deeply.

"I know that what you are saying is most probably true, Lacklan. It makes a lot of sense. I know the reputation of the Regiment. Hell, our own Delta Force was modeled on it, after Charlie Beckwith served with you guys in Malay. But for crying out loud, Lacklan! His prints *are* on the gun. They *are* in the bedroom and they *are* in my living room! How do you account for that?"

I shook my head. "That is not conclusive, Charles. It's far from an impossible frame."

He thought for a moment, frowning deeply. "Look here, I have a proposition to put to you. I have nothing personal against your man. I don't even know him. But what I want is for my wife's killer to be caught. Do you think you can do that?"

"Yes."

"Then let me employ you. We'll call you a consultant, with specialist knowledge of the accused's background. I carry some weight in this town and I'll tell Jackson to cooperate with you, give you access to their investigation and their file, share what information they have." He sat forward and stared hard at me. "I'll get you anything you need. Find my wife's killer, Lacklan."

"You have a deal. What I need is to see the crime scene."

His face went pale. "It hasn't been touched since that night. I'll show you."

"You don't have to do that. Just tell me where it is. I'll find it."

He hesitated. "It's up the stairs. There is a galleried landing. The master bedroom is down on the left. It still has the police tape..."

He looked suddenly old and drawn, grateful to put off for one more day having to confront the room. I sighed.

"I'll need you to show me the drawing room and walk me through what happened."

"I know. Yes. That's not a problem. I just can't bear to think what she must have gone through."

I left him there and went back to the checkerboard hall. It was a red-carpeted oak staircase that split into two right angles after ten steps and then rose on both sides to a gallery that looked down over the entrance hall under a domed cupola. Two passages fed off the gallery into each wing of the house. I followed the one on my left into the south wing.

The master bedroom was the last door on the right. It

was dimly lit, and crisscrossed with shadows from the arched window at the end of the corridor. A strip of yellow police tape was strung across it. I pulled it down and opened the door.

I have seen my share of carnage in my life, more than most people. What I saw, and smelled, then, stopped me in my tracks. It was a large room. Dim, gray light filtered in from a tall, glass-paneled door on the left that led out onto a small terrace. Another door on the right opened to an en suite bathroom. The floor was parquet, and strewn with Persian rugs. There were two hand-carved, free-standing wardrobes against the wall. Directly in front of me, about fifteen or twenty feet away, was a heavy, oak, four-poster bed.

At first I thought that the duvet and the sheets were burgundy, but as the stench hit me, I realized that they was saturated with blood. In the two weeks since the killing, he had not had the room cleaned, and in the intense humidity preceding the storm, the bedding had not yet fully dried. I closed the door behind me and stood absorbing what there was to see, and smell.

There was a lot of blood, too much, so much that it had spilled onto the floor. I could see where the handle and the glass on the terrace doors had been dusted. There were prints, presumably hers, Carmichael's, and Bat's.

I approached the bed. The quilt and the sheets were drenched from shoulder-height down to about mid-thigh. Slightly more than two feet down from the pillow, the mattress had been punctured. That in itself was odd. I examined the perforations and decided they looked like closely grouped bullet holes, though they had later been torn in order, I guessed, to extract the slugs. On an impulse, I took my Swiss Army knife and cut a piece of the blood-soaked sheet and put it in my wallet.

I pulled the duvet back over the sheet and found the same holes, only neater. There were four of them, very closely grouped. Whoever killed her was a good shot, and his hands had not been shaking. He had control of his weapon, and of his emotions. He had not shot her in the head, though he was clearly capable of it. He had deliberately shot her in the belly. One of the slowest, most painful deaths possible.

If it was an execution, it was a personal one.

I looked around a bit more, then went back downstairs and found Carmichael where I had left him. He looked embarrassed and kept his eyes on the tabletop.

"I haven't..." He sighed noisily through his nose. "I haven't been able to..."

"I know, it's hard to face. You want me to take care of it?"

He glanced at me and frowned, but there was gratitude in his eyes. "No. No, thank you. Sooner or later, I have to face what has happened. I'll take care of it today."

"James will help you if you let him."

He nodded.

I said, "I need to see where you exchanged fire."

He stood. "It's through here."

The doors to the drawing room were opposite the library, and made of the same, highly polished walnut. The room was long and broad, running from a large, bow window at the front of the house to tall French doors at the back. These led onto the same, ample lawn I had seen from the breakfast room. There was a large Georgian fireplace set into the far wall, surrounded at a distance by comfortable, modern armchairs and a sofa. There were original impressionists on the walls and an eclectic selection of antique furniture. On a credenza beyond the fireplace there was a silver tray with a collection of decanters and glasses.

I looked around. It didn't take me long to find the bullet holes in the walls. One had gouged out a chunk of the chimney breast, about seven feet off the ground. Another had narrowly missed what looked like an original Chagall over the credenza.

"Those two were mine," he said.

"You want to walk me through it?"

"It was about eleven forty-five. I'd been into town for dinner. Sarah was out. She was a great lover of jazz. I don't enjoy it myself. My taste runs more to the baroque and the renaissance. So, I had been out. When I got home, I came into the drawing room, intending to have a nightcap. I stepped in and switched on the light. He was there."

He pointed down toward the Chagall.

"How was he dressed?"

He stared at me a moment in surprise. "Um... He was wearing dark pants, jeans perhaps. A dark sweater, or a sweatshirt, I am not sure. It was very sudden and unexpected. And he had on a ski mask or a balaclava. I remember he was armed with a revolver and he fired at me. There is the shot, in the wall."

He pointed behind him. The bullet hole looked about right for a .38. It was above and to the right of the door, about a foot from another painting. I pointed at it and frowned.

"That's an original Picasso."

"My grandfather was a fanatic of modern art. He bought that before Picasso was world famous. I have no idea what it is worth now." He looked back at the sideboard, where the shooter had stood. "I was slow to react. To be honest I was stunned. My mind was reeling. He fired again before I could draw my weapon."

"You were armed."

"I always carry. The second shot is over here..." He walked toward the bow window and pointed to a hole in the wall, about eight feet off the floor. I followed and stood next to him. I ran my hand over the wooden frame of the bow, and examined the small panes of glass.

"How old is this window, Charles?"

Again he looked surprised. "It's original, from when the house was first built for my great, great..." He made an 'and so on' gesture, "Back around the time of the War of Independence. A little earlier than that."

"Superb."

He nodded. "So, I managed to react. I pulled my piece and let off three shots. One over the fire, another narrowly missed the Chagall and the third knocked out one of the panes in the French doors, missing him in the process. He got out that way and made off across the lawn, into the woods. My first thought, as you can imagine, was Sarah. I ran upstairs and..." He blanched. "There she was, in that ghastly..."

"I have to ask, Charles, forgive me. Did you check to see if she was dead?"

"Of course, immediately. It was my first thought. But she was, quite obviously, dead. I called Jackson. I believe it was eleven fifty-five, according to the police report."

I went and stood by the door, recreating the scene in my mind. The killer would have been six feet from the fireplace, just beyond the armchair, with his back to the drinks tray, about twenty or twenty-five feet from Carmichael. He let off one shot. Carmichael dodged to the killer's right, he let off another shot, then turned and ran. Meanwhile, Carmichael had pulled his own piece and fired once, hitting the fireplace, twice, missing the Chagall, three times, missing the killer and shattering a pane of glass in the French doors.

"If it had been Hays, the moment you stepped through the door he would have double-tapped you in the chest. The higher the pressure—the more intense the situation—the more automatically the training kicks in. It's like Pavlov's dogs. Surprise him and he will double tap to your chest, without thinking. It's an autonomic response." I gestured at the walls. "Forgive me, but this shooting is shit. This is the wild shooting of a panicking amateur."

He looked embarrassed. "I... It's been a long time..."

"You're not a professional killer, Charles. But Bat Hays is."

He nodded. "I get it."

"Who were your wife's enemies, Charles?"

He spread his hands wide and shook his head. "That's what Jackson asked me. I want to say she didn't have any, but obviously, she did. Everybody loved her, Lacklan. She was an angel. She was the sweetest, kindest, most humane person I have ever met."

"She was younger than you?"

"Considerably." He walked over to the fireplace and dropped into one of the large armchairs. "I'm fifty-nine. She was forty, and looked five years younger."

"She used to go to jazz clubs on her own."

"I know, I know what you're thinking, and don't imagine you are the first person to say it to me—especially in a community like this. But I trusted her implicitly, and if there had been anything going on, believe me, in *this* town, I would have heard about it." He shrugged. "But long before I heard about it, she would have told me. We had that kind of relationship." He smiled, then laughed. "I knew when I married a beautiful woman twenty years younger than me that sooner or later, she would feel tempted by a younger man. That was something I just had to accept. As it turned out, that never happened. We were in love. It's that simple."

I leaned on the back of the chair opposite him, looking down into his face. "It's that simple for you, and maybe it was that simple for her. But if some guy was in love with her, maybe it wasn't that simple for him."

He nodded. "That's what Jackson said. He believes that Hays fell in love with her, that she turned him down, and he killed her."

"Maybe his theory is right, but his suspect is wrong." I looked at my watch. "I need to get back. Listen, does James live on the property?"

"Not exactly. James has a cottage on the grounds, at the back of the house. Sally, the maid you saw earlier, lives in town."

"He didn't hear anything?"

He shook his head. "No, he's somewhat less than a quarter of a mile away."

He promised me again that he would talk to Detective Jackson about cooperating with me. Then he called James and had him drive me back to the Soniat. On the way, I asked him, "You didn't hear anything that night, James, nothing odd or out of the ordinary?"

He looked real upset. "I sure as hell wish I had, Cap'n. But that house is made of solid stone. Whatever goes on in there, stays in there. Only thing I heard that night was a pig squealing like it was being murdered—if you'll forgive the term."

"A pig?"

"Yeah, a pig, screamin' like hell."

"What time was that?"

"Oh, that would have been about eleven o'clock. Before any of this stuff went down. Besides, it was out by the corrals, where they keep the livestock."

I thought about it. "What time did you go home?"

"Mrs. Carmichael went out 'bout six, and Mr. Carmichael said he was gonna eat out, so he sent us home just before eight."

Outside the hotel, he opened the door for me and I climbed out. I paused, looking up at the sky.

"A pig?"

"It was a pig, Cap'n, screamin' like crazy. Didn't last long, just a few minutes. But I'm pretty sure it ain't nothin' important."

He smiled and I nodded.

I watched him drive away, back toward Dauphine Avenue, and wondered about Sarah. The sky was still black, and the temperature felt like it was climbing.

SIX

I WENT UP TO MY ROOM AND STOOD UNDER THE shower for five minutes. Louisiana is never what you'd call cold, if you come from New England. But the close humidity and the climbing temperatures in Burgundy right then were what you'd expect from the equator, in summer.

I changed my clothes, had some lunch, and drove to the police station. The winds had dropped and there was an eerie, claustrophobic stillness in the air.

Detective Jackson was expecting me. The desk sergeant told me to go right ahead.

His door was open and he looked up as I stepped in. He leaned back in his chair and sighed.

"You're determined to make my life a misery, Walker."

"I'm determined to make sure Hays doesn't go down for a murder he didn't commit."

"Yeah, yeah, yadda yadda. Siddown." He pointed to the chair opposite him and I sat. He picked up a file. It wasn't very thick, and he tossed it across the desk to me. "I don't know how you did it, Walker, but you sold the old man on your story."

I opened the file and started leafing through it. I spoke as I scanned the pages.

"If Hays had done this job, you would have a double homicide on your hands, and no suspect. It's that simple."

I paused, reading. The revolver had been recovered in the woods at the back of the house. I laughed quietly.

"What's funny?"

I looked up and held his eye. "Tell me something, the slugs you recovered from the mattress and the slugs you pulled from the wall in the drawing room, were they from the same weapon?"

"Yeah, ballistics showed they were a match."

"So here's something I'm having trouble with, Jackson."

"That's Detective Jackson to you."

"Yeah, yeah, yadda yadda. Here's our killer. He gets into the house, he climbs the stairs, gets into her room where she is sleeping, back pretty early from the jazz club, and, in the dark, he puts four beautifully grouped rounds into her belly. At this point, he is cool enough and composed enough to have a steady hand and make four perfect shots. Now he goes downstairs, into the drawing room and is, presumably, about to make his escape through the French doors. But Carmichael gets home and disturbs him. And now, with the light on, facing an as-yet unarmed man at twenty feet, he shoots high and wide, twice. That sound to you like a special ops veteran with ten years of experience and over two dozen kills to his name?"

He sighed and spread his hands. "What can I say?"

"You can tell me why he was cool upstairs and shaking

like a virgin in a whorehouse downstairs. You can tell me why, instead of wearing gloves, he left his prints all over the crime scene and the weapon, and you can tell me why he thoughtfully left that weapon for you to find in the woods, instead of continuing for ten minutes and pitching it into the bayou."

He didn't say anything so I kept leafing through the file. I spoke as I turned the pages.

"You know, if Hays had wanted to, he could have walked into a six-figure job with MI5, MI6, the CIA—or the Mob for that matter—as a professional assassin." I looked up at him. "There are only about six hundred of us at any one time. We are not the best, Jackson. We are selected from the best. Am I beginning to get through to you?"

I paused. I had seen something that caught my eye. He noticed it and frowned.

"What?"

"Sarah Carmichael had a sister?"

"Yeah. Simone, Simone D'Arcy. She'd been visiting with her that evening."

"I thought she'd gone to a jazz club?"

He shrugged and made a face. "So she told her husband she was going to a club. Maybe she planned to go with her sister. They used to go out a lot together. They were both into jazz. But instead it looks like they stayed in, talking. Then Sarah went home early. She must have been home by eleven or eleven thirty. Her sister says she left just before eleven. It ain't that far."

"Nobody saw her arrive?"

"Nope."I read on, talking half to myself. "And her sister didn't go with her, she drove herself."

"Uh-huh. She left her sister and went home alone in her own car."

I looked up. "Where does Simone live?"

"About two miles from here. South on 61, just before you come into Hardwood. You gonna see a turn on your right, before the gas station. You follow that to the end, you'll come to a set of gates. That's Simone's house."

"She's got money, too, huh?"

"They all got money. Old money."

I nodded and kept leafing. "So the general consensus on Sarah Carmichael is that she was an angel. An angel who frequented jazz clubs without her older husband. You going to tell me the truth or stick to the party line?"

"I don't know if you're a cynic, a wiseass, or both, Walker. I know I don't like you and I know you're here to cause trouble to protect your Limey friend. Fact is Sarah Carmichael was a wonderful person, she was faithful to her husband, and if there was some gossip at one time because she used to go out without him, it passed, because she never crossed the line. She was a good woman, and after Katrina, she did a lot, and spent a lot of her own money, to rebuild communities and the environment around here. So in future, keep your wiseass comments to yourself."

I studied his face a moment. He looked sincere. I dropped the file on his desk.

"Noted." I stood. "Thanks for your help, Jackson. I'll try to stay out of your hair." I stopped at the door and turned back to face him. "By the way, I don't like you either." I pointed at the badge he had hung from his belt. "And that badge, you don't deserve to wear it. You're either bent or incompetent. I don't know which yet. But either way, you're going down."

The desk sergeant was still watching the weather. Havana was being torn to shreds, but Sarah was not moving, neither south nor north.

I stepped out into the clammy afternoon and climbed into the Zombie. I hit the ignition and the two big engines came silently to life. I slipped out of the lot and, unlike the hurricane, I headed south. The roads were empty under the leaden sky and I hit a hundred, letting the air batter my face through the open windows. Outside Hardwood, I turned right and cruised through the woods until I came to the two tall, cast iron gates. They were open and I slipped silently between them.

The house was Creole, and though you could see it had once been magnificent, now there were subtle signs that the cash just wasn't there to maintain it. The gardens that surrounded it were running to seed, the lawns were overgrown, and the paint on the white walls and the veranda was beginning to peel in small patches here and there.

She was sitting at the top of the steps that led from the front lawn to the porch, watching me approach. She was wearing white jeans and a white shirt with the cuffs turned up, and she was smoking a cigarette. The brilliant white of her clothes made a stark contrast with the darkness of her skin.

I pulled up and climbed out into the sultry air. She half smiled and half frowned at me as I walked toward her. A trail of smoke rose from her lips. To say she was beautiful would be only half the story. She was graceful, effortlessly elegant in her movements and gestures, and there was an indefinable quality of depth to her smallest expression. She was extraordinary.

"How did you free-wheel down a flat drive, mister?"

"I was drawn by the power of destiny. I'm looking for Simone D'Arcy."

"You found her. It must have been your destiny."

"You're Sarah Carmichael's sister?"

"You sound surprised."

I nodded. "You're black and she was white. You don't see that often."

"She was my stepsister. Now you know who I am, how about you tell me who you are?"

It was said without hostility, without challenge, more as an invitation. For a moment, I had to avert my gaze.

"My name is Lacklan Walker. I was Bartholomew Hays' superior officer when we were in the army together."

She didn't so much narrow her eyes, as half close her lids and raise her chin slightly. "You mean you're his friend."

"Yeah, I'm his friend."

"You feel guilty about that?"

I was surprised by the question. "No..." But I said it without conviction and wondered if I was lying.

She heard that in my voice and smiled. "Your body language says otherwise, Lacklan. Why are you here?"

Again, what could have been hostile came across more as an invitation.

"I'd like to ask you some questions about your sister." I hesitated. "Hays is accused of killing her, but I know he didn't do it."

She seemed to study me for a moment, biting her lip. "Do you know that, think it, or feel it?"

I gave a small sigh. "I don't want to play word games, Ms. D'Arcy..."

"Neither do I, Lacklan. I would like to know whether what you have is knowledge, a suspicion, or a hunch."

"It's knowledge. I know Bat Hays didn't kill her. Can we talk?"

She spread her hands and there was amusement in her eyes, bordering on mischief. "It's what we're doing." She stood. Her body wasn't perfect. Perfect was banal compared to what her body was. Maybe her breasts were a bit too large, maybe her hips and her ass were a bit too curvaceous. Maybe her legs were too long; but when you put it all together, it was insane.

"You want a beer, Lacklan?"

"Yeah. I could use a beer. Thanks."

I followed her onto the veranda where there was a white, wooden table against the wall with two white chairs facing out, to the garden. A small, brass bell stood on the table beside a glass ashtray. She rang it as she sat.

I rested my ass on the railing and pulled a cigarette from my pack. While I was lighting it, the door opened and a woman in her fifties stepped out. She had blond hair turning to gray, tied in a knot at the back of her head.

"Yes, ma'am?"

"Two beers, Inga. Nice and cold, my love."

Inga left without saying anything and Simone watched me watching her while she held her lower lip with very white teeth.

"I'm trying to figure out what made Sarah tick."

"Really?" She looked amused, but not in a flattering way.

"That's pretty vague. She wasn't a clock. Can you be more precise?"

"I don't know. Everybody is telling me she was an angel, that she and Charles adored each other..." I shrugged with one shoulder. "But her behavior, as far as I can make out, doesn't tie in with that."

She sucked on her cigarette and squinted through the smoke. "You want me to tell you she had a dark secret, and that was what got her killed?"

"I don't want you to tell me that, Simone. But so far it's the only explanation that makes any sense."

The door opened again and Inga came out with two frosted glasses of beer on a tray. She set them on the table and left. Simone picked up a glass and sipped.

"It seems insane, frosted glasses in November, but this heat is almost oppressive. It's tropical." She gazed out at the restless trees. "That made her tick. Not so much climate change, but the effect it was having on Louisiana, on the local environment."

I raised an eyebrow. I couldn't keep the irony from my voice. "Is that what she was doing in the jazz clubs on her own, campaigning for the environment?"

She sighed and again dropped her lids over her huge eyes. "Cheap, Lacklan, and I suspect not worthy of you."

"How do you know what's worthy of me?"

"You're here, aren't you? You're in your friend's corner, talking to the sister of the victim, fighting his cause. That's the kind of man you are, isn't it? Loyal, committed, true..."

"We were talking about Sarah."

She puffed her cheeks and blew. I picked up my beer and pulled off half.

"What can I tell you, Lacklan? She was a good person, like you. She cared. She cared about people, about communities of people. She cared about suffering and unhappiness. She was not only a good person, but a beautiful person. And she cared about Charles." She crushed out her cigarette, streaming smoke from her nose. "But people aren't just one thing. You know your Shakespeare? Othello was a good, honorable, decent man. But jealousy is triggered in his soul by Iago's wicked manipulations, and Desdemona's simple naivety. So, which one is Othello? The good, honorable man, or the crazed, jealous monster?"

"I don't know."

She spread her hands. "He is a woven fabric, made of both threads."

"Is that what Sarah was, a woven fabric?"

"It's what we all are."

"So what was she doing in the jazz clubs while her husband was at home, or dining in restaurants?"

"Listening to jazz."

"Did she have an affair with Bat Hays?"

"Not that I'm aware of, Lacklan."

"Was she having an affair with anybody?"

She shrugged. "Same answer. I was not my sister's keeper."

"You're stonewalling me."

She closed her eyes, smiled, and sighed again. "Look, Lacklan, I understand you want to help your friend. But if doing that means dragging Sarah's name and reputation through the gutter, I am not going to help you do that. We all have our loyalties."

I looked down into my beer. For the second time in just

a few minutes, she'd made me feel ashamed, for reasons I couldn't quite fathom.

"That's not what I intended to do."

"But it's what you would have done, if I'd let you?"

I looked into her eyes.

She held my gaze, like she was reading a text inside my head. "That's what you do, Lacklan, isn't? You see something that needs to be done, and you storm in, guns blazing, leaving death and destruction in your wake, and tell yourself it's what you had to do to get the job done."

"How could you know that?"

"Isn't Bat Hays the same? Isn't that what all men like you do?"

"You're making a lot of assumptions, Simone, based on very little." I took a drag and we were both silent for a moment. I looked at the burning ember on the tip of my cigarette and wondered how much truth there was in what she'd said. I thought probably it was all true. "Hays' life is over if I can't help him. He doesn't deserve what they will do to him. I don't want to put a slur on Sarah's memory. I don't want to hurt you, or anybody. I just want to know the truth."

She gave a small laugh that was almost bitter. It was the closest thing I had seen in her to an ugly emotion. "You want to know the truth without hurting anybody. Good luck with that."

She stood and came close beside me, looking out at the garden, and up at the heavy, motionless ceiling of cloud.

"Synchronicity," she said.

"What is?"

"It's a Jungian concept. Not an easy one." She glanced at

me, like she was wondering if I would get the concept. "Sarah, she is threatening to destroy us all: Sarah the storm, and Sarah, my sister. There can be no causal link between the two, yet there is a connection in meaning." She gestured up at the sky. "Both Sarahs have unleashed a destructive force, one from the sky..." She paused and seemed to examine my face, with little darting movements of her eyes. "The other from the earth."

I wanted to tell her that I was not a destructive force, that I did not want to hurt her, but the words seemed paralyzed in my throat. She was standing close, so close I could feel the warmth of her body.

She closed her eyes and turned away from me, leaning back against the wooden pillar that supported the veranda. I was suddenly hungry for her and had to fight the urge to take hold of her body and crush it to mine. She opened her eyes as though she had sensed my thoughts.

"She'd grown tired of him. She loved him, but he'd become an old man, not in years, but in his mind. In his soul. She was young, alive, hungry...."

"So she was having an affair."

"I told you, I don't know. But she was thinking of divorce." She shook her head. "I think he knew, but don't let your imagination run away with you, Lacklan. He's a kind, gentle man."

"Like Othello?"

"No, not like Othello."

"That night, was she with you or was she at a club?"

Her eyes trailed down from my face, to my chest and to my hands. "Can I have one of your cigarettes?"

I pulled a Camel from the pack and handed it to her. She

put it between her lips and I flipped the Zippo. She leaned into the flame and inhaled. She leaned back as she let out the smoke. "She was with me. We were going to go to the Blue Lagoon."

"Bat played trumpet there."

"He's good. She liked to listen to him. He was playing that night."

"But you didn't go."

She shook her head. "We stayed and talked. She was upset. She didn't know what to tell Charles. They'd started sleeping in separate rooms." There was something quietly tragic in her expression. "Servants gossip. I think the whole of Burgundy knew, except poor Charles. He couldn't accept it, but she couldn't bring herself to be with him anymore. She thought... she *knew*, he had realized. She knew she was going to have to tell him. But she still loved him, as a friend. More than a friend. Family."

"There was somebody else."

"I keep telling you I don't know."

"And I keep not believing you."

She shrugged, like she didn't care. "A lot of the time she said she was going out to listen to jazz, she wasn't. At least not in the clubs."

"What do you mean?"

"When our parents died, we inherited two houses. This one, which belonged to my stepfather, and another, smaller one, which belonged to my mother. I got this one as my home, because Sarah was married and already had that monstrous mansion, and she got the smaller one. Charles never knew about it."

I frowned. "Why?"

"She always thought of it as mine because it had belonged to my mother. So it just sat there, closed up. When things started to go wrong with her and Charles, I advised her to use it as a studio. She was a talented watercolorist. Not great, but good. It was a place where she could get away from a relationship that had become a prison; a place where she could be creative, be herself, listen to music. A place where she knew she was emotionally safe."

"You talk like a psychologist."

"A psychiatrist."

"So she came to you for help."

"I advised her to create a space for herself, where she could make a wise choice about the future, about what she wanted to do."

"Did you go there with her?"

"Once or twice, not often. It was her space. Don't ask me if she took lovers there. I don't know."

"Where is this house?"

"On the Sara Bayou, in the woods north of here. Over the bridge on Tunica Road. It's called Solitude."

I felt the heat of the cigarette on my fingers and stepped over to the table to crush it out in the ashtray. As I did it, I asked on impulse, "Are you married, Simone?"

She took a moment to answer, watching me. "And that is relevant how?"

I smiled without much humor, not sure how to answer. "Another perspective..."

"You asking or telling?"

"I don't know. Are you? Married?"

"No. There are no men in my life."

I had nothing left to ask her, but I didn't want to leave.

We stood a moment staring at each other, her still leaning back against the wooden column, with the flaking white paint, the cigarette smoldering in her fingers.

I said, "Thanks for the beer. Thanks for being honest. I'll think about what you said, all of it."

She watched me go down the steps to my car. As I opened the door, she said, "That's the most dangerous thing of all, you know?"

I looked up at her. "What is?"

"A destructive force that thinks."

I didn't answer. I got in the car, turned silently around, and headed back the way I had come.

SEVEN

THAT EVENING I MET BAT AT THE BLUE LAGOON ON Desiré Street, a small cul-de-sac off St. Claude Avenue, in the heart of town. He wasn't working that night. Harry, his boss, had told him he didn't want him working there till the trial was over. People can be helpful like that.

Despite the hour—it was after eight—the temperature had not dropped and it was still unseasonably warm and humid, and half the patrons were out, drinking on the sidewalk. Above, the clouds were dense and a luminous, smoky orange, reflecting the lights from the town.

We shouldered through the crowd, made our way to the bar and ordered an Irish and a Scotch, then carried them to a table in the corner. For a moment, we drank in awkward silence. Then, I said, "I went to see Simone."

He stared into his drink, tipping it this way and that. "Oh yeah?"

"It seems Sarah was not as happy in her marriage as most people thought."

He arched his eyebrows, but aside from that made no expression with his face at all. "Oh, right."

"Seems she was planning to divorce him."

He finally looked at me, shook his head and sighed. "I wouldn't know anything about that, sir. Like I said, I barely knew her."

I gave one nod and after a moment went on, "Also, Carmichael had a change of heart."

"What does that mean?"

"He sent a car for me this morning. Seems he thought about what I said and believes I'm right. He's employed me to find out who killed Sarah."

"That's a bit fuckin' weird, innit?"

"Is it? Not really. He saw the logic that a killer of your experience would not leave his fingerprints and his weapon all over the place for the cops to find."

He stared at me a moment. "Oh."

"So I examined the crime scene, or, more accurately, the crime scenes."

"What do you mean, scenes?"

"She was killed upstairs in her bedroom, but he attempted to kill Carmichael downstairs, in the drawing room."

He frowned, nodded, and said, "OK, and?"

I thought about it a minute. "Let me give you my impressions first, then we'll try and make sense of them. First thing that struck me, there was a hell of a lot of blood. It was a through and through wound to the belly, four shots, but it was more blood than I have ever seen from that kind of wound."

He looked uncomfortable and took a swig of his whisky.

"What else?"

"The shots were accurate at about twenty feet, well grouped. But downstairs, the guy couldn't shoot to save his life. Literally. At twenty feet he shot twice, three or four feet wide and high. Then he ran. Carmichael got off three rounds, but he was just as bad. Carmichael was a Marines Gunnery Sergeant."

That caught Bat's attention and he stared at me. "And he couldn't hit a target at twenty feet."

"Maybe it's not as odd as it sounds. He was in the Corps about thirty or forty years ago. He was shocked and it was a moving target."

He wasn't convinced but he said, "OK, if you say so."

"So, I'm turning this around in my head and here are my initial thoughts. I'm trying to visualize what happened. Sarah has been out visiting her sister. She comes home early and Carmichael is out, having dinner at a restaurant. She goes upstairs and by eleven she's in bed, presumably asleep."

"You got this from Simone?"

"Partly. You know her?"

"Just, you know..." He made a coming-and-going gesture with his hands, like they had crossed each other sometimes in the bar.

I nodded. "Sure. Anyhow, at some time around eleven, the killer gets into the house, either through the front door or through the French doors at the back. The police report says they could find no forced entry. He goes upstairs to the bedroom and enters without waking her. And here is where it gets complicated."

"How?"

I sighed, still turning it over in my head and wishing I could light up a cigarette. I took a swig and sighed again.

"Because he takes out the gun that you have previously left your prints on, and he does not leave his prints over the top, which means he is wearing latex, surgical gloves. He puts four rounds into her, very tightly grouped, then he leaves your prints on the bedpost and on the door handle, which means he has taken the trouble to make latex copies of your prints." I paused, watching his face. He looked depressed. I continued. "He then left the room and went downstairs to the drawing room. Presumably he came in that way, via the woods, and planned on leaving that way. But as he's making his way toward the French doors, Carmichael comes in and turns on the light. The guy panics, lets off two rounds and runs. Carmichael goes upstairs to check on his wife and our guy makes good his escape across the lawn and into the woods, where he carefully leaves the revolver for the cops to find."

I sat back and he stared at me, incredulous. "He made fuckin' latex copies of my prints?" He waited a moment, trying to read my face. "Are you having second thoughts? Are you thinking I done it?"

"No. I am convinced you didn't. Stay with me, Bat. Questions: one, what made this guy choose you for the frame? Two, what makes a guy shoot with such accuracy one moment, and then miss wildly the next?"

He drained his glass. "Well," he said, smacking his lips and placing it carefully back on the table. "The prints and the shooting all point to a pro—a real pro. Real pros don't go to pieces because the lord of the manor comes home. So the bad shooting on both parts was a fake, which means that

Carmichael was in on it, or employed this bloke to do the job."

I signaled the waitress for two more drinks. "That was my first thought, and the obvious conclusion. But it has a weakness."

"What?"

"Everybody, including Carmichael, thought Sarah would be out that night till late, as she usually was when she went to listen to jazz. She told him she was going out for the night. They were coming here, in fact, to listen to you. She went to her sister's to pick her up, but they got talking about Sarah's problems with her husband, and in the end they didn't come. Sarah went home to bed instead."

"So who knew she was home?"

The waitress brought the drinks, and when she'd gone, I flopped back in my chair and sighed. "On the face of it, Simone. Not exactly an ace hit man."

He spread his hands and shook his head. "Well, then, what the fuck?"

"Right now, Bat, there is only one way it makes any sense to me."

"There's no way it makes fuckin' sense to me, sir. 'Scuse my fuckin' French."

"Think about it. Everybody loves her. She does good works for the community and the environment. At first, I thought maybe there was a jealous lover, or her husband. But when this woman goes out to listen to jazz, apparently that's not a euphemism. She really did go out to listen to jazz."

"I told you that, didn't I?"

"Yeah, you did. So nobody wanted her dead, and nobody except her sister knew she was there at that time..."

I saw his face clear as the penny dropped. "Fuck. She wasn't the target. He was."

"That's the way my mind is going, at least."

"A man like that might have enemies."

"You don't make that kind of money without treading on some toes. So..." I watched him.

He waited.

I said, "What made the killer choose you?"

He sighed. "Honest, I have no idea."

"I can't help you, Bat, if you don't level with me."

"I am!"

"I know you're hiding something, Bat."

He looked away, toward the door, where the crowds were gathered, laughing.

"I can't force you, pal. But you are not doing any of us any favors by hiding stuff from me. Hell, Bat, what? You don't trust me?"

"It ain't that. You know it ain't."

"What, then?"

He stared at the tabletop a while, then said, "So what you going to do?"

"You mean apart from giving you a sound thrashing and throwing you in the Mississippi?"

"Yeah, aside from that."

"I'm going to tail Carmichael for a couple of days. I figure if he was the intended victim, whoever it was is going to have to try again. If that's the case, then they will probably be watching him. So I am going to try to watch the watcher.

I also need to find this guy who set you up. But that is going to be hard if you won't talk to me."

He looked mad for a moment. "I am talkin', in't I?"

I put my elbows on the table and stared him in the face. "Why you?"

He looked away.

"No, Bat, you're not talking. You're bullshitting me and I am trying to save your life. I don't appreciate it."

"I'm sorry."

"I'm not stupid, Bat. I know what you're doing. But you're making a mistake."

He shrugged and held my eye. I could see there all the obstinacy that had got him into the Regiment in the first place, the obstinacy that had made him one of the best of the best. He had made up his mind, and I knew that nothing I could do would make him budge.

"OK, pal. We'll do it this way. But you have to realize, sooner or later, whatever it is you are hiding will come out."

"Yeah, maybe, but not through me it won't."

"OK." I slapped him on the shoulder. "You want to get some food?"

We ordered a couple of burgers and while they were being fried, he asked me, "So, what do you think of Simone?"

I smiled. "She's as hot as a Carolina reaper. Smart, too. What about you?"

He shook his head. "Nah, not my type. Too fuckin' dangerous. Too deep."

"You got that right. What's your type, then, Bat?"

We'd had the same conversation a hundred times, from the deserts of Iraq and the mountains of Afghanistan to the rainforests of Colombia, but it was a good place to revisit and remind ourselves that we were allies, comrades in arms, *contra mundum*.

He sat back, a lopsided smile on his face, gazing up at the ceiling. "English rose. That's my type. Peaches and cream complexion, demure, real cut glass accent, like Kate Beckinsale, know what I mean? Bit of class, faithful, shy, blushes easy. But a right fuckin' daemon in the bedroom!"

We laughed out loud and spent the rest of the evening talking about the old times, remembering old friends, some —not many—dead in action. All of them unique, singular men, because the SAS has a policy of recruiting eccentrics and creative thinkers. We even sang a few songs, and when the band started to play, Bat pulled out his comb and a piece of paper, and jammed with them from where he was sitting at our table, getting more applause and cheers than the band.

At two AM, we stepped out and I walked him home, arm in arm, singing obscene army songs under the angry sky, defying the world to do its worst. We were the Clan, invincible.

At his door, I gripped his hand in mine. "Stay strong, Bat. We'll win. We always do."

"Who dares wins, right?"

"Right, who dares wins."

He went inside and I made my way down Congress toward Chartres Avenue and the Soniat, turning over in my head his description of the ideal woman. I had a feeling I could not shake that, bar the cut glass Beckinsale accent, he had described Sarah Carmichael down to a T.

EIGHT

Next morning, I was up at six and went for a run before breakfast. It was pitch black and as warm as a summer day. The TV in reception was saying that the NWS' worst fears were confirmed. Hurricane Sarah had turned north and was now headed across the Gulf straight for New Orleans, causing havoc and leaving utter devastation in her path. The death toll was high, and rising, and the damage to property was already being calculated in the billions.

She was coming, and bringing death with her.

I ran for two miles out of town, through the forest along Tunica Road. I crossed the bridge over the Sara Bayou and came to some open parkland at the junction with Solitude Road. North, the landscape opened up into farmland, but south, where it followed the bayou, the forest grew dense and dark.

I trained for an hour as the horizon in the east turned from black to a menacing, leaden gray. Then I headed back. As I ran, a small column of trucks and cars, laden with their essential possessions, was pulling out of Burgundy, headed north.

Back at the hotel, I stopped at reception, drenched in perspiration, to collect my key. Luis was still glued to the News Channel.

"You're not leaving?" I asked him.

He made a face and shrugged, reaching for my card. "They saying it's gonna blow itself out over the Gulf. New Orleans gonna get the brunt of it, but it'll be a tropical storm by then, you know what I'm sayin'? It ain't gonna hit Baton Rouge, never mind Burgundy. People panicking, but we a hundred miles from New Orleans, ain't nothin' gonna happen this far north."

"Hope for the best, prepare for the worst."

He gave me a look. "You know what, Mr. Walker, sometimes you *prepare* for the worst, and you *make* the worst happen."

I showered and dressed, and by eight fifteen I was sitting in my car in the Burgundy High School parking lot, across the road from the gates to Carmichael's property, drinking black coffee from a flask. Nothing happened until twelve fifteen. Then Carmichael's black Lincoln sedan pulled out of the gates onto Route 61 and turned south. I gave him a minute and followed.

I stayed well back, where even if he took the trouble to look, he wouldn't spot me in his mirror. I trailed him through St. Francisville and on, east and south for another twenty miles through farmland and suburbs into Baton Rouge. We stayed on the Scenic Highway, past the vast Exxon Mobil refinery, till we came to Chippewa Street. We followed that down past the Capitol, with the vast, dark mass of the Mississippi on our right, till we came to Main Street. There, we followed the one way system for four blocks. Just past the Capital One building, I saw them pull into a lot on the right, so I parked outside St. Joseph Cathedral. I watched James open the door for Carmichael. He got out, said something to him, and walked through the lot and into the Gras Tower Plaza, an elegant, two-story red brick office block. James pulled out of the lot and headed east, toward the I-110.

I got out and went to have a look at the brass plaques outside the entrance. There were two. One was Guy Woodbridge, a gynecologist, the other was Dane, Schuster and Wilberforce, attorneys at law. I figured he hadn't come to see Guy Woodbridge. I went back to my car and waited.

At one thirty, four men in suits came out. One of them was Charles Carmichael. The other three I had never seen before, but they had the look of attorneys. Two of them were non-descript suits, the other was a short, rotund man, completely bald on top and very emphatic in the way he spoke. They walked and talked their way into the parking lot, pausing every few steps for the rotund guy to stress a point, and eventually climbed into a dark blue Cadillac.

I called Hirschfield.

"What?"

"Dane, Schuster and Wilberforce, you know them?"

"That's a fatuous question. I know *of* them. They died like a hundred years ago, of old age. Dane and Schuster only had girls. They married money. Wilberforce's great grandson, or great-great grandson, is now the senior partner. I know *him*. We play golf."

"Could you have a conflict of interests here?"

"What is today, Stupid Question Day? A: how could I possibly know if I don't know what you're talking about? B: of course not!"

They pulled out of the lot onto Main Street and I followed.

"Carmichael just got into a Caddy with three attorneys from Wilberforce's firm."

"Well, that's not surprising. They specialize in real estate transactions, property law, trusts, that kind of stuff. He probably uses them all the time. What do they look like?"

"Two suits and a short, fat bald guy."

He laughed. "That's Wilberforce. Say hi from me."

"Yeah, right."

I hung up and followed them east along Main Street till we joined the I-110. Eventually we pulled on to Route 61 headed north, and I thought at first we were going back to Burgundy, but at the cement works, they turned east on to Route 68, headed toward Jackson.

There was practically no traffic on the road, so I fell right back and trailed them for perhaps six miles, then saw them slow and turn in to what looked like a tree-lined driveway, just past Par Road. For a moment, I was undecided. I didn't even know for sure why I was here or what I expected to find. I just had some vague idea that Sarah's killer might be stalking Carmichael. But so far I had seen no sign of that.

I made a decision and turned onto Par. About a quarter of a mile along, parallel with the house where they seemed to be headed, there was a dense woodland. I left the Zombie there, concealed among the trees, took my binoculars from the glove compartment, and made my way on foot, through the forest, toward the house.

This was neither Georgian nor Creole. This was a modern mansion, probably not more than twenty years old. It belonged squarely in the new millennium. It was a stack of four, white, concrete rectangular cuboids piled on top of each other at forty-five degree angles with huge, plate glass windows, spiral exterior staircases, stepped gardens, and a stream that seemed to run through the house. It was spectacularly ugly to look at, but probably just spectacular on the inside.

I eventually found them in the top cuboid, which seemed to be one vast space with a central, copper fireplace and large, minimalist Scandinavian style furnishings. It was like IKEA on steroids. I settled on my belly among the ferns and watched them.

They were all animated and talked a lot, especially Wilberforce and Carmichael. They had their attaché cases open and, while they sipped what looked like cognac, they studied documents which they handed back and forth while they spoke. You didn't need to be Patrick Jane to work out they were discussing a big deal, and that they were happy about it.

Wilberforce made a couple of phone calls. After that, the exchanges became more relaxed. There was a lot of laughing and less exchanging of documents. The hours slid by and the sky grew darker, but the clammy heat did not grow less. At six, in the cuboid beneath the party, I saw a man in a white jacket, and a couple of girls in French maid uniforms, setting a table and lighting a fire. It looked like this was going to be a long night.

By six thirty, it was pitch black and the house formed an eerie, luminous spectacle in the midst of a field of darkness. I watched the four men rise from their seats and descend to the glowing dining room. They ate and drank wine against the dancing light of the flames, toasting often. They were celebrating something, that much was clear.

By half past eight, they were having more cognac and I was contemplating throwing in the towel and going back to the hotel for a late dinner, when they got up from the table and started making their way down. I watched them through one luminous cube after another until the spotlights came on outside. At that point, I swore profusely and started to run.

I made it to the Zombie and pulled out of the woods in time to see their headlamps moving north along Route 68, away from me and toward Jackson. I left my lights off and accelerated after them. As I have mentioned before, the Zombie is totally silent and will do 0-60 in less than two seconds. Its top speed is as yet uncharted territory, but I figure it will do 200 MPH without breaking a sweat. It didn't take long for me to place myself within a hundred and fifty yards of them. Then I slowed and tailed them.

After five miles, we came to the junction with Route 10 and they turned left, as though to enter Jackson. As I took the corner, I put my headlamps on. They crossed the town along Charter Street. It was still and silent, each house bathed in a dead glow of streetlight. We came out the other side and they kept going for another five miles until we came to a bend in the road where there was the glow of a bar or a club. Here they pulled off into a parking lot and I cruised slowly past.

It was a club, set back from the road among the trees. A large neon sign outside spelled out *The Full Moon* in yellow script. Above it was a golden disc, and below, two blue squiggles suggested the sea. I drove on for a quarter of a mile, did a U-turn and came back. When I pulled in to the lot, I saw the Caddy was gone. They were obviously planning on making a night of it. I left the Zombie in the darkest corner I could find and went inside.

It was full, and the air had the close warmth of too many bodies crammed together in a confined space. There was a clamor of voices straining to be heard over each other, and over the sound of the band. The band was a trumpet, a bass, and a piano, picked up through mics and amplified. The overall effect was that you could not hear either the talk or the music. I shouldered my way through to the bar, scanning the tables for Carmichael and his pals. They weren't there.

I leaned on the counter next to an empty stool and ordered a double Irish. While he was pouring it, I asked him, "You got any private bars, members only…?"

He glanced at me and shook his head. I turned and looked around. At the back, past the stage where the band was playing, I could see a couple of doors. One of them led to the toilets, the other said 'Private'. Two got you twenty that Carmichael and his pals had not gone to the can.

"Buy a girl a drink?"

She was short and cute, with Afro-Caribbean hair that had gone out of fashion when red and black posters of Che were still all the thing. She had black hair, black eyes, black chocolate skin and very white teeth, and she had appeared on the stool next to me. She was wearing blue satin shorts and no bra under her T-shirt. The overall effect was good.

I smiled. "If you'll let me."

"Well, sure. I'll have a rum and Coke."

She leaned forward as she said it and I could see her pupils were like two vast black holes. She laughed as though I'd said something funny. I called over the barman and ordered her drink. While he was mixing it, she tried to focus on my face.

"Who are you?"

"I'm whoever you want me to be."

She laughed again. "That's my line. The guys come here looking for a party. I'm the party girl! And when they ask me who I am, I say what you said, 'I'm whoever you want me to be.' My name is Trixy."

"Seriously?"

"No. But I ain't gonna tell you my name now, *am* I?"

"I guess not. So where do you party, Trixy?"

She crooked her finger at me and I leaned close. I felt her lips and her warm breath on my ear. "Through the door by the can, and up the stairs." She sat back with a look of mock wonder on her face. "There's a whole 'nother club up there. *Private!*"

"And what goes on up there?"

"Parties, poker, roulette. You name it, baby! It's wild."

I grinned. "And how would a guy from out of town become a member of this private club?"

She gave a sexy little whoop and leaned against me, laughing. "You pays your money, and they let you in. It ain't cheap. But if you get in, you gotta take me." She leaned close to my ear. "They got the *best* blow up there. Promise?"

"I promise."

"You got money?"

"More than you can imagine."

Her eyes went wide. "Hey, we can get some stuff from Ive. You wanna come back? We can party at home?"

I looked across the crowded room at the door marked 'Private'. They'd be up there till the small hours, celebrating their deal. I was tired and hungry. I smiled down at Trixy. She looked warm and sweet. I could use warm and sweet right then, but I could use a steak and a beer more.

"How much?"

"Hundred bucks if you get some coke!"

She said it like it was the deal of the century, and maybe she was right. She craned her neck to look around the room. "He's always here, man. We'll get some stuff from him and go to my place."

I took two bills from my wallet and put them in her hand. Cute as she was, I felt suddenly tired and I knew I wasn't going anywhere that night. I bent over and kissed her cheek. "Maybe some other night."

I stepped out of the club and a wall of warmth hit me. The sound of frogs was loud on the air. I went and sat on the hood of my car and lit a Camel, blowing smoke up at the clouds, stained orange by the Full Moon. I could still hear the trumpet wailing from inside.

I looked at my watch. It wasn't nine yet. I thought about Simone, in her large, empty house. I had memorized her number from the police file. I reached in my pocket, took out my cell and stared at the screen. If I asked her to dine with me, I knew she'd say yes, and I knew she'd stay the night. If I went to her house, I knew she'd let me in.

I hesitated a moment too long, then put it back in my pocket, climbed in my car, and drove silently into the night, back toward Burgundy.

NINE

IT WAS AN EIGHT AND A HALF MILE DRIVE BACK TO Burgundy, because the road took a big detour south through St. Francisville before heading north again. As I passed Simone's gate, I slowed and looked in. There was a dim glow seeping from her windows, touching the lawn and the trees. I sighed, softly thumped the wheel and accelerated on toward town.

But as I approached the exit for Dauphin Street, on a sudden impulse, instead of turning right into the town, I kept going north until I came to Tunica Road. There I took the left fork over the bridge into the forest, where I had been running that morning. The dark was impenetrable, and even the powerful beams from my headlamps struggled to push back the dense gloom. I crossed the bridge over Sara Bayou and came to Solitude Road on the left. I turned into it and crawled south with the window open, scanning the dense, black wall of trees on the far side of the blacktop.

Then I saw it, a gap in the blackness, where the orange

ceiling of cloud shone through, and there, like a stencil against the flame-colored sky, the spiked arch of the iron gate.

I pulled across the road and parked. I killed the engine and the lights and climbed out. The gate was padlocked. I pulled my flashlight from my pocket and played the beam over the gate and the walls. There was no sign of an alarm system. I took a hold of the iron bars, pulled myself up, and vaulted over. I hit the ground silently and remained motionless for a count of one hundred and twenty, listening for dogs. There was nothing, so I ran the five hundred yards down the drive, staying close to the dense gloom under the trees.

The building was Creole, like Simone's, but much smaller. It was on one floor, with five steps climbing to a raised veranda that encircled the house. The windows were dark, like eyes closed in sleep, or death. My breathing was heavy from the run. The air was dense and clammy. There was no breeze, no whisper in the branches, only an absolute stillness and a silence that even the sigh of the bayou, not fifty yards away, and the incessant sawing of the frogs could not penetrate. It was a silence that seemed almost to scream from the dark house.

I climbed the steps and tried the door. As I had expected, it was locked. The windows and the back door gave the same result. I always carry a Fairbairn & Sykes commando knife in my boot, and a small Swiss Army knife in my pocket. A couple of minutes with the smaller blade had the front door open and I slipped inside. I tried the light switch and five lamps around the room came on. I wasn't worried about the light being seen. The house was completely surrounded by dense forest.

The room was large and ran from the front of the house to the back. Over by the right wall, there was an upholstered bamboo sofa and two chairs nested around a rough-hewn coffee table. A number of other small tables stood here and there against the wall, supporting table lamps of curious design and color. The floors were wood and strewn with rugs that looked African or Caribbean in design. Overhead, a ceiling fan had started to revolve when I switched on the lamps. On my left, I could see a sideboard and on it a collection of bottles, gin, martini, whiskey, and an old-fashioned soda bottle. A couple of long, low bookcases held a wide range of books, from glossy hardbacks on the great masters, to well-thumbed dime thrillers.

The walls were wooden too, and hung with watercolors that, as Simone had said, were not great, but were good enough to hang. There were also four Voodoo masks on the walls.

The room was bisected by a couple of thick wooden columns, and beyond them, under a second ceiling fan, was a long dining table with six chairs. Beyond that, against the far wall, was a tall artist's easel. On it there was a large canvas.

I crossed the floor to the table, pulled my Camels from my pocket and lit one. I stood looking for a long while at the painting. It was done in oils, with thick, aggressive brush strokes. The style was not original, late impressionist, impasto, Gauguin and Van Gogh meet Bonnard, but without their genius. Even so, it was good. Beside the easel, there was a wooden tea trolley, but instead of a tea pot and cups, it held a palette, a collection of brushes and tubes of paint, and bottles and dirty jars of turpentine. The smell was strong and oddly erotic.

The painting was of a black woman, nude. She was lying on a bed among tangled sheets with her left arm above her head and her right across her belly. It was honest and unashamed. Whoever had painted it had captured her, the exquisite figure and the features of her face, with the seductive hint of excess: the exaggerated hips, the over-full breasts, the generous lips.

There was only one bedroom, over on the right. The door was ajar. I moved to it and pushed it all the way open. The light from the dining room leaned in at a crooked angle and lay across the bed. It was the same bed that was in the painting, only Simone wasn't lying in it, and the sheets were not twisted and tangled. It was neatly made, with fresh, fluffed-up pillows and a new, clean duvet.

I snapped on the light. It came from two lamps on the bedside tables. I let my eyes travel over the room. There was an ashtray on the bedside table on my left, caught in the pool of amber glow from the lamp. It had two butts in it. I went over and examined them. One was a Sobranie Black Russian, the other was a Marlboro. Next to the ashtray there was a ring, left by a glass. It was about tumbler sized.

I went around to the other side and found what I expected, another ring, only smaller. This one would be the base of a wine glass, maybe champagne. There was an en suite bathroom and I stepped inside and switched on the light. One tooth mug, one toothbrush, and all the toiletries you would expect from a rich, privileged woman in her late thirties.

It wasn't dirty, but it wasn't especially clean, either. I got on my knees and leaned over the bath to peer into the plug-hole. There was the usual matting of hair gathered around the holes. I opened out my Swiss Army knife again and carefully scraped out the fluff and dropped it in the palm of my hand. Then I sat on the floor and sifted through it. Most of it was light, thin blonde hair. There was no doubt in my mind that that belonged to Sarah. But there was other hair too, short, strong, black, and tightly curled.

Across the dining room, directly opposite the bedroom, was the kitchen. It was large and open. I rummaged in a couple of drawers and found some freezer bags and popped the hair into one, sealed it and put it in my pocket.

On the draining board, I found a whiskey tumbler and a white wine glass. A picture of Sarah's last night in this house was beginning to take shape. It was a shape I didn't like.

I went back to the living room, poured myself a whiskey, sat on the sofa, and lit another cigarette. I sat smoking and drinking, trying to find an alternative explanation for everything I had seen. I couldn't, every scenario I played out in my mind ran up against the same obstacle. Finally, I crushed out the cigarette and went back into the bedroom. I got down on my hands and knees and examined the rush mat on which the bed was standing. It wasn't clean. It was pristine. I stood, grabbed a hold of the heavy, wooden bed, and heaved it to one side.

I felt a rush of anger well up inside me. Where the legs of the bed had been standing, there were no indentations, no marks, nothing. The mat was brand new. I ripped away the bedclothes and hurled them on the floor. The mattress, like the mat, was new. I grabbed the bed frame and lifted it savagely, tipping it on its side, knocking over the bedside table and sending the lamp crashing to the floor. I got on my hands and knees and scoured the mat. Then I ripped up the mat and scoured the floor. It was luck, but I knew there was a chance and it paid off.

If you fire a .38 at somebody's belly, on a mattress, the chances of the slug exiting at the back are slim, you'd need to be at the right distance. A human belly is dense and strong. But the chances of it penetrating the mattress after the belly are almost negligible. And that told me that there was a chance, a slim chance, but a chance nonetheless, that when they changed the mattress and the bedding, one of the slugs might have dropped to the floor. And there it was, under the left side bedside table, up against the skirting board. It was a .38.

Somebody had been shot in that bed, at close quarters. The mattress and the bedding had been changed, as had the rug under the bed. It had been done in a rush, maybe even in a panic, because they had brought a brand new mat, a new mattress and new bedding, but they hadn't bothered to clean the rest of the bedroom, or the house; they had cleared away the glasses and washed them, but not the ashtray, and they hadn't hung around long enough to take the glasses out of the draining board. Whoever it was did not want to be seen at this house. Did not want to be associated with Sarah Carmichael and her studio.

Somewhere, there was a blood-stained mattress and a blood-stained rug, maybe there was a body with it. Maybe not. I picked up the slug and dropped it into another bag, and then into my pocket, then went to the dining room and opened the back door. The air on the veranda was humid and warm. The sound of the bayou and the frogs assaulted me. There were no prizes for guessing where the mattress and the rug were. By now they were on their way to the Gulf of Mexico.

Why?

I had answered some of the questions I had asked myself at the Carmichaels' house, but those answers had just raised more questions, harder ones to answer. Like, if he had taken the trouble to drag the mattress and the rug down to the bayou, why the hell had he not thrown in the .38 with it? Was it the same .38? Had he kept it for a second victim, for Sarah? I thought about the blood-stained mattress. I thought about the other blood-stained mattress at the Carmichael mansion.

And then the answer was there before me, clear and obvious.

Carmichael was at the Full Moon. James would be in his cottage.

I didn't bother putting the bed back or hiding any signs of my presence. I left and made my way back through the oppressive darkness, up the driveway that wound through the dense woodlands, climbed over the gate, and leaned on the roof of my car. I looked up at the scorched, orange clouds, sagging low over Burgundy. I had made a career out of killing for ten long years. Bat Hays and I had worked together as professional killers, soldiers and assassins, and sooner or later, both of us would have to account for what we had done, for how we had lived, and killed. Did it matter? Did it matter how you killed, or who you killed? Was killing evil in itself, irrespective of who the victim was? Was killing a sadistic monster just as bad as killing a woman, an angel, like Sarah Carmichael?

Were Bat Hays and I evil men? Was I struggling to find justice, because in my heart I knew that I was evil? In trying to redeem Bat, was I really trying to redeem myself? Was that why I was living in hell?

I climbed into the Zombie and went and did what I knew I had to do.

TEN

IT WAS ALMOST TEN BY THE TIME I GOT BACK TO the hotel. Hirschfield was still in the dining room with a bottle of Rotem & Mounir on the table. He was smoking a long, black cigarette and hailed me with a fat, happy smile on his face as I came in.

As I sat, he showed me the cigarette and said, "I convinced the manager that I would sue him for a breach of my human rights and make a class action of it, but assured him that if he was fined for allowing me to smoke, I would pay the fine and testify in his favor."

"You're a good man."

"Besides, I have it on good authority that only Jackson and the sheriff remain in Burgundy, everybody else has fled north. I am waiting for suckling pig. Will you join me?"

I nodded and pulled out my cell. I called Hays.

"Yeah, Captain. All right?"

"You eat?"

"Kind of."

"We need to talk. I'm in the dining room with Hirschfield."

"Five minutes."

I hung up and Hirschfield sipped and cocked an eyebrow at me while he did it.

"You look mad."

"I am mad."

"Have a drink."

I called the waiter over. "Give me a martini, very dry. And another one of these damned Cotes du Rhone. And get me a steak. Two, there'll be somebody joining us."

He looked vaguely surprised at my tone of voice and hurried away with my order.

Hirschfield smacked his lips and sighed.

"Something tells me you have something I ought to know about."

I pulled a Camel from my pack and lit up, blowing smoke at the ceiling. I chewed my lip and stared at Hirschfield.

"Sarah Carmichael had a place on the bayou that her husband didn't know about."

He raised his eyebrows real high at his glass, like it had been a really impertinent glass, and sighed through his considerable nose. "That would explain her immaculate reputation."

I nodded. "It does."

He looked at me. "It does? As a fact?"

I reached in my pocket and pulled out the cellophane bag of hair and the slug. I dropped them in front of him.

"There were two kinds of hair in the sink hole in the bath, hers and a black guy's."

He eyed it and grunted, but he didn't touch it.

"We need DNA profiles on them, and we need a ballistics comparison on the slug."

He took the bags and looked at them. "I'll see what I can do. There is a lab in Fort Worth that can do it in a couple of days. I'll have them driven over. It's not cheap."

"Whatever it costs, Hirschfield. Get it done." I hesitated. "There's more."

"Are you having doubts about Hays?"

"I don't know."

"If you don't know, that means you are."

I studied his face a moment while he studied mine back.

"I won't know until he gets here." We sat in silence a moment. "Is there anything I should know about Wilberforce?"

He looked surprised. "Like what?"

I told him what I had seen.

He looked impatient. "That little scenario has probably been played out a hundred times over the last ten years. We engage in the warfare of business so that we can have these little celebrations of triumph. Read nothing into it. He has made a deal, nothing more."

I stared at him. I didn't like what he was saying. I stared at the walls and I stared at the waiter as he brought me my martini on a tray. Then I stared at the martini for a moment before I took a sip.

"It doesn't make any sense, Hirschfield. None of it makes any sense. Why...?" I hesitated and stopped.

He raised an eyebrow at me. "You kill... *have killed*... professionally, Lacklan. So you do it efficiently, pragmatically. But murder is not like that. Murder is emotional. The people most likely to murder each other are people who are in love. Logic goes out the window. If he was in love with this woman, and he killed her, you may be sure that he was out of his mind when he did it."

I sighed again. "*Shit!*"

I watched Bat enter the dining room. We were the only table occupied. He saw us, hesitated a moment as he saw the look on my face, then came and joined us.

"Mr. Hirschfield, Captain." he sat. "I've seen you looking happier, sir."

I looked away. The waiter approached. Bat ordered a Scotch on the rocks. As the waiter left, I locked eyes with Bat and said, "How long were you fucking Sarah Carmichael?"

His face went like stone, and without him saying anything, I knew that what had upset him was not being found out, but the way I'd phrased it. I waited. He just stared at the table. Finally, I said, "Goddammit, Hays! You don't need to tell me anything! I already know! I told you! If you didn't come clean, it would come out sooner or later! Well it has! You were meeting her at her studio, on the bayou, in the woods. I've seen the house, I've been inside, I found your damned hair in the plug hole."

I grabbed the bag from the table where it was sitting in front of Hirschfield and threw it at him.

"You don't need to confess, you don't need to betray her. We're past that. How long was it going on?"

He sighed and buried his face in his hands with his elbows on the table. Suddenly, Peggy Lee started singing about black coffee. Black anger welled up in my gut.

"Cut the bullshit, Bat. We've been through too much

together for these games. You were protecting her reputation. That's admirable. Now it's over. Talk to me."

He peered at me over his fingers as the waiter put a large tumbler of whisky in front of him.

"It was..." He sighed deeply and put his hands on the table. "It was twice, no more. She came and talked to me one night, after I'd been playing. She liked the way I played. She was knowledgeable, very, about jazz. She liked me, said I was good. We had a great evening, talking. About midnight she left. She always left about that time, twelve, one. But she gave me her number, asked me to call in half an hour. I did. She told me where she was, her place on the bayou. I went there. It was amazing, the paintings, the place, her..." He shrugged. "I fell in love. It's that simple. I was head over heels. I'd always liked her, she was my type. Demure, classy... We spent the night together. Two or three nights later, she come back. Same thing. I went to her place by the river. Even better than the first time. It was magic. She was funny, you know? Good sense of humor, classy. I was nuts about her... Still am."

He paused and looked away.

I said, "But?"

"In the morning, she told me that was it. No more." He turned to face me and his eyes were full of anger and reproach, like it was my fault what had happened. "We was done. She told me she had a thing about black men. It was just sexual. She was turned on by black guys. She'd had me, she liked me, she'd like to be friends, but not lovers no more. She'd met some other bloke." He paused, looking down into his drink. "I asked her if she was going to spring the same surprise on him in a couple of days, and she said she most likely would. She loved her husband, but he was past it. Couldn't get it up for her anymore. So she was playing the field, shaggin' black blokes..."

There were tears in his eyes.

"So you killed her?"

His face creased up. "Don't be fuckin' stupid all your fuckin' life! 'Course I didn't fuckin' kill her."

Hirschfield snorted. "Tell that to the prosecution. Tell it to the jury."

"I'll tell it to whoever you fuckin' like, mate. She broke my fuckin' heart, but I didn't kill her. That was..." He heaved another sigh. "That was two, three nights before she died." He shrugged. "I left, went home, went to work. Life goes on, right?"

I leaned forward. "Why wouldn't you tell me any of this, Bat?"

He shrugged. He looked almost embarrassed. "Because she was the most perfect woman I had ever met. I didn't want her memory... *sullied.*" He shrugged again. "I dunno, she was perfect, a lady..."

"Who was this other guy?"

"Dunno."

"Bat, for crying out loud! Stop saying 'I dunno'! Make an effort will you? You are looking at life—the rest of your fucking life! Maybe the death penalty! Who was this guy? He is probably the guy who killed her!"

He met my eye. "I don't know. After that, I tried to block her out of my mind, ignore her. It might have been any number of blokes. She didn't discriminate..." There was a sudden bitterness in his eyes and in his voice. He was aware of the irony of what he had said. "As long as they were black, she didn't care. No shortage of black blokes in Louisiana. I don't know how many of us she fucked! Could be hundreds..."

"You're not helping, Bat..."

"Yeah, well, that's the way it is."

I snapped, "No, goddammit, Bat! It isn't the way it is! Who is trying to frame you, for crying out loud?"

The waiter came with two steaks and set them in front of us. He opened another bottle of wine and filled our glasses.

When he'd gone, Bat stared at me for a long moment. "I don't know," he said. "I honestly have no idea."

"Was she in here that night?"

"No."

"What about her sister?"

"No." He shook his head.

"What do you remember from that night, Bat?"

"Nothing. It was just a night like any other."

"No!" I snapped again. "It wasn't! Because that night Sarah did *not* go out! That night she went to see her sister and spoke to her about wanting to divorce her husband. That night, instead of going on the town to listen to jazz, she went home..." I paused, hesitated. "Only she didn't, did she?"

Hirschfield was frowning down at the tablecloth. "No..."

I went on. "She didn't go home. She went to her studio. And there she met..." I looked at Hays, who was staring at me. "Who? Not you. What did Sarah smoke, Bat?"

"Fancy foreign things."

"Sobranie."

He nodded.

"So she met a black guy... A black guy who smokes Marlboro. What do you smoke?"

"Fuckin' hell, sir. I smoke Marlboro. But 'round here? 'S'like sayin' a black bloke who wears jeans. Every other bloke smokes Marlboro."

I cut into my steak. "How'd he know to meet her there?"

Hirschfield said, "She called him."

I chewed and looked at him. "Her phone."

He was looking at the table cloth. "Not mentioned in the police report."

I pointed across the table at Hays, who still hadn't touched his steak. "You know something. Maybe you don't know that you know it. But you saw that son of a bitch because he was in your club that night, and maybe you didn't see him, but he was watching you. What time did you leave?"

He frowned and became abstracted. "Well, it was me night off. I wasn't supposed to be there at all, only she said she wanted to hear me play that night. She called me. We arranged to meet there, and then I'd play a number. But she never showed, did she."

"So what time did you leave?"

He shrugged. "'Bout ten, I suppose. I waited an hour, and when she didn't turn up..." He shrugged. "I was beginning to feel like she was playin' silly buggers, playin' with me. I don't like that, so I left. Now I know she wasn't. She was..."

He looked away.

I thought about it for a moment. "Whoever killed her, Bat, saw you leave." I shook my head. "At the very least they knew it was your day off. Whoever killed her was watching you, knew your history, your daily routine... Somewhere in your head, Bat, you know who this is."

Hirschfield was watching me. After a moment, he said, "So what's next?"

I hesitated, unsure how much to tell him. In the end I said, "I still have some questions I need to answer in my own mind, things I am not clear about. I'm going to have a word with Jackson tomorrow. Meantime, there's something I need you to look into, Hirschfield."

He raised an eyebrow at me. "What's that?"

"I need to know the terms of Sarah's will. I also need to know the terms of Carmichael's will."

He frowned. "*Carmichael's* will? Charles Carmichael?"

"Yeah, Charles Carmichael. Who inherits if he dies?"

ELEVEN

By next morning, the wind had picked up again and everywhere I looked, as I drove through the empty streets, things were being dragged, thrown, and tossed by gusts of wind that were bowing and twisting the trees. Above my head, shreds of low-flying cloud were being torn and stretched across the heavy, gray ceiling of a very angry sky.

The Burgundy Police Department parking lot was empty but for one unmarked Ford. I parked in front of the main entrance, climbed out of my car, and stood a moment, listening to the mounting gale whistling and moaning in the trees. This was the outermost tail, the fringe of the storm. The eye was five hundred miles south, over the Gulf. I wondered for a moment where Marni was, if she was wondering about me, or if the fracas in Tucson and Washington had made her give up on me completely. But it was just for a moment. I put the thought out of my mind. I had no time for that now. First I had to deal with Bat and Sarah, then I could get back to Marni.

The desk sergeant looked up as I stepped in. "It's comin'," he said. He shook his head. "My heart goes out to them poor folks in New Orleans. It's gonna hit them hard. Real hard."

I nodded. "Yeah. Is Jackson in?"

"In his office."

I found him sitting behind his desk, staring out the window at a row of trees that looked like a green ocean in a storm. He turned and eyed me as I stepped in.

"What the hell do you want?"

I threw a pack of Camels on the desk as something like a peace offering and sat in the chair opposite him.

"I work for Carmichael, remember?"

"I don't know what idea you got, Walker, but working for Carmichael doesn't give you the right to come in here insulting me. So if you're bringing me more of your attitude, you can get the hell out of here. Carmichael or no fucking Carmichael."

"I hear you."

"What do you want?"

I scratched my forehead. "The blood. The blood at the scene."

"What about it?"

"There was a lot of it."

He shrugged. "She was shot four times in the belly with a .38 at close range. She took a long time to die and bled out. What of it?"

"Did you have the blood tested?"

He looked at me like I was crazy. "What the hell would I

do that for? She was lying in a pool of her own blood, why the hell would I have it tested? It's her blood!"

I stared at him a moment, then shook my head. "Yeah, see, I don't think she was killed there."

"What?"

"I'm not sure, but I don't think she was killed there. I think she was killed somewhere else."

He sat forward and put his elbows on the table. "That is the *stupidest*, the most fucking *ridiculous* thing I have ever heard in my entire, fucking *life!*"

"Will you humor me?"

"*Humor you?* You want me to fucking *humor* you? You come in here playing fucking detective, exploiting the vulnerability of a man whose wife was murdered in his own house, insulting people, playing the fucking wiseass special ops hot shot, and in the end you ain't nothing but an asshole! Check the fucking blood? Humor you? You're lucky I don't throw you in my fucking jail!"

"Take it easy, will you?"

"Take it easy? Get out of my fucking office. That's the second time I've thrown you out and it's the last. Don't come back, Walker, I'm warning you."

"I'm going." I didn't move. I sat looking at him for a moment. "What do I have to do to convince you to have the blood tested?"

"Nothing. It's a stupid idea. It's the most stupid idea I ever heard. I am not going to do it. It is not going to happen. Get out." I hesitated a moment and he narrowed his eyes at me. "Do you have information pertinent to my investigation? Are you withholding information?"

I thought about it for a full five seconds while I stared at his face. In the end, I shook my head and stood. "No, no information. You're probably right. But you should test the blood. I'm pretty sure she wasn't murdered in her room at Carmichael's place."

He made a face like I disgusted him and flapped his hand at me. "Yah, get out of here you fucking clown."

Outside, there was a steady whistling from the wind blowing through the overhead power cables, and a sighing and groaning from where it was surging through the trees and the buildings. I crossed to my car, battered by the air, wrenched it open, and clambered in and slammed the door, leaving the howl and bluster outside.

I dialed Simone's number, and while I was waiting for her to answer, another call came through. It was Carmichael.

"Lacklan, we need to talk."

"What's the problem?"

"The DA has been in touch. He's a friend. Just come over, will you?"

"Sure, I'm on my way."

As I fired up the engines, I was aware of the alarm bells going off in my head, I just wasn't sure exactly what they were telling me. But whatever it was, I knew it wasn't good.

I was shown into his study. He looked unhappy as he stood up to greet me. He shook my hand and gestured me to one of his chesterfields. As I sat, he sat across from me.

"Lacklan, the DA has been in touch with me. They are ready for the preliminary hearing. He is satisfied that it will be a slam dunk. I don't know what to say..." He sighed. "I put your concerns—*our* concerns—to him. He dismissed them out of hand. I asked him for more time, but he believes I am being foolish. Jackson feels the same way.

It's..." He shrugged and sighed again. "It's an open and shut case."

"Do you believe that?"

"Let me ask you. Have you made any progress? Have you found anything?"

I nodded. "Maybe."

His face cleared. "Then by all means, fill me in. Give me something I can take to him; something we can adduce at the preliminary hearing."

I thought for a moment. "Give me a second, will you?" I pulled out my phone and called Hirschfield.

"What?"

"Good morning, Hirschfield. Listen, don't ask questions, just answer. Can you legally get access to prosecution material evidence?"

"Like what?"

"Like a blood sample from the crime scene."

Carmichael frowned.

Hirschfield said, "Access how?"

"To have our own tests carried out."

"Of course. But why would we?"

"I want the victim's blood tested."

Carmichael went white and stood, staring at me.

Hirschfield said, "*What?* Have you gone *insane?*"

"I have my reasons. Can you do it?"

"Yeah, I can do it, but why the hell should I?"

"Because I'm asking you to, and I have just told you I have my reasons."

He sighed heavily. "I'll file the request."

I hung up. Carmichael had moved to the window and was looking out at the silent, tossing trees.

"What is this, Lacklan? Why can you possibly want to test the samples of my wife's blood?"

"Because I don't believe she was murdered here."

He turned from the window. His face had turned from ashen to crimson. His voice was choked with emotion. "I *found* her! The bed..."

"I know, Mr. Carmichael, I saw it. But there are too many things that don't square up." I hesitated a moment. "Are you able to answer some tough questions for me?"

"I hope they are not all going to be as... *bizarre* as that one..."

"I think you should sit down, Mr. Carmichael."

He frowned at me like I'd said something outrageous, but came around the chair again and sat. "What is all this about, Lacklan? This is not what I expected when we spoke the other day."

"If the answer was predictable, you wouldn't have needed me. Jackson could have taken care of it. The very nature of this murder is telling you it is something unpredictable, something out of the ordinary, isn't it?"

"What's your point?"

I was trying to read him, but all I could get was anger and pain. Finally, I asked him, "Did you ever visit Sarah at her studio?"

He clenched up his face, like he thought I was going crazy. "What the hell are you talking about? What goddamn studio? Walker, I am beginning to think Jackson is right..."

I ignored him. "The one she inherited when her parents died. Simone got the house, she got the smaller place on the bayou." I pointed in the general direction. "In the woods on Solitude Road."

His mouth sagged. "You're out of your mind."

"Am I? What makes you say that?"

"There is no studio, no house... If she had inherited anything I would know about it!"

"So you had no idea that she owned a place in the woods where she used to go and paint?"

He shook his head. "I don't believe you."

"I was there last night."

"How...?"

"Simone told me about it."

"Why did she keep it a secret from me?"

I felt for him, but I had no choice. "I think you need to level with me, Mr. Carmichael. Things were not perfect between you and Sarah, were they?"

He averted his eyes, looked at the cold fireplace. "All couples, Lacklan... We had our small problems. You can't live with someone day in, day out without small problems arising."

"I guess that's true. Only in this case it had gone beyond that, hadn't it?"

"No." He still wouldn't look at me. "That isn't true. We just needed to talk things through a little more."

"Did you know she was thinking of divorcing you?"

Now he looked at me and his face was savage. "You're lying! How could you possibly know that?"

"She discussed it with Simone the night she died."

"Simone is a lying bitch!"

"Is she? What makes you say that?"

His mouth worked, like the words wanted to come out, but he was fighting them. Eventually, he looked away. "She is a dissolute woman, decadent. She poisoned Sarah's mind."

"You think she was lying?"

"In all probability."

"Either way, she was at the studio. It's where she painted."

"Painted?" He narrowed his eyes at me again, like I was talking crazy, but I went on.

"Your wife was a talented watercolorist, and it seemed she was moving on to oils."

"This is madness!" He stood again and walked across the room, staring around as though he was searching for something that made sense. "I don't know this woman you are talking about! My wife had no interest in art! She never even spoke about it! Search the house! Where are the books, the paintings, the watercolors, the brushes? Where are they?"

"At her studio."

He swallowed.

I went on, "There was also a brand new duvet on her bed, brand new sheets, and a brand new rush mat under it. So new the bed legs had not even made an indentation. You should sit down for what I am about to tell you next."

His breathing was heavy. He returned to his chair and sat.

"What cigarettes did your wife smoke, Mr. Carmichael?"

"Sobranie, why?"

"What about you?"

"I don't smoke. The odd one, socially, whatever is going. I don't buy them."

"What was her drink?"

"White wine! Are you going to tell me what this is about?"

"Yes. I found an ashtray on her bedside table. It had two

cigarette butts in it. A Sobranie Black Russian and a Marlboro. There were rings on the tables, from a whiskey glass and a white wine glass. I found the glasses washed up in the kitchen, on the drying rack."

"Oh no..." His face crumpled and he shook his head. "Oh no, Lacklan, no. Don't do this to me."

He buried his face in his hands. Either it hurt or he was a damn good actor. I couldn't help wondering about where he had spent the night, at the Full Moon, but I guessed that didn't mean much. People have crazy ways of dealing with bereavement.

After a bit, he pulled a handkerchief from his pocket, dried his eyes and blew his nose.

"Forgive me, Lacklan. This has been a devastating shock. Do you mind if we continue another time?"

"I'm sorry, Mr. Carmichael, I'm afraid we aren't done yet. Time is one thing we haven't got." I reached in my pocket and pulled out the slug in the freezer bag. I dropped it on the table. "This was under the bed. It looks to me like a .38."

He gaped at it, picked it up, and examined it closely. "But you have to give this to Jackson. This changes everything." He frowned, shaking his head. "I don't understand."

I leaned forward, took it from his fingers and dropped it back in my pocket. "I am not giving this to Jackson. I can't put my finger on exactly why, but I don't trust him. He's too damned keen to ignore facts and go for his slam dunk." I sat back and tried again to read his face. It said he was really confused. I said, "Somebody was shot in that bed. The bedding and the mat were removed and probably dropped into the bayou."

"You think Sarah was killed *there?* That doesn't make any sense."

"Right now, nothing makes any sense. Bat Hays smokes Marlboro, but why the hell would he shoot Sarah at the studio and then come and frame himself at your house? None of it makes sense." I stood. "I have some things I need to do. When is the preliminary hearing?"

He seemed to gather his thoughts. "The day after tomorrow, the storm permitting."

TWELVE

OVERHEAD, THE CLOUDS WERE STARTING TO BOIL and twist, trailing long shreds and spitting rain. I climbed into the Zombie and caught a glimpse of Carmichael staring after me through the window. I pulled out of his drive onto Route 61 and turned right. I drove slowly, thinking.

The wind gusted and battered the car. I pulled out my cell and called Simone again. She still didn't answer.

Two minutes later, I pulled into her drive and parked in front of the steps to her veranda. The wind was strong enough to make me unsteady on my feet. I climbed the wooden steps and hammered on the door. She didn't answer, so I hammered again. I was pounding a third time, considering picking the lock, when the door opened. She didn't say anything. Her hair was rumpled and her eyes were puffy, and she was wrapped in a white satin robe.

"We need to talk."

"You need to talk. I need to sleep."

She turned and walked away, but she left the door open,

so I followed her into an airy room with broad windows and low, modern furniture. It should have been bright, but it was heavy with gloomy, gray light, and in the garden the silent trees bobbed and waved like dancing shrouds. She moved over to a bamboo and wicker trolley and started mixing herself a gin and tonic.

"I'm guessing it's too early for you," she said.

"Who was Sarah's lover?"

She froze with the bottle of Beefeater half way to the glass. Then she continued to pour.

"I told you she had no lovers."

"You lied."

"You have no manners." She added the tonic and turned to face me. "How dare you come into my house accusing me of lying?"

She said it without much feeling and sank into a large peacock chair. She had a small table beside the chair. On it, there was a pewter box. She opened it and took out a cigarette, placed it in her mouth and lit it with a match.

When she was done, I said, "I was at the studio last night."

Her face hardened. She avoided my eye. "Who let you in?"

"Me."

"So?"

"There had been a man there."

"How can you tell?"

I ignored the question. "He smokes Marlboro. Who is he?"

"I don't know what you're talking about."

"Maybe..." I paused. I walked to the couch and sat,

placing my elbows on my knees, studying her. She sipped and sighed, like it was doing her good. "Maybe you don't fully understand," I said.

She looked me over and waited.

"My friend is facing life in prison, or worse, for a murder he did not commit. This is a man I owe my life to several times over."

"Spare me the brothers in arms act, Lacklan. My sister just got murdered, remember?"

"And I'm trying to find out who did it, remember? And you and I both know you're lying and hiding something from me. But if you think I am going to stand aside and let Hays go down, just because you don't feel like talking..."

"What? What will happen if I think that?" It was a challenge, but it was a lame one.

I shook my head. "Don't do it. There is nothing—are you hearing me?—*nothing* I will stop at to save his life. You had better think this through, Simone. You want me on your side. You don't want me as an enemy."

She raised an eyebrow and sucked on her cigarette. "Am I supposed to be afraid?"

"You'd be wise to be."

She looked worried but tried to hide it.

"Work with me, Simone. Who was it? Who was her lover? Was it Hays?"

She rubbed her eyes and sighed. "You son of a bitch..." After a bit, she opened her eyes and studied me for a moment. "I'm sorry. I didn't mean that. Of course you want to help him, he's your friend."

"Was he her lover?"

"There was more than one. Satisfied?"

"Was Hays one of them?"

"I don't know. She didn't tell me about them."

"Why?"

She frowned. "What the hell do you mean, 'why'?"

I felt a pellet of anger start in my belly. "Come on, Simone! Snap out of it! You're her sister, her friend! She's telling you about her sex life with her husband, that she's considering divorcing him. You advise her about the studio and being creative, making a space for herself... You're intimate! For crying out loud! Why would she *not* tell you about her love affairs?"

She stared at me for a long moment, then looked away at the ashtray while she tapped ash. "God, you're relentless."

"Get used to it. Now answer the damn question."

"It's not relevant."

"I'll decide that."

"No! You will *not!*"

I raised my voice. "Sweetheart, I have the meanest son of a bitch attorney in Louisiana on my payroll. If you are worried about protecting your sister's reputation, you better get with the damned program. Because if I give him the studio on Solitude Road and her lovers, the yellow press are going to have a feeding frenzy right there, in the gutter. Now *talk!*"

Her eyes blazed. "You piece of..."

"*Yeah! I'm all that! What are you hiding from me, Simone?*"

She turned away. I could see the muscle in her jaw working. She stood and carried her glass to the window. I saw the glint of a tear on her cheek.

"I was very close to Sarah..."

"You were her sister."

"No, more than that. I..." She stopped, hesitated, took a deep breath. "When my mother married Geoff, her father —you know, normally, stepsiblings resent each other. There is a lot of jealousy and rejection. But Sarah wasn't like that. She had the sweetest, kindest nature you could imagine."

She turned to face me and sat on the sill.

"She missed her mother. They were very close. Geoff was distant, moral, upright... Just the kind of man my mother would go for."

"You're losing me. Where is this going?"

She sighed. "Sarah was lonely. So was I. When our parents married and we all moved in together, Sarah and I immediately formed a bond. We became friends, sisters. But as time went by I..." She held my eye for a long moment, willing me to understand and save her the shame of saying it. I didn't. I waited. Finally, she said, "I began to have feelings for her."

She stared down into her glass. She looked humiliated. My head was reeling.

"Was it mutual?"

She shook her head. "No. She had no idea."

I gave her a moment, trying to think it through. "So how is this relevant?"

"She had no idea until recently, when things started to fall apart between her and Charles. She used to come over in the evenings to talk. Sometimes we'd go out to listen to music. Sometimes we'd stay in, have dinner. She used to say I was her rock. She didn't know what she'd do without me." She heaved another huge sigh and finally looked at me. "You know, it's a lot easier for women to express affection to each other. A bit too easy sometimes."

She drained her drink and went back to the trolley. She stood dropping ice cubes into her glass. Then a slice of lemon. Then she poured the gin and the tonic. When she'd finished she stayed, staring down at what she'd put together, like she was wondering what it was doing in her hand.

"She was a very loyal woman. Very loyal and faithful, and she loved Charles. It was traumatic for her to realize that she was no longer in love with him. She used to cry, and I would comfort her. We hugged a lot."

She turned to face me. "If I had been a guy, I have no doubt we would have made love, even if she regretted it afterwards. One night, a few weeks back, a couple of months maybe. We were a bit drunk. She was tearful, telling me how much I meant to her. I misread the signs and tried to kiss her. She freaked."

I rubbed my face. "Holy shit... It wasn't complicated enough."

"What? You want me to apologize? I didn't just lose a sister..."

"I know. I'm sorry. What happened?"

"We made up. I apologized and she was all sweetness and understanding. But it was never quite the same again. She went a bit crazy. She said she wanted to reinvent herself, discover who she really was. She started painting more, spending time at her studio." She paused. "She also started seeing men. But, for obvious reasons, she never told me about them."

I asked the obvious question. "If she didn't tell you about them, how do you know?"

She gave a small, ironic laugh. "She told me she needed to see men. They were never more than one or two night stands. She would often ridicule them or put them down, as though she was trying to soften the blow for me, or tell me that I was somehow more special than they were. It was complicated, an emotional briar patch. The point is, she never named names."

I stood and went to the trolley. I poured myself a large whiskey. I stared out the window. It was barely midday but the sky was as dark as early evening, and growing darker.

"You think she was beginning to have feelings for you?"

I heard her voice, sullen behind me. "No. I don't think so. I think she was in shock. I was all she had left and I had abused our trust. She was desperately trying to find some firm foothold, some way of making sense of it. Like she said, she was trying to find out who she was."

I turned to face her. She was watching me. I said, "So, what about the painting?"

"I told you, that started shortly after..."

"Don't be cute, Simone."

She frowned. "What do you mean?"

"The big canvas. The nude."

Her frown deepened. "She didn't paint on canvas. She did watercolors."

"Simone, cut it out. There's a seven foot canvas at the studio. A nude."

She didn't answer for a bit. Her eyes flicked over my face. "You think it might be her killer?"

"I hope not."

"Why?"

"Because it's you, Simone."

Her hand went to her mouth and for a moment I thought she was going to collapse. She shook her head. "Don't say that. Please, Lacklan..."

I put down my glass and walked over to hunker down in front of her. "Simone, I don't know what the hell was going on between you and Sarah, and frankly it's none of my business. But one of these men that she was seeing murdered her and framed my friend. You may not realize it, but you know who it was. Somewhere in your head there is a clue to who did this."

They were the same words I had used with Bat the night before, and the irony of that fact did not escape me.

She got to her feet and walked away from me, standing in the middle of the floor, blinking away her tears, like she didn't know which way to turn. I came up behind her and held her shoulders in my hands, speaking close to her ear.

"You said she mocked them, ridiculed them. There must have been clues in the things she said, hints as to who they were. There can't have been that many of them..."

She leaned against me and rested the back of her head on my chest. "They were all black."

"Like Hays."

"She said it was an act of defiance against Charles. He is old school..." There was bitterness in her voice. "He still believes in segregation."

"But you didn't believe her."

"At first I did. But now that you've told me about the painting..." She turned around, keeping her body close to mine, and faced me. She placed one hand on my chest. "Maybe she was projecting her feelings for me onto them... Could it be...?"

"Who were these men, Simone? Try to think. There has to be some hint, something you remember."

Her eyes were distracted. Her body was pressing up against mine. I could smell the lemon from her drink on her breath. She frowned at me and touched my cheek with her fingers.

"Harry, one of them was Harry. She let slip that he ran a club. It had to be Harry."

Her fingers went up into my hair. My belly was on fire and my heart was pounding. When I spoke, my voice was thick. "Simone, don't do this..."

"Shut up and hold me," she said, and her mouth closed on mine.

THIRTEEN

I LAY STARING AT THE CEILING. THE OVERHEAD FAN turned with a throb like a slow pulse, but did nothing to cool the thin film of perspiration on my skin. Outside, I could hear the clatter and rattle of random objects, lifted up and dragged this way and that by the mounting gale. A moaning, wailing voice howled out of the sky, warning that bad things were going to happen.

Simone's head lay on my chest. She was snoring softly, her body clinging to mine, her bare skin hot under my hand. I taught myself a long time ago that guilt is a useless emotion. Sometimes remorse can lead you to fix something that you have done wrong, but all guilt ever does is twist you inside and make you bitter.

All I felt, then, was regret. She was the most beautiful woman I had ever known, and I had wanted her badly. But not like that, not then.

I slipped my arm from under her and made my way to

the bathroom, where I stood under a cold shower for five minutes, like I was trying to wash away my mistakes. But by the time I got out and toweled myself dry, they were still there. All of them.

She was awake, lying with the twisted sheet coiled around her like a snake. I stood in the bathroom doorway, leaning on the jamb, watching her watching me.

She said, "I'm sorry."

"Don't be. It is what it is."

She gave a humorless laugh. "You're not the romantic type, right?"

I picked my jeans up off the floor and pulled them on. "Are you?"

She sat up, dragged the sheet up around her to cover herself. "I don't know. I never had the chance to find out."

"I'm sorry. I was never the man to find out with."

"Do you regret it, Lacklan?"

I bent down and picked up my shirt. "Do you?"

Now she laughed with more humor and I smiled. It was a nice laugh.

"*I'm* the psychiatrist, remember? I'm the one who is supposed to answer every question with another question." The smile faded. "Do you regret what we have done?"

I pulled on my shirt and started buttoning it up.

"No. But I wish we had done it at another time, for another reason."

She looked sad and turned away. "If it's any consolation, so do I. Maybe..." She watched me pull on my boots. "Maybe when this is over..."

"Yeah, maybe then."

. . .

I WENT DOWN to my car with anger twisting inside that I did not understand. I hit 100 MPH going back up 61 and wound through the empty streets of Burgundy till I came to St. Claude Avenue. I parked outside the Blue Lagoon and walked down Desiré to the entrance. I was surprised to find it open, and pushed through the door. It was empty, except for Harry polishing glasses behind the bar. He flashed me a grin.

"We're closed, my friend, and I don't know if we gonna be open tonight. But seein' as you braved Sarah to get here, I guess I have to give you a drink. What'll it be?"

I sat on a stool and put my elbows on the bar. "Give me a Bushmills, Harry, straight up. Make it a large one."

He put the tumbler in front of me and a bowl of peanuts, uncorked the Irish and poured me a generous measure.

"You Bartholomew's friend, right?"

"Yup. Lacklan."

"That's bad, what they doin' to him."

I nodded. "I know he loved her," I said. "But I also know he didn't kill her." I shrugged and took a sip. "When you serve with a man as long as I served with Bat, you get to know him. Besides..." I put a smile on the right side of my face, where it looked rueful. "He's a trained assassin, Harry..."

He looked at me like I'd just said he was from Mars. "Bartholomew? A trained assassin?" He burst out laughing. It was a high-pitched screech of a laugh. "What you tellin' me?"

"Eight years in special ops."

"Well, I knew he was in some British special ops unit, but a trained *assassin?*"

I nodded. "The SAS is not just a military regiment. It does a lot of..." I paused to give it meaning. "*Specialized* work. If Bat had wanted to kill her, he would have made a clean job of it. This..." I shook my head in disgust. "This is amateur. This is a mess."

"Man. You're serious."

"Sure I am. Say, what kind of woman was this Sarah? I heard she slept around a bit?"

He grinned. "I ain't no gossip. And she was discreet. I'll give her that. She had class, know what I'm sayin'? She was never scandalous. Never made a scene. She'd come in, listen to the jazz. And you always knew when she had chosen some dude. She'd let it be known, know what I mean? She'd let it be known real cool, with a look or a smile. And after a bit, she would leave."

I smiled. "You're kidding. Really? And how would they know where to go? I'm guessing she didn't take them home. She was married, right?"

"Oh, she was married all right, and Mr. Carmichael ain't none too fond of colored folk. He was civil enough, but he believed in segregation."

I frowned like I didn't understand. "Segregation? What's that got to do with it?"

"Oh, man, she didn't like white boys. The woman had taste!" He laughed. "She liked her men of the dark persuasion. You wouldn't stand *no* chance!"

He laughed again and I smiled. "How about you? You ever get the wink and the nod?"

He was still laughing his high-pitched laugh. "She would

discreetly slip you her number. An' you would call, and she would tell you where to go. It was kind of exciting."

"So you did, you old dog!"

He slammed the bar with his palm. "Man! She was hot. I went once. You never went more than twice. That was the word. I went once."

"When was that?"

His laughter died away. He chuckled a couple of times and then wagged his finger at me. "Uh-uh, no way, man. No way! I see what you're doin'. I see where you're goin'. No, uh-uh. I'm gonna ask you to *leave* now."

"What's the matter, Harry? We're just sharing old war stories. You were one of the privileged few. When did you go see her?"

His face had gone like stone. "Get out, man."

I shook my head. "No, Harry. I'm afraid not. You're going to talk to me, and you are going to tell me what I need to know. Don't fight me, 'cause this is only ever going to end one way. Be smart."

He leaned under the bar. I knew what he was going to do before he knew it himself. As he swung the shotgun over the counter I slammed it down with my left hand, then yanked savagely on it and gripped the barrel under my arm, making him lurch forward. At the same time I caught the side of his head in a right cross that made his mouth sag and his eyes dilate.

His legs had gone to jelly. He was struggling not to fall. I vaulted over the bar, grabbed the hair at the back of his head and smashed his face down on the bar twice. I heard him gasp, "Oh God..."

I leaned close to his ear and snarled, "Now, this can go

one of two ways, Harry. You choose. I can stick that shotgun up your ass and blow your brains out of the top of your head, or you can talk to me. What's it going to be?"

"Don't hurt me anymore, man, I'll talk to you. Just don't hurt me no more."

I grabbed him by the scruff of his neck and dragged him from behind the bar to the nearest table. I sat him down, then collected my whiskey and the shotgun and went and sat opposite him.

"When d'you sleep with her?"

"It was about a month ago. I don't remember exactly. It was difficult for me." He gestured at the room around him. "I have the club..."

"So who else? Was there anyone who got real sweet on her?"

He swallowed and looked scared. "Bartholomew. He was pretty sweet on her, man. She invited him over twice. She liked him, too. Liked the way he played the horn. I thought they was gonna get serious."

"Yeah, I know about that. Who else?"

His eyes became abstracted. "There was that guy. I can't remember his name. He wasn't from round here."

"You shining me on?"

"No man, I's serious. He was from out of town somewhere. Not from Burgundy. He came in most nights for a couple of weeks."

"How long ago?"

He frowned. "Now you mention it, it was just before she died. But she wasn't here that night. Neither was he."

"I know. What was this guy's name? What did he look like?"

"He was tall, real tall, maybe six three or four, slim, but you could tell he was strong. Like whipcord, know what I mean? What was his name? It wasn't his real name. It was a nickname, like Snake or Blade, somethin' like that."

"And Sarah liked him?"

"She liked him a lot. I think she liked him because he looked dangerous. A lot of women go for that. He had them black glasses, like Ray Charles, and that big grin with all them real white teeth..." He snapped his fingers. "Ivories, or Ivory, that was his name. Ivory. I remember now. On account of his teeth. 'Cause they was so white."

"Ivory."

"That was his name. She was into him, big time. I think she saw him more than twice." He frowned again, like he was trying to remember something. "I think him an' Hays was friends. He was askin' me about him one night, and they got talkin'."

"No kidding. Where can I find this grinning snake?"

He shook his head. "I swear I don't know. He came into town for a couple of weeks. Then he vanished. I never seen him before or since."

"If I find you are lying to me, Harry, bad things are going to happen. Do you fully understand what that means?"

He nodded several times at high speed. "I never seen him before and I never seen him since. I swear, man."

I broke open the shotgun, took out the shells, and put them in my pocket. I shoved the weapon across the table at him. "This wasn't necessary. We could have gotten here without the violence. I just wanted to ask you some questions."

He spread his hands. "Sorry, man. I thought you wanted to put me in the frame..."

"Water under the bridge, but Harry? Don't ever pull a weapon on me again. I have no more questions I need answering. You understand me...?" He looked queasy as the meaning of my words sank in. I nodded and put a hundred bucks on the table. "Let's be friends instead. Be smart."

I stepped out into Desiré. In the alley it was almost as dark as night, still and quiet aside from an occasional breeze that moved the trash on the ground. But on St. Claude Avenue, at the end of the cul-de-sac, there was an unearthly whistling and howling. Somewhere, a shutter had come loose and it was hammering with an incessant rhythm. To me in that moment, it sounded like a daemon trying to break out of his infernal cell.

I walked to my car, leaning into the battering air. This was not the hurricane yet. This was just the gale. The real storm was yet to come. I got behind the wheel, closed the door and fired up the powerful engines.

Ivory.

The guy who'd asked about Bat at the bar, the guy who'd offered him the job and taken him to the warehouse, the guy who'd tricked him into putting his prints on the murder weapon. But I was remembering, I'd heard his name somewhere else. I'd been too tired and preoccupied at the time to register it. I was real mad at myself. I could see Sergeant Bradley's crimson face in my mind's eye, scowling at me and roaring in his Kiwi accent, "*It's sloppy, fucking carelessness like that, Walker, that gets men killed! Get your fucking act together!*"

He wasn't kidding. I moved down Main Street and

turned left onto Route 61, into the storm. Get your fucking act together, Walker. I remembered where I had heard the name. Only it wasn't Ivory, it was Ive, and a cute babe with Afro hair had told me he sold coke, at the Full Moon.

I wondered if Simone would have called that Jungian synchronicity.

FOURTEEN

I PULLED OFF THE ROAD ABOUT A MILE FROM THE Full Moon, in the lee of a wall of bowing trees and, with my clothes and hair flapping around me, I went to the trunk. I opened it and pulled open my kit bag.

Kenny had been my father's manservant and butler as long as I had been alive. He was family to me, more than family, because where my family had all turned their backs on me, he never had. He had stayed the course and been a true, loyal friend. When my father had died, I had inherited his house and his fortune, and Kenny had come as part of the package[1]. He was happy about the arrangement, and so was I.

I had asked him to prepare me a kit bag, and he knew what that meant. There were my two Sig Sauer p226 Tacops, a Heckler & Koch assault rifle, my take-down hickory bow with twelve aluminum broad-heads, the Smith & Wesson

1. See *Dawn of the Hunter* and *Double Edged Blade*

500, a couple of cakes of C4, and enough ammunition for a short war, plus a couple of bugs and tracking devices. The man knew me better than I knew myself.

I selected a Sig, checked it was loaded, and removed the safety. Then, I slipped it under my jacket in my waistband and climbed back in the car.

Like the Blue Lagoon, the Full Moon was still open for business, but there was practically nobody there, save an old guy sitting in the corner over a beer, and the barman. I leaned on the bar and he came over.

"What'll it be?"

"Give me a beer. Surprised you're open. Everybody seems to be closing shop and running north."

He shrugged. "We've had these scares before. These storms, they hit the coast and stay there. It's gonna be rough on New Orleans, maybe Baton Rouge will get some damage. But not all the way up here." He cracked a bottle and handed it to me. "You want a glass?"

I shook my head. "They're saying it's the worst storm in history."

"Sure. Two hundred and thirty mile an hour winds. But by the time it hits land, it's gonna be a tropical storm, lots a'rain, but only gale force winds."

I nodded like he was wise. "Hope you're right. Say, I'm looking for Ive, he around?"

"Who's askin'?"

"Name's Walker. I was in here last night. I had a drink with a cute chick, short, Afro hair..."

He shrugged and made a face that said I was boring him. "There are a lot of cute chicks in this bar. We're famous for it."

"She said Ive was the man to see for a bit of blow."

"Come back tonight. I don't know who the hell you talkin' about, but all kinds of people show up here at night. You know what I'm sayin'?"

"Sure."

He eyed me sidelong while he washed some glasses.

"You're new in the district. I ain't seen you around."

I grinned. "I came down for the storm."

He looked at me like he wanted to hit me. "You came down for the storm?"

"Climate change. It's the big thing, man. My editor wanted me to cover it."

"You're a long way from the storm, friend. Storm's in New Orleans."

"Yeah, and you got every network and paper in the country covering it. What you're going to find in the *New York Times* is how climate change is affecting the lives of people who live on the periphery. How is the storm affecting *your* life and business..."

I gestured at his empty bar.

He looked skeptical. "You're with the *New York Times*?"

I nodded. "You know, you're right. The storm will drop from hurricane to tropical storm when it makes landfall, but..." I counted out on my fingers. "One, it's out of season by two months. Two, it's diameter is *one thousand miles*, so even if it drops to tropical storm from hurricane, it isn't the wind you need to be worrying about. It's the rain. Now, I ask you, how is severe flooding in Louisiana in November going to affect..." I counted out on my fingers again. "Cotton, pecan, sugarcane..." I gave a humorless laugh. "And I don't need to remind you that Exxon is right there, *on* the

Mississippi in Baton Rouge. So the point my editor wants to make is that, wherever you are in Louisiana, this storm is going to affect you." I nodded several times. "Let's face it, wherever you are in the U.S.A., this storm is going to affect you."

He watched me throughout the speech, a cloth in one hand and a glass in the other. When I'd finished, he went back to polishing.

"I hadn't thought about it like that."

I drained my beer and laid some money on the bar. "Thanks. I'll see you tonight."

"Yeah, man."

My cell rang as I was reaching the door. It was Hirschfield.

"Yeah."

"I got the sample."

I frowned. "That's too quick. It's less than twenty-four hours."

"I know. I called the DA and asked him what the hell is going on. He blamed the storm. Said there's not much work coming in to the lab. I told him bullshit and he said that, as well as that, Carmichael has influential friends—him among them—and they want to expedite things. He heard about your crackpot theory and wants you to prove to yourself that it's horseshit."

"You believe any of that?"

"I believe they have a reason for us to get the sample fast. They don't want delays. They want the conviction in the bag."

I thought about it for a moment. "Who'd he hear it from?"

"My guess is Jackson."

"Yeah. Where are you?"

"At the hotel."

"I'm coming over."

"Suit yourself."

I drove fast. The roads were empty and I made it in a few minutes. As I stepped through the door of the Soniat into the internal patio, Luis called to me, "Mr. Walker, Mr. Hirschfield, he is waiting for you in the bar."

I found him at his usual table, behind the fern.

"Have a drink, talk to me."

"No. Where's the sample?"

He scowled, pulled a padded manila envelope from his hip pocket and handed it to me. "What are you going to do with it?"

I didn't look at him. I opened the envelope and looked inside. There was a glass vial with blood-stained cloth in it. "I'm flying to Washington. I'll be back tomorrow or the day after."

"Flying? In this weather?"

"I'll fly from Jackson, Mississippi."

He sighed heavily through his nose. "This is getting complicated, Lacklan. We need to talk."

I shook my head. "You need to talk. I don't."

"I just told you this is getting complicated. You know what that means?"

"Yeah, Hirschfield, I know what it means. It means people are getting involved that you didn't expect to get involved. People you play golf with."

"Don't be a smartass."

"You tell me what it means, then."

"It means this is more than just a guy killing a woman out of sexual jealousy."

"I know that. I'm glad you realize it now." I hesitated. "Stay onside, Hirschfield. You don't want me as an enemy."

He looked mad. "Take a hike, Walker, and don't be so damn fast to insult and threaten people. I'm scared of you!"

I nodded once, then left.

I stepped out into the wind and the dying light again, climbed in my car and hit the ignition. There was a short, staccato blast of a siren, and the inside of my car was flooded with red and blue light. I looked in my mirror and saw a patrol car behind me. I killed the engine and opened the window.

Jackson climbed out the passenger side of the car, and hugging his flapping jacket to his chest, leaning into the wind, he walked around to talk to me.

"Get out!"

"Why?"

"Because I'm telling you to! Come inside! We need to talk!"

I sighed and followed him into the shelter of the hotel entrance.

"What do you want, Jackson?"

"I want to know where you're going."

"What goddamn business is that of yours?"

"I can make it my business, Walker. If I look through your vehicle and find..."

"It'll be the last thing you ever do as cop. You want to know where I'm going? I'm going to D.C., to talk to friends and have this sample analyzed." I held up the manila envelope for him to see. "It's the blood from the crime scene. You got any more questions for me, talk to my attorney. He's in the bar. Now get out of my way, Jackson."

I went to move and he put his hand on my chest.

"Wait a minute." He jerked his head at the envelope and narrowed his eyes. "What the hell do you think you're going to find?"

I held his eye for a count of three. Then, I shook my head.

"It's too late for that, Jackson. You had your chance to be a cop and you blew it. Now you're no more than paid muscle with a badge. I told you before, when I bring your masters down, I'm bringing you down with them. Next time you put a hand on me, I'm going to break your arm in three places. Now get out of my way."

Jackson, Mississippi is north of Burgundy. I took Main Street to Route 61 and headed south toward Baton Rouge like I had all the hounds of hell snapping at my ass. It took me fifteen minutes to reach the outskirts of the city. The wind was crazy and getting crazier the further south I went. That meant the roads were deserted. At Southern University, I turned onto the I-110 and hit 120 MPH through the city. Nobody tried to pull me over. There was nobody there to try. It took me three minutes to reach the Horace Wilkinson Bridge, and less than thirty seconds to cross it.

Then I floored the pedal, heading west along the I-10. It was two hundred and fifty miles of straight road to Houston, and I aimed to do it in two hours.

FIFTEEN

On the way, I called a private lab I'd heard about in Houston. I knew that getting DNA results from forensic labs was not like the movies. Through official channels, it would take four weeks minimum. I didn't have four weeks. I didn't even have four days. I needed to cut corners, whether it meant pulling strings or bribing people, I didn't give a damn. I could feel the hyenas closing in and I needed to act fast.

I talked to three labs without success and finally, after half an hour, I found a place on South Voss Road, the CCD Lab, in the west of the city. They claimed they could produce results in one to two days. I told the girl I was willing to pay well over the odds for a fast result and she put me through to Dr. Glendinning, the head of the lab. I explained to her that my case was urgent, and that whatever the lab's normal fee was, I was willing to pay double if they could get me results in twenty-four hours.

She was quiet for a moment, then said, "What is your name, sir?"

I hesitated less than a second, then told her, "Captain Lacklan Walker."

She liked the rank and I heard the smile in her voice. "Just give them your name at reception and I'll come and meet you myself."

I hung up and took a deep breath. I was flying by the seat of my pants, but so far I hadn't crashed.

I followed the I-10 onto the Katy Freeway, past the Memorial Park, and took exit 760 onto Voss Road. It was five PM and raining. I drove south for three miles and finally came to the building—an eight-story glass and concrete monolith set in its own parking lot.

The CCD Labs took up the whole of the eighth floor. I rode the elevator to the seventh floor and stepped out into a lobby that would have looked more at home in a Hollywood representation of a palace in Atlantis. The floor was dark green marble under a vaulted ceiling. The walls were white marble and there were Greco-Roman frames around all the doors. My boots were loud as I crossed the large, echoing space and leaned on the green and white marble reception desk. I smiled and told the pretty Texan girl behind the desk that I was Captain Lacklan Walker, there to see Dr. Glendinning.

She picked up the phone and smiled at me with very white teeth. While she waited for Dr. Glendinning to answer, she told me she hoped I was having a nice day. I told her not really and she creased her eyes, like I'd said I was.

"Dr. Glendinning? Captain Walker is here for you."

She appeared after a few minutes through tall walnut

doors. She was about five ten, with red hair and a nice body. She was wearing a white lab coat and an expensive blue suit underneath it. When she saw my jeans and my sweatshirt, the twitch of her eyebrows told me that in her world, captains don't dress like tramps.

I raised an eyebrow to her twitch and we shook hands.

"Dr., can we talk somewhere in private? This is a very urgent matter."

Again the frown, but she nodded and said, "Sure, let's go to my office."

I followed her among echoing footfalls, through the same walnut doors into a less glamorous world of beige carpets and functional furniture. She showed me into the cubicle she called her office and sat behind her desk. I sat opposite her and pulled out two samples: the one Hirschfield had given me, and the one I had taken myself from the bed where Sarah's body had been found.

"Dr. Glendinning, I don't care how much this costs. I need this done by tomorrow afternoon. I can't tell you what it's about, but I can tell you that a man's life depends on getting the results immediately. If you need official confirmation, I can give you a number at the Pentagon that you can call." I took Ben's card from my wallet and put it in front of her. It was a bluff, but she had no way of knowing that. When she'd taken it in, I smiled and said, "But then the price will be capped."

She smiled back for a moment without speaking, then she said, "The simplest way I can think of to do this, Captain Walker, is if I take you personally as a private client. I will still have access to the full range of forensic tools that we use here. Does that sound acceptable?"

"It sounds perfect." I pushed the two samples across the desk to her. "I need to know if these samples match, and I need the DNA profile on each one of them." I pointed at the one Hirschfield had gotten from the DA and said, "I'd like you to label that one 'DA', and this one," I pointed at my own, "Walker. When will you have the results?"

"Tomorrow afternoon. About three. If you give me a number, I'll call you."

"Can you email me the preliminary results when you have them?"

She nodded. "I can do that." Then, she smiled a little ruefully. "But I was kind of hoping you'd come and pick them up yourself."

Obviously, she'd decided she liked the way captains dressed in my world. "I'll remember that next time I'm in Houston."

I walked through the drizzle down to Westheimer Road and found a small Italian restaurant. I found a table by the window and had a beer and a pizza. As I sat and ate, I tried to organize my thoughts. A voice in my head kept telling me that there were things that made no sense. But then I reminded myself, they made perfect sense to somebody, somewhere—they made perfect sense to Sarah's killer. What didn't make sense was the way I was looking at it. I had to look at it in a different way. I had to try and see it from the killer's point of view.

I'd been focusing too hard on the question of whether Bat had killed Sarah. But that wasn't the real question. Why? Because I already knew that he hadn't. I was going over the same ground in different ways, trying to find new ways to prove what I already knew.

So what was the real question? Who killed Sarah?

I took a pull on my beer and stared out at the wet road and the steady flow of traffic. Somehow, that didn't feel like the right question either. I asked myself why not? I leaned back and stretched out my legs. Because.

Because...

I circled around it for a while and finally settled on it. Because in my gut I could feel that she was not the intended victim. I had felt it almost from the start.

Then something clicked.

Simone. Simone had said that Carmichael and Sarah were sleeping in separate rooms. But the body was in the master bedroom. Carmichael was in denial about the break up of his marriage. He wanted everybody to believe they were fine. So he had made no mention of the fact that she was not in her own room, to do so would have been to admit they had problems. Maybe the poor sap wanted to believe she had finally returned to their conjugal room that night for a reconciliation. Who knows? Maybe she had. But the fact remained, she should not have been in that bed. He should.

Had the killer known that? According to Simone, all of Burgundy knew it. My head was reeling. It meant something, but I couldn't see what. I tried to consider it from all angles.

I had called him a poor sap, but Simone had insisted that Sarah loved her husband, even if she'd stopped being in love with him. Had she then, after all, after her crisis with Simone, after the shock of discovering that her stepsister—the woman and friend on whom she relied emotionally—was in love with her, had she decided to attempt a reconciliation with Carmichael? Had she gone willingly to his bed, to wait for him to return? Was that the reason she had gone home early and not gone to the jazz club?

If that was right, then those four shots were almost certainly not intended for Sarah, but for Carmichael.

So far that made perfect sense, and if it was right, the question became not who wanted Sarah dead, but who wanted Carmichael dead? For a moment, my mind strayed to the Full Moon, and Ivory. Did Carmichael have associates there who had reason to want him eliminated? Had he upset people there? Had Ivory heard about Bat's past from Harry and decided, if he could not employ him, to frame him for the murder he intended to commit? Had he then entered Carmichael's house and, thinking he was shooting him, shot his own lover instead?

It was possible, but it left unexplained what had happened at Solitude, at the studio. Who had been shot at the studio? Who had changed the mattress, the bedding and the mat, but left the glasses and the ashtray? And how did they come to use the same gun that had killed Sarah?

It was not synchronicity, Jungian or otherwise. This had to be the same killer's hand at work. Whoever had killed Sarah, wittingly or not, was responsible for cleaning up a similar crime scene at Solitude.

Two crime scenes, only one body that I knew of. One crime scene incompetently cleaned up, the other incompetently attempting to frame Bat, with excessive amounts of blood, and displaying shots both highly accurate and incompetently wild.

I looked down at the pepperoni pizza growing cold on the plate in front of me, picked up a piece, and took a bite. What was the real question? What was the question—what were the questions—I should be asking? Not did Bat kill Sarah. Not who killed Sarah. But, was Sarah the intended victim? Was Charles Carmichael the intended victim? And, what happened at Solitude?

I looked at my watch. It was after six PM and already getting dark outside. I paid my check and stepped out into the evening rain. As I walked up South Voss, my mind went back to the Full Moon. Maybe I was clearer on the questions I should be asking, but there were still two big, glaring coincidences that did not fit into any explanation I had come up with yet.

One was the second, apparent murder scene at Solitude. The other was that on the day I had tailed Carmichael, he had wound up, late that night, secluded in a private bar at the very club where Ivory sold coke. Ivory, who had tried to recruit Bat Hayes, Ivory whom Bat had refused to implicate, Ivory who had been Sarah's lover just before she died—Ivory who was rapidly climbing the scales as my number one suspect.

One thing at least was clear. Maybe I didn't know what to ask, or what the likely answer would be, but I sure as hell knew *who* to ask.

If the road leading out of Baton Rouge had been practically empty, the road leading in was totally deserted. Ninety percent of the traffic out was headed north. But there was literally zero traffic in, from any direction. Except me.

The I-10 from Houston to Baton Rouge is pretty much a straight line all the way. So, as I came out of the city, past Hog Island, I floored the pedal, delivering one thousand eight-hundred foot-pounds of torque to the back wheels, and felt the surge of power crush me back into the seat as I watched the needle rise from 70 MPH to 170, in little more than a second. She wanted to do more, but I wanted to arrive alive.

The Zombie hurtled through the night, its powerful beams punching two amber cones through the darkness. What started out as light rain in Texas, grew heavier as we approached the Mississippi. After an hour, I could feel the wind, screaming in off the Gulf, battering the car, threatening to drive me off the road. Eventually, I had to slow, or risk being overturned by the gale. Even so, I made it in two hours.

I slowed to 100 MPH over the Wilkinson Bridge and sped through the desolate city, north toward St. Francisville. There, the tires screamed as I slowed to 60 MPH and turned sharp right at the crossroads onto Jackson Road, and covered the six miles to the Full Moon in less than five minutes.

I pulled into the lot with my heart pounding. There were trucks and cars there, but not many. The wind was easily gale force and mounting, and though the rain was less than it had been down by the Gulf, it was enough to wet my face and soak my shirt as soon as I climbed out of the car. The sky was black, but shaded with orange in the west, and through the darkness, lights winked across the fields where the trees and hedgerows were bowed across them by the wind. I pulled up my collar and headed for the bar.

That was when the door opened and four guys stepped out.

SIXTEEN

They were big, and not the kind of guys you'd want your sister to bring home. They came down the steps and spread out with the rain glistening on their faces. I glanced at each one in turn and calibrated them.

When guys surround you planning to give you a beating, you can always be sure that the one who stays in front of you is Alpha. Take him down and you have a psychological advantage over the others. This Alpha was six-three with a chest like a beer barrel and arms that were grotesquely deformed from working out in a gym. If he got you in a bear hug he'd crush your ribs. His hips were narrow and his legs were thin compared with the rest of his body. He probably had no staying power, but he wasn't going to need it, not where I was sending him. He stood in front of me in the drizzle, bending his little knees.

Two of the other guys peeled off to my left. They were big, too, but not as big. The one who headed behind me liked his beer. He had a gut and I knew he would be slow.

The other one, the one who stayed on my left flank, was slim, but muscular. Athletic. He had a black goatee and you could tell by his eyes and the way he moved that he liked to use a knife.

That left the guy on my right. He wasn't black, he was Latino, shorter than the others, aggressive and wanting to prove himself. He was going down second, then the Gut. Goatee would be last.

I said, "What's this about, guys? Is there a problem?"

Alpha answered, wiping trickles of rain from his eyes, "You the problem, man. We gonna put an end to that problem. Got a message for you. Go home. Get outta here."

I smiled. "Oh, you're not going to kill me? That's a mistake. Who's the message from?"

He telegraphed it long before he did it. It was in the expression of contempt on his face, it was in the small step he took with his left foot, and the way he dropped his hand to his right pocket. By the time he'd said, "I ain't got time for this shit..." I had already run two steps toward him.

I guess they'd expected me to run away after he'd taken the blade from his pocket. Instead, I ran toward him before he'd had the chance to pull it. He was frowning in surprise as I made the scissor kick and smashed the heel of my boot into his jaw. He went straight over backward, with a big *whoomph!* in the mud. I turned as I landed. I knew Latino and Goatee would react first. Goatee was more athletic, but Latino was more dangerous, because he had the attitude. They came at me from both sides while the Gut lumbered forward through the puddles.

Goatee had a blade in his right hand, held low, and Latino was swinging his right fist at me in a wide arc. I caught the glint of brass on his knuckles and stepped inside the arc of his punch with my left raised and rigid. As his fist slammed behind my back I wrapped my arm around his, pressing his elbow hard against my side and bringing my hand up under his armpit. His face was just a couple of feet from mine and I rammed the heel of my hand into his chin. I heard the crunch of teeth and saw blood ooze from his lips. Goatee was already on me and I swung Latino viciously around into his path, shoved hard and gave him a kick in his solar plexus for good measure.

While they stumbled against each other, the Gut came rolling up and hurled himself at me. A take down is most men's preferred way to fight, so nine times out of ten, they will grab hold of you with both hands to try and drag you to the ground. That is their most vulnerable moment, because they have no weapons, and you have all of yours available.

The Gut charged me and grabbed hold of my jacket. I took a big step back, pulling him with me, and jabbed hard with my knuckles into his windpipe. His eyes bulged when he realized he couldn't breathe. I shoved him aside as he bent double, clawing at his throat. I'd come back for him later.

Goatee was pushing Latino out of the way so he could run at me. I shoved my left hand at his face so he wouldn't see the kick coming from my right foot. I smashed the heel of my boot into his kneecap, and as he bent double with the pain, I grabbed his right wrist and twisted his arm, pressing the palm of my left hand against the joint. He didn't want to let go of the knife so I rammed my left forearm into his elbow and broke it.

Then, he dropped the knife and let out a small, gasping scream. But by then, I had his hair in my left hand and I'd pulled the Fairbairn and Sykes from my boot. I keep it razor sharp and it slipped easily through his jugular and out through his windpipe. He gurgled and bled out in a few seconds.

Latino was recovering, staggering to his feet. I took a single step toward him and rammed the blade hard into his fifth intercostal, on his left side. He went into spasm for a moment, as his heart seized on the blade, then he slid off the knife.

The Gut had collapsed onto his face in the mud and was writhing in pain, so I broke his vertebrae with a kick to the back of his neck and ended it for him. That left the big guy. I stepped over to him and finished the job with my knife. Not much blood drained into the puddles beneath him, where the neon sign for the Full Moon danced and rippled in the rain. He was probably dead already. A kick like that can break your neck.

I collected their watches, their knives, and Latino's knuckle dusters, plus a few other tokens, put them in my pocket, and stepped into the bar.

It wasn't crowded. There was no band tonight, but there were maybe a dozen people there, or a little more. The bartender looked surprised to see me, but not in a good way. Maybe he'd thought I was going home. I smiled at him.

"That wind is getting pretty crazy out there. Gimme a beer, will you? Say, is Ive in yet?"

He cracked a bottle for me and put it on the bar. Now he looked worried. "Yeah, he's in back. But you can't go in there."

I gave him an idiot grin. "I can't or I mayn't?"

He made a face like brain-ache. "*What?*"

"Well, you see? I may not, means I have no permission. I can't means that physically, I am not able." I held his eye. "I'm pretty sure that physically I am able. What do you think?"

He swallowed. "It's private, members only."

"How do I become a member? See, I'm in the mood for a hand of poker or two." I leaned across the bar, leered at him and spoke in a very quiet voice. "I'll tell you what's going to happen, pal. Either you can let me in to the back room, so I can play cards with the boys, or I can tear your heart out of your chest and sit here and eat it while I blow your patrons' heads off. Now, I'm telling you that Ive will want to see me, because I have things I need to discuss with him. So you make a smart decision about what you're going to do next."

He stared at me for what seemed like a long time, but was probably no more than four or five seconds. Eventually, a voice from down the bar, calling for a beer, seemed to bring him around. He glanced at the guy, said, "I'm coming," and stepped out from behind the bar to look out the front door. I turned on my stool and watched him gaze out into the wind and the rain. He turned back to stare at me. Now he looked scared.

I said, "How about it?"

I followed him across the room, past the stage, to the door marked private. He opened it with a key and stepped in and spoke quietly to some people I couldn't see. I stayed close, with my hand on the butt of my Sig behind my back. After a moment, he glanced at me and left without saying anything. I stepped through the open door.

The room was maybe twenty feet square. There were

two girls on the right, sitting on a couch at the foot of some stairs that climbed to the next floor. They had a coffee table in front of them with a small, dusty mirror on it. There was another mirror on the wall beside me, in a steel frame. On my left, there was a window.

Ahead of me, there was a red, vinyl bar backed with more mirrors, and a coat rack with four coats; and between me and the bar there was a large, round table with six men seated around it. They were all watching me, they were all smoking, and each one had a glass of either rum or whiskey. Ivory was hard to miss. He was facing me just as Trixy had described him, like a snake. Sitting in front of him was a box of Marlboro cigarettes.

I glanced at the other men around the table. They were all between forty and sixty and well dressed. One of them was black, the other four were WASPs.

I hooked the door with my heel and slammed it closed. I saw a few eyebrows twitch. I nodded at the table.

"What's the stake?" Nobody said anything. I pointed at the snake. "You Ivory?"

"This is a private club, mister. You ain't been invited."

"What's the stake?"

He glanced at his companions. They were getting nervous. He grinned suddenly. His teeth were very white. "Five grand. If you got that much on you, pull up a chair."

"Is that all?" I took a couple of steps over to the table, between two of the suits. "I figure I'd like to raise the stakes, Ivory."

I reached in my pocket and pulled out the four watches I'd taken from his goons. I dropped them on the table and looked around. They were all frowning at the timepieces, except Ivory. He was looking at my face.

"What would you say these watches are worth, Ivory?"

"They ain't worth shit. If they were, they wouldn't be on my table."

One of the WASPs, a guy with permed, silver hair, shrugged. "A grand, at most."

I smiled at him and pulled out the three knives and the knuckle dusters, tossed them on the table. "How about if we throw these in, Ivory? That increase the stake at all?"

The permed WASP scowled. "What is this? Who is this clown?"

Ivory said, "Don't talk, Bill." To me, he said, "Your stake still ain't worth squat. I suggest you turn around and go home before you find yourself out of your depth."

I looked at the black lenses of his sunglasses and saw myself reflected there. I thought of Bat Hays, waiting back at his house, waiting to know whether he would spend the rest of his life behind bars, whether he was to have his own life taken from him; waiting to find out exactly what this son of a bitch had done to him, secretly, behind his back, slithering and hissing in the dark corners of his world.

I reached in my pocket again and pulled out four blood-stained thumbs. I tossed them on the table. A couple of them bounced once and settled. There was a second of absolute silence, then a collective gasp and the four WASPs backed up and stood. A chair keeled over and hit the floor. Bill said, "Holy shit!"

Ivory and the guy I knew was his right hand man looked at the thumbs and looked serious. There was a sudden bustling and the four WASPs made for the door, grabbing their coats, blustering about how they didn't need this kind of shit and Ivory had better get his damned act together. They wrenched the door open and stormed out, closing it behind them.

"How's that stake doing, Ive?"

"You out of your depth, Walker."

I shook my head. "Ive, you have no idea. I am the ocean. You? You're a babe in arms lost at sea. I am going to give you a chance. Tell me what happened to Sarah Carmichael, tell me what your connection is with Charles Carmichael, tell me what happened at Solitude, what happened that night, and I won't kill you."

His companion grinned. Ivory leaned back and opened his big mouth. His teeth really were very large and very white. He laughed a long, wheezing, high-pitched laugh. Then, he flopped his head forward and giggled quietly. Finally, he grinned at his companion.

"Yo-yo, it seems that Sarah is going to take all kinds of people down with her. She is one mother of a *bad* storm." Then, he turned to me and his smile faded. "Get the hell out of here."

I gave my head a small shake. "You made the wrong choice."

I left the club and stepped out into the black storm. The four bodies were still there, saturated by the rain with their wet clothes flapping in the wind. Ivory was right about one thing. Sarah was going to take a lot of people down with her.

SEVENTEEN

By the time I got back to the Soniat, the rain had started in earnest. All the way there, the windshield wipers had been beating a rhythm like a panicking heart, trying to push away the deluge. But they were overwhelmed at every sweep by the torrential downpour. The road was practically invisible and I had to crawl the eleven miles back to Burgundy. A journey that should have taken ten minutes took over half an hour. All the way, I was thinking I should have taken Ivory right there, broken every bone in his body, one by one, until he confessed. But I knew that his testimony would have been worthless if extracted by torture. I had got what I had gone there to get: confirmation that Ivory was my man. Now I needed to plan my next steps.

I finally parked outside the front door on a flooded Chartres Street, barely lit by streetlamps that reflected not so much off wet cobbles, as off the streaming water. I climbed out of my car and ran the three strides to the door, ducking into my collar. As I stepped into the patio, the sound of drumming water overhead was almost deafening. Luis made hand gestures at me, pointing up, above his head. "The tarpaulin, we have to put it up, or we are flooded! It's crazy!"

I looked at my watch. It was after nine. "Am I too late to eat?"

He flapped his hands at me. "No, no, everything upside down, don't worry. Mr. Hirschfield is in the dining room. He likes to eat. He likes to take his time. This storm...!" He sighed loudly.

"What's the latest?"

"Is not a hurricane no more." He held out his hands like he was holding two giant melons. "But biiiig motherfocker tropical storm. *Big* flooding! They expect landfall in New Orleans in twenty-four or forty-eight hours. Is gonna be bad. Those poor people... poor city!"

I leaned over his desk to look at the screen of his TV. It looked like the apocalypse.

I muttered something that wanted to be sympathetic and made my way into the dining room, removing my jacket. Hirschfield hailed me. He was half way through demolishing a cheese board and had a bottle of cognac open on the table. I gave my jacket to the waiter and said, "Bring me your biggest steak, and a bottle of wine."

He hung up my jacket, goggled at the Sig in my waistband, and hurried away to the kitchen. As I sat, Hirschfield raised an eyebrow at me. "Unless something spectacular happens to you when you put your Y-fronts on over your pants, you have not been to Washington, D.C."

"Correct."

"I am offended. I have served some of the greatest criminal minds in America, and I have been loyal to every one of them. Why won't you trust me?"

"Don't get sensitive on me, Hirschfield. I trust you as much as I trust anyone, and I don't trust anyone when they're having their fingers removed with pliers."

He spread his hands and raised one shoulder. "Fair point. Where did you go?"

"I'll tell you tomorrow after three. Have you any news for me?"

"Good and bad. First, Baton Rouge is *closed!* Any hope that New Orleans would take the brunt of the storm and spare the capital has been abandoned. Baton Rouge is going to get hit, and hard. This means the trial is postponed. If you are thinking of smuggling Hays out of the country, now is the time to do it."

"No."

"Good. Now, you wanted me to find out who the beneficiaries of their wills were. I had to pull some strings, but that's my specialty." He scratched his head. "She was the sole beneficiary of his will. If he died, she got everything. I don't know what you were hoping for, but whatever it was, I am not personally surprised by these terms. It was a safe bet. He's crazy about her, *ergo* he leaves her everything. They also had substantial insurance on each other, as you would expect."

He raised his eyebrows and stuck out his bottom lip. "Her will was a little more surprising. I was not able to get the precise terms because the will is being contested and it is *sub judice*."

I frowned. "Contested?"

"Don't ask me by whom, because I do not know. I can only surmise."

"Her sister?"

He shrugged. "That would seem logical."

"Correct me if I am wrong, but the grounds for contesting a will are pretty limited."

"The grounds, and the people who have *standing*. That means the people who are entitled to contest it. It's either a person who *would* have inherited something if she had died intestate—without leaving a will—*i.e.* family. Or a person who was named in a previous will, and the will was changed. In either case, what the challenger is trying to do is prove that the terms of the will they are challenging are invalid, that they don't reflect the true wishes of the deceased."

The waiter brought me my steak and poured me a glass of wine. I sat staring at them both without seeing them. After a moment, I raised my eyes to meet Hirschfield's.

"Either Charles Carmichael is contesting a will in which Simone is the beneficiary, or Simone is challenging a will in which Charles Carmichael is the beneficiary. The chances of it being anybody else...."

"Nonexistent. Nobody else has standing."

"Are we looking at a side issue or motive?"

He raised his eyebrows high on his forehead and spread his hands. "Search me. You're the one playing detective, and you won't make me a party to what you know. So until after three PM tomorrow, you are paying me to sit here and eat cheese."

"What about the slug?"

"I'll have a full report in a couple of days, but I hope

he'll give me a call tomorrow at some point with the preliminary results."

I cut into the steak and stared at him while I chewed. Finally, I said, "I found Ivory."

He slowly raised an eyebrow.

"And when were you planning on telling me this? It is good news."

"I'm trying to figure out what it means."

"It means we have some corroboration for Hays' story! For crying out loud, Lacklan! Keep me in the goddamn loop or there is no point in employing me at all! Let me do my job!"

I nodded. "I'm sorry. But it's complicated. When I called you and asked you about Wilberforce..."

"Yesterday."

"Yeah, yesterday. I followed him and Carmichael and a couple of suits to the Full Moon, a club six miles southeast of St. Francisville."

He shrugged. "You told me, and I said then that there is nothing very special in that."

"Yeah, well, it turns out Ivory operates out of a back room there, a private club where they play poker, snort coke, and have a bit of bad boy fun. The day I followed them, that was where they went, to Ivory's back room."

He grunted.

I went on. "I went there again tonight to talk to Ivory..."

"Wait a minute. Let's take this one step at a time. How did you know Ivory was there? How did you know it was him in the backroom?"

I hesitated. For now, at least, I wanted to keep Sarah out of it. "I had a chat with Harry at the Blue Lagoon. He told me the guy who'd been talking to Bat was called Ivory. Bat had told me the same thing. The night I followed Carmichael and Wilberforce, a cute young girl at the Full Moon asked if I wanted to buy some blow from Ive, in the back room. I put two and two together."

"OK, Ive was Ivory. And that's where you've just come from?"

"Yeah. I left word I wanted to talk to him, so he was expecting me. Four of his boys had a reception committee ready."

His eyes flicked over me, looking for cuts or bruises.

I ignored him. "I killed them."

"Jesus!"

"Then I went in to talk to Ivory. He was there, just like Bat and Harry described him. He was playing poker with four guys who looked like businessmen, attorneys, surgeons... You know the type: German car, permed hair, Italian suit."

"I know the type. The Carmichael type."

I nodded.

"So you're thinking maybe he got into trouble with Ivory or some of his friends and, as you suggested before, he was the intended target."

"Yeah." I sighed. "She wasn't supposed to be in that bedroom. I heard from Simone that they were sleeping in separate rooms. She'd moved into a guest room, and apparently that was common knowledge, thanks to the staff gossip machine. But her body was found in the master bedroom."

"So somebody with a personal grudge against her would not have expected her to be in that room."

I sipped my wine. "So, on the one hand it suggests the

intended victim was Carmichael, on the other, it raises the question, what the hell was she doing in that room?"

He grunted. I ate in silence for a bit while he thought.

"The problem is," I said when I'd finished my steak. "It's a nice, simple theory that doesn't explain everything it should explain." I reached for my glass, drained it, and refilled it.

He was nodding, staring at the tablecloth.

I went on, "Like what the hell she was doing in that room, and who the hell got shot in the bedroom at Solitude."

"The difference between a policeman and a soldier," he said, unexpectedly, "is how you view killing. Soldiers kill because they are told to. Their motive is simply that it is their job. You kill a man, or a woman, simply because they are your enemy, even though you may not know why. But a policeman knows that outside of the army, people kill for one of two reasons, sex or money. And the motivation is either loss or gain. You want to avoid losing sex or money, or you want to acquire sex or money."

I thought about that. Soldiers killed so that other people could get more sex and money, usually fat men and fat women in suits. I said, "Yeah, and people usually want money so they can get more sex, so maybe Freud was right after all. It's all about sex."

In Sarah's life, it seemed to be looming large.

He sighed. "You and Hays are trying to protect Sarah's reputation. That is very noble of you, Lacklan, but I am not stupid. I have been around the block a few times. If she was seeing men at her studio, at Solitude, it is more than possible that one of her lovers got shot there, and most probably dumped in the bayou along with the mattress and the bedding. With the flooding from the storm, the chances of finding that body, or the bedding, are negligible."

I said, "She's with a lover, Ivory finds them and kills the lover. He leaves and she goes home. For some reason she goes to the master bedroom. Maybe she's in shock from the killing and needs comfort. Perhaps the horror of what has happened has driven her back to her husband. But he's out having dinner. Ivory arrives intending to kill him, for reasons as yet unclear, and kills her by mistake."

He stuck out his lip and nodded. "That's a very plausible theory. Now you just need to prove it. Have you told any of this to Jackson?"

I shook my head. "I don't trust him."

"What are you going to do?"

"What I am good at."

He frowned. "What's that?"

I treated him to a very small smile. "Cry havoc, and let slip the dogs of war."

EIGHTEEN

I CLOSED THE DOOR TO MY BEDROOM AND PULLED off my jacket and my shirt. It should have been cold, but it was warm and the humidity was off the chart. Even with the door closed, I could hear the drumming of the deluge on the awning they'd stretched across the central patio. The wind rattled the shutters and dashed rain against the window.

I looked at the shirt in my hand, and for the first time became aware of the blood on it. I dropped it in the wastepaper bin and opened the tall French windows onto the small terrace that overlooked the street out front. The flowing water was spilling onto the sidewalks and, down the road, it had got into one of the street lamps and was making it buzz and flicker on and off. It didn't look like the apocalypse. It looked like something else, something more final, more hopelessly terrible.

I picked up the phone and called room service. It rang for a long time before he answered.

"Bring me a bottle of Bushmills, will you?"

"Of course, Mr. Walker."

"I'll be in the shower. Just leave it by the bed."

"Of course."

I pulled off my boots and my jeans and went into the bathroom. There, I stood under a hot shower for ten minutes, trying to wash away the filth of the day: the mud, the cruelty, the lies and, above all, the blood.

I had killed four men as a matter of course. I had done it efficiently, without passion, without hatred. I hadn't even done it to survive, it had never crossed my mind that they would take me down. I had done it because it was expedient. They were the enemy, so I killed them.

It was the reason I had left the SAS. Somewhere inside me, almost out of earshot, my soul, or what was left of it, was calling out, warning me, that I was losing my humanity. Life and death were losing their meaning. And when life loses its meaning, what's left?

As I stood under the hot jets, letting them cleanse my skin, I realized I had lathered my head, my face, and my body for the fourth time. I stopped, tried to relax, and let the streams of clear water wash away the tension in my muscles. But the voices in my mind would not relent, and the pictures kept rising up again and again in the darkness of my mind, the astonished eyes of one man after another as they realized they were going to die.

By my hand. By my killing hand.

And I had not even done it for Marni. I had left my small home in Wyoming, come back to the world, returned to the killing, for what? To honor a promise to my father, and to protect the only woman I had ever really cared for. But this, what I had done tonight, I had not done for them.

I had done it for Bat Hays, and for the Regiment.

I turned off the water and stepped out of the cubicle. I grabbed a towel and dried myself. I was suddenly exhausted and craving sleep; and a large Irish to numb the aches in my body and in my mind.

She was sitting on my bed with a glass of whiskey in her hands. She didn't say anything smart or witty. She just watched me. For a moment, I thought about sending her away. For a moment, I thought that I wanted to be alone. But the words died on my lips and I knew that what I really needed was to hide in her warmth, in her skin, and hold her in the darkness.

She held out the glass to me and I saw that there was another on the bedside table. I took it.

"What are you doing here?"

"The storm has arrived."

"I noticed."

"I need to talk."

"I need to sleep."

"We can do both."

Her smile was hesitant and I could see I had hurt her. I sighed. I took a swig of whiskey. It burned, but it felt good. I pulled on a fresh pair of jeans and finally said, "I'm sorry. It's been a hell of a day."

"You want to talk?"

I walked over to the small balcony and stood looking out at the flood. Cool rain spattered my face and my bare feet.

"Do you miss her?"

She didn't answer for a moment, there was only the hiss and the incessant splatter of the water falling on the road. Then her voice came, quiet, subdued.

"Sometimes, it hurts so much I think I'm going to go crazy. Other times it's more like something is missing, something familiar. Like when you're a kid and you lose one of your teeth. You keep expecting it to be there, but there is just an empty space."

"Is that why you're here, to fill an empty space?"

Again the silence, filled only by the rain.

"What if I were? Would that be a bad thing?"

I shrugged, shook my head and took a drink. "That would be fine by me."

"Is there anyone, Lacklan? Anybody you need?"

"I forgot how." I turned to face her. I gave a smile that had no humor or happiness in it. "You know what Sinatra said, 'I'm for anything that gets you through the night.'"

She gazed into the bottom of her glass. "Lately it's felt as though it were night all the time. I don't believe it will ever end, Lacklan." She looked at me for an answer, but I didn't have one. "Are you any closer?"

"To what?"

"To finding who did it?"

"Maybe."

"What will you do when you find him?"

"Make him confess. Get Bat off the hook."

"What if he won't confess?"

I held her eye a moment, considering the unlikelihood of what she was suggesting. "He will."

"Will you torture him?" She looked a bit sick.

"If I have to. But with most people, the threat of torture is enough."

"You are ruthless, aren't you?" She said it with no particular inflection, just stating a fact. "Will you kill him?"

"You want me to."

It wasn't a question and she looked away, as though she felt ashamed.

I sat in the chair by the window and took another pull on my whiskey. I swallowed and enjoyed the burn. After a moment, I said, "Somebody else was killed that night. Do you know who it was?"

She looked at me sharply. "What are you talking about?"

"At Solitude, in her bedroom, in her bed. Somebody was killed."

"*That night?*"

I shrugged. "I don't know. I'm guessing." I raised an eyebrow and smiled. "That night surprises you, but not the possibility of another body? Who was it?"

She seemed to squint at me, like I was crazy. "How the hell should I know? What makes you think there was one?"

"The bedding was pristine, the mattress, and the mat under the bed were brand new. I told you about the cigarette butts..."

"It's hardly conclusive!"

"...and there was a .38 slug under the bedside table."

"Jesus...! A .38?"

"Yeah. I'm waiting on ballistics, but it's probably from the same revolver that killed Sarah."

She was frowning. Her eyes were abstracted and seemed to dart back and forth between images she was seeing in her mind. "So, he finds somebody in her bed, kills him, then goes to her house and kills her..."

"Doesn't make a lot of sense, does it? If she has a lover in her bed at Solitude, what is she doing in..."

Something made me falter a moment.

She was watching me carefully. "What?"

I stood and went to refill my glass. When I was done, she held out hers for me. I poured in a measure. She was still watching my face. As I put down the bottle, I said,

"She wasn't in her room, Simone."

"What?"

"She was in the master bedroom. In their bed."

"No. That's impossible."

"Why is it impossible?"

"It's just... She wouldn't!"

I felt a flash of anger and irritation that surprised me. I was suddenly half shouting at her. "Come on, Simone! Get real! It happens! People are fickle!"

"Shut up!"

"You want to know what happened?"

"Shut *up!*"

"She loved you! You freaked her out when you tried to kiss her! She was confused and it was like you said, she projected her love for you onto a string of men. None of them satisfied. They lasted one or two nights and she moved on to the next one, looking for satisfaction. Looking for the love she felt for you, and the sexual fulfillment she wanted from a man. But she never stopped to think!" Suddenly, a rage was building inside me that I knew had nothing to do with Simone or Sarah. "She never stopped to think, the way nobody ever stops to think, of the pain they might cause the people they play their games with!"

Her eyes fastened on mine. We stared at each other a moment, my breathing was harsh and my heart was hammering on my chest.

"She didn't stop to think about how her sexual *rampage*

might hurt you! She didn't stop to think that, even if for her it meant nothing, some of those men, those *toys,* might be capable of love! Might develop feelings for *her!* Well, Hays did! Hays fell in love with her! Because Bat Hays is a man with a heart and a soul! And the way she used him, hurt him! So how many others did she hurt? This saint? This *angel* of yours?"

"Stop it..."

"I'll tell you what happened. She was fucking some poor schmuck in her bed and one of her other male, black harem walked in, was enraged, and shot him. She fled, cured of her sexual fantasies by a powerful dose of reality. So she ran back, looking for the loving arms of her husband, because all of a sudden she was in love with him again! Not you, not the string of sexy studs she'd been playing with, but with the man who gave her *security!*" I spat the word at her, like it was her fault that human beings sucked. "Well here's a news flash, sister! People kill over sex. They do it all the time. And this animal followed her home and..." My voice, like my anger, trailed away. "And killed her, in her husband's bed..."

I turned and went back to the window. The wind was howling like a damned banshee. By contrast, the room was still and silent. I expected at any moment to hear the door close as she left, but it didn't.

"That's a lot of bitterness, a lot of anger, Lacklan."

"Yeah?"

"Who betrayed you...?"

"Save it. I'm not looking for a therapist." I turned to face her again. "What happened that night, Simone? The truth."

"I told you. We talked. She left."

"Why did she wind up in her husband's bed? Who was killed at Solitude?"

"I don't know, Lacklan. Please believe me. If I knew, don't you think I would tell you? I want her killer caught—perhaps more than anyone."

I sighed. She put her glass down on the floor, stood, and came over to me. She took hold of my shoulders and smiled at me.

"Lacklan, she may have been flawed, damaged, confused..." She shrugged. "Who isn't? You should know that better than anybody. But she *was* an angel. There was no cruelty or unkindness in her, and if she hurt people, she never did it intentionally. Don't judge her."

She stroked my face and stepped past me. She went to the balcony and leaned against the wall, looking out at the storm.

"You know what her dream was?"

I took a sip and felt the warm spirit burn my lips and my tongue. "What?"

"The Sara Bayou Park."

"The what?"

"The Sara Bayou Park. She owned a large stretch of forest and marshland on the banks of the bayou. It stretches from the studio for about a mile along the river, and for about half a mile to either side. She wanted to convert it into a nature reserve, a park, to protect the fauna of the bayou, alligators, snakes, birds... and encourage research into how the natural habitat is suffering from climate change and urban encroachment."

It sounded familiar. I asked, "What stopped her?"

She shook her head. "Nothing. She was in talks with the

State and with the university, to start the Louisiana Regeneration Project."

"How'd Carmichael feel about that?"

She shrugged. The light from the flickering lamps outside touched her skin. "He loved her for it. He wanted to be involved. She said he wanted to take over."

"Is that why you are contesting the will?"

She looked me over, then back out at the rain. "Yes."

"You hate him, don't you?"

"Yes."

"Enough to kill him?"

She smiled, but she didn't look at me. "No, not enough for that." After a moment, she added, "Most of us, don't you know. It takes a special kind of man to kill somebody."

I turned out the light. The rain glowed silver outside and gave her black skin a strange, luminous sheen. I went and stood close to her, turned her around to face me. Her eyes were huge and dark. Slowly, deliberately, I started to remove her clothes.

NINETEEN

When I woke up in the morning, she'd gone. I wasn't sure if I felt relieved or if I missed her. I made my way to the bathroom and stood for five minutes under the shower, switching from scalding to cold and back again.

When I felt awake, I stepped out, toweled myself dry, dressed, and went down to the dining room for breakfast. It was eight AM and Hirschfield was already there, eating eggs and bacon. He was looking at his tablet beside his plate and breaking a bread roll as I came in. He waved at me without looking up, like he had eyes in the top of his head, and pointed to the chair next to his.

I told the waiter, "Black coffee and toast," and made my way to his table.

As I sat, he said, "The wifi keeps cutting out and the internet is patchy to say the least, but I have news for you."

"Good."

"Ballistics, we'll have a full report in time, but I have the preliminary results. The bullet you found at Sarah's studio, Solitude, is a match for the bullets that killed her."

I grunted. "No great surprise, but at least it's a solid fact."

"Yes, indeed, and it tells us that the situation is not as cut and dried as Jackson would like us to think."

I nodded. "I just wish we knew when that slug was fired."

"Hmm..." He devastated one of his eggs with his knife and fork, speared a chunk of toast with bacon on it, and stabbed savagely at the yolk before stuffing it into his mouth. He chewed methodically and dabbed his lips with his napkin. "And at whom. That would be a useful piece of information. Nobody, as far as I am aware, has been reported missing."

"I know. I grilled Simone last night, but she seems genuinely to know nothing."

He raised an eyebrow at me, but said only, "Indeed." He drained his cup and refilled it. "One thing seems to be clear, Lacklan, and I can't help feeling it is time you discussed it with Carmichael."

I made a question with my face, but I knew what he was going to say.

"It seems pretty clear that you are right, and she was not the intended victim." I studied his face a moment. He spread his hands and raised his eyebrows. "Somebody was killing off the competition!"

The waiter brought my coffee and a basket of toast. I filled my cup and glanced at Hirschfield. "That's an interesting way of putting it."

He gave a complacent shrug. "All human stories boil

down to one of two situations, Lacklan. Somebody is trying to get hold of something, or somebody is trying to get rid of something. It's one or it's the other. Often, it's both. What can I tell you? In this case, it looks like somebody was trying to get rid of the competition, maybe so they could get Sarah. Either way, I think you need to bring it to Carmichael's attention."

I bit into my toast. "You're right. I'll go over there this morning. How bad is the storm?"

"The rain is a diluvium, but the winds for now are just gale force. The power keeps failing, so it is hard to know what is happening in Baton Rouge and New Orleans, but if it's this bad here, it must be terrible there."

Fifteen minutes later, I was crawling along Main Street at 20 MPH, leaning across the steering wheel, trying to peer out into a desolate world of torrential rain and bowing, bouncing trees, seen through a dense mist of spray.

I came to the gas station at the junction with Route 61 and crawled through six inches of water onto the main road. There wasn't another vehicle or another person to be seen. As I crossed over the blacktop toward Carmichael's drive, the Zombie was rocked by the force of the gale. The only sounds were the deafening drumming of the water on the roof and the hood, the hiss from the road, and the wild screaming of the wind in the pylons and the trees.

I pulled up outside his Greco-Roman portico, and in the five seconds it took me to climb out of the car and run up the steps to his door, I was drenched and almost blown off my feet. I rang on his bell and hammered on the knocker. After a few moments, it was wrenched open by James. He looked astonished to see me.

"Cap'n! What in the name of all that's holy...?"

"Good morning, James. I need to see Mr. Carmichael. I'm guessing he's in."

"Sure! He's in his study. Right this way..."

"I know the way, James. It's fine."

He watched me cross the checkerboard floor, knock on the door, and step in without waiting for an answer.

The fire had been lit and Carmichael was sitting in one of his chesterfields. He had a silver coffee pot and a china cup on an occasional table beside him. He was staring at the flames and blinked and looked up after I had closed the door.

"Lacklan. I didn't expect you today."

I approached and leaned on the back of the other chair. "I need to talk to you."

"By all means." He gestured at the chair I was leaning on and I came around and sat.

"Coffee?"

I shook my head. "I'm not sure you have been totally open and up front with me, Mr. Carmichael."

He frowned, but he kept his eyes on the fire. "What are you talking about?"

"Your relationship with Sarah. You knew it was in trouble. You knew it wasn't as good as you made it out to be."

"This again? We were having a few difficulties, like any couple. Clearly, they affected her more than I thought."

"That's fine as far as it goes, Mr. Carmichael. But when you hide the fact that she had started sleeping in a separate room, that can seriously hinder the investigation, Jackson's and mine."

He glared at me, but turned his gaze back to the wavering flames. "It was temporary. It wasn't relevant."

"I disagree. Amongst other things, the crowd she was hanging out with and..." I hesitated a moment. "Going to jazz clubs with, they all knew you were in separate rooms."

He closed his eyes and the color drained from his face. "How much of this humiliation do I have to endure?"

"The sooner we get to the truth, the sooner it will be over."

"Yes, we were sleeping in separate rooms. She said she wasn't clear in her mind about... us."

I nodded. "And Bat Hays knew that, Mr. Carmichael. Do you see why that is significant?"

He turned to look at me, frowning, with tears in his eyes. "He wouldn't..." He let the words trail away. I finished for him.

"If he had intended to kill Sarah, he would not have gone to that room." I gave that a moment to sink in, then went on. "In fact, nobody from that crowd would have expected her to be in the master bedroom."

His breathing had quickened and his eyes were staring. "No..."

I watched him carefully. "I need to know that you understand what this means, Mr. Carmichael."

His breath shuddered, his face clenched like a fist around his pain and he leaned forward into his hands, sobbing. "Oh God, no, how could I have been so stupid?"

I gave him a moment longer, until his breathing had settled. "Mr. Carmichael, Charles, do you understand that you were probably the intended target?"

He nodded, then leaned back into his chair. His cheeks

were wet, and when he spoke, his nose was blocked, as though he had a bad cold.

"I didn't think the pain could get any worse, but now..."

"You can't think that way."

He turned his head toward me. "It's my fault she's dead. It should have been me in that bed. It should have been me..."

The wind rose from a howl to a scream, a squall lashed the glass in the window, and the flames wavered in the grate. His eyes seemed to cling to me, and for a moment, I was reminded of a man clinging to a raft in a storm, knowing that in just a short while, he would have to release his grip and drown.

"Charles, try to think. Who? Who would want to do this to you?"

He gave a damp, shuddering sigh, wiped his eyes with the back of his hand, and reached in the pocket of his cardigan for a handkerchief. He dried his eyes, then blew his nose noisily.

I stood and went by the fireplace, where I was in his line of vision.

"Charles." I said it again and his eyes, almost resentful, finally focused on me. "You are going to have to face this. I'm going to tell you something. The possibility that you were the target was on my mind from day one. It struck me that the killer might still be stalking you, so I followed you."

He scowled.

I ignored him. "I followed you to your attorney's place in Baton Rouge, then to his country house where you celebrated some deal, and then to the Full Moon, where you went into the back room. I am guessing that there, you played poker and relaxed with business associates."

His face had gone hard. "How dare you...!"

"I dare, that and a lot more. Don't waste time on that. You have to face the reality of this, Charles. Get a grip!"

His covered his eyes with a shaking hand. "Jesus! What a mess..."

"For crying out loud, Carmichael! I'm on your side! I'm trying to help you!"

"I know..."

I spotted the tray of decanters on a sideboard against the far wall and went over. I poured him a stiff bourbon and brought it to him. He stared into my face for a moment, then at the glass, and finally took it in a trembling hand. He took a slug and it seemed to steady him. He said, "Let me think. Give me a minute to think..."

I went and poured myself a measure of whiskey and rested my ass against the sideboard while I waited. Rain lashed the glass and outside, trees waved through the mist of spray. For a second, my mind drifted and I wondered where Marni was at that moment. Was she in the same storm?

Carmichael's voice drew me back. He seemed to be talking to the fire, half in a trance.

"Regeneration," he said. "Regeneration has become big business in Louisiana. Katrina, now Sarah..." He took another sip and stared into his glass as he swallowed. "We have seven thousand, seven hundred miles of shoreline. Did you know that? It's disappearing at a faster rate than anywhere in the United States. That is just one of the side effects of climate change." His voice sank into a sullen mumble. "Everything in life has a knock on, Lacklan.

Nothing ever happens in isolation, especially in…" He waved his hand at the rain-spattered windows. "Especially in the ecosphere. Sarah would have told you that. You re-introduce a wolf into its old habitat, and within six years, rainfall has increased and you have forests growing where before there were plains…" He turned to look at me as though I might not believe him. "That happened, in Yellowstone Park in 1995. Did you know that?"

I shook my head. He looked back at the fire. "It did. You introduce a predator into an ecosystem, it changes the whole system, down to the physical geography. By the same token, change the physical geography, and it affects everything else."

"What are you telling me?"

"Wherever there is change, you will find speculators looking to make a buck. Change always means winners and losers, you know that. And winners and losers are people who can be exploited. So the changing ecosystems of Louisiana mean business opportunities for speculators."

"And you are a land developer."

"Sarah and I had a dream. To regenerate the rivers, the bayous, and the forests of Louisiana, and encourage the state and the university to invest in the project and use it for research. We had generated a lot of interest. But a project like that needs a lot of backing, a lot of money. So we were also encouraging investors to put money into land development."

I returned to my chair and sat. "Go on."

"There was one potential investor, from out of state, Grumman. A cool customer with a lot of money to invest, but he was aggressive, very aggressive. He didn't give a damn about the vision, the broader picture. He wanted the land we were offering, on his terms, and he also wanted to exploit the land that we were intending to develop as natural habitat. If we had given in to his demands, he would have had a damn Disneyland there, with alligator theme parks and God knows what else. He said if we did it his way, it could be worth hundreds of millions of dollars."

"You upset this guy?"

He shrugged. For a moment, he looked like a sulking child. "I'm a plain-talking man, Lacklan. You know that. I told him there would be no compromise on the natural park. It was my way or the highway. He didn't like that, but I didn't think he would go to this kind of extreme."

I frowned. "What would he gain by killing you?"

"Perhaps he thought that he could manipulate Sarah more easily. There were several investors who liked his ideas. Sarah was very influenced by my opinions. Our love life was going through a difficult time, but she still loved and respected me."

I took a deep breath and considered my whiskey for a moment. "Did you take Grumman to the Full Moon?"

"It was Wilberforce's idea. He's a bit of a character. His view is that businessmen are the modern day knights and warriors, and they need to let off steam just as the warriors of old did." He shrugged and gave a rueful smile. "Wine, women, and song. Maybe there is some truth in that, after all."

"From what I saw, the Full Moon is into a lot more than wine, women, and song."

"Yeah, well, we are all grown ups, right? I stayed clear of the drugs and the whores, but a lot of our investors enjoyed a bit of that and expected it. It happens, from Anchorage to

Tierra del Fuego. And a happy investor is a generous investor."

I waited. He just sat slumped, staring into his glass, then shifted his eyes to the burning logs. Finally, I prompted him.

"So did Grumman meet Ivory?"

He went very still.

"Ivory?"

"Don't bullshit me, Carmichael. So far, I am on your side and I am a good ally. Let's keep it that way."

"Yes, he met Ivory. Ive runs the club at the back, the poker games. He also provides the coke and the girls, and any other services..." He swallowed. "Are you telling me that he...?"

"Ivory framed Bartholomew Hays for Sarah's murder."

"Jesus Christ..." He closed his eyes and sat very still. "I may as well have put the gun to her head and pulled the trigger myself."

"Charles, you will have time for self-recrimination later, and nobody is going to save you from that. You will just have to go through it and find a way to deal with it. But right now, you need to man up and fix this mess. If Grumman is responsible for this, I need him and Ivory to confess, or at the very least, incriminate themselves."

He put down his glass and rubbed his face with his hands. "Yes. Yes, of course, I see that. I'm sorry, Lacklan, this has been... This has all been such a..." For a moment, he couldn't talk and looked away. He took a couple of deep breaths. "You need a trap. We need to trap them somehow."

"Is that feasible? Can we do that?"

He nodded. "I'll think of a way, just give me a minute."

I ignored his request and asked, "Charles, who is contesting her will?"

He flashed a glare at me. "Is there anything you don't know?"

I narrowed my eyes. "Is there anything I shouldn't know? If you don't volunteer, I need to get it myself."

"Simone. But we are resolving it amicably. Wilberforce has it in hand."

"What are the grounds? What's her standing?"

"As her sister, she feels she is entitled to something. I am not averse to that, within reason. It just seems at the moment that everybody is trying to steal Sarah from me."

He levered himself to his feet and for a moment he looked like a very old, broken man, but the emotion drained from his face and he glared at me.

"We can do this," he said. "But on one condition."

I frowned. "What condition?"

"We'll get the evidence to get Hays off the hook, but I want Grumman and Ivory dead."

TWENTY

I FOLLOWED HIM ACROSS THE ROOM TO A mahogany door. He pulled a set of keys from his pocket and unlocked it, pushing it open onto a small room, maybe fifteen feet square. The walls were lined with mahogany and glass cabinets from floor to ceiling, each lined with green baize. These were constructed over sets of drawers, each about four feet in width and a foot in depth.

The cabinets contained firearms. I counted twenty-four rifles, ranging from antique Winchesters to the latest model HK416 A5 assault rifle, by way of some badass shotguns. There was also at least double that number of handguns: antique flintlocks and Colt revolvers, as well as Glocks, a Browning Hi Power, CZ, two Smith & Wesson 500, the snub nose and the long barrel, and the 357 Magnum Dirty Harry made famous. And more besides.

He pointed at the drawers. "I have more in there, and plenty of ammunition. Some of them are registered, not all.

This federation is founded on the right of every man to carry a weapon with which to defend himself against tyranny, whomever that tyrant might be. If ever Burgundy needs to rise up, I'll be able to arm a couple of hundred of them." He paused a moment, staring blindly at the cabinets. "You've opened my eyes today, Lacklan. From what you have told me, Grumman and Ive are two just such tyrants. They have taken from me that which I most loved." He gazed at me with tears in his eyes again. "I can't bring her back, but I can punish the men who took her, and ensure they don't ever do this to anybody else, ever again. Will you help me?"

I nodded. "Yes. I will. What's your idea?"

"It won't be easy, with the storm."

"Where is Grumman?"

He seemed to think about it for a long moment. "Last I heard, he was sitting out the storm with Wilberforce in his country house. What we need is to get him and Ive together, talking."

"I can bug Ivory's room at the club."

He eyed me. "You can? Have you bugged me?"

I half-smiled. "Not yet."

"I'll get a message to him, from an anonymous email address, purporting to have knowledge of Jackson's investigation, claiming that evidence has come to light connecting Grumman and Ive to Sarah's death, and that Hays is no longer a suspect."

I shook my head. "No. It needs to be something they can act on, we want them discussing a plan. The email will claim to have information connecting Grumman to Ivory, and thereby to Sarah's murder. That information is for sale. If they won't buy it, it goes to Jackson or the sheriff."

He nodded. "OK, that's good. We tell them to be at the Full Moon, in the back room, at a given time tonight to negotiate a pay off."

I finished it for him. "They'll meet there long before the arranged time, to discuss their options and how to handle the situation. We record their discussion, and once we have enough evidence to convict them..."

"We execute them."

I gave him a moment, then asked, "Have you got the stomach for this, Charles?"

He looked at me with dead eyes. "Yes. This is something I need to do."

"Fine. Give me a couple of hours. The place is bound to be empty right now. I'll go and set it up. If I can get a signal, I'll send you a message when I'm done. Either way, I'll come back to get you. We don't want your vehicle seen anywhere near the Full Moon tonight."

He nodded. "Agreed. What about you? Your car is easily recognized."

"Yeah, but it's silent, and if it comes to the worst, I have friends who can get me out of trouble."

He stared at me a moment, then frowned. "Hasn't Hays got the same friends?"

"No. And in any case, this isn't worst case yet."

I thought I saw a flicker of fear in his eyes, but he turned and stepped out of the room. I followed him back into his study and he closed and locked the door. I went and stood by the fire. Carmichael sat back in his chair.

I said, "Don't drink any more until after it's done. I need you sharp. You need to put Sarah out of your mind until we get back."

He nodded. "I don't want any more."

"What about Jackson?"

"What about him?"

"He warned me off. I got the feeling he was protecting them."

He shrugged and his gaze was lost in the fire again. "I'd be surprised, but I guess it's possible. If he is involved, they are bound to incriminate him. If he's there, we kill him. If he's not, I'll make sure he spends the rest of his life in prison."

"OK, I'm going. Stay focused. Don't go to pieces on me."

He looked at me again with those same dead eyes. "I won't. Not till it's over."

I stepped out into the screaming gale. The driving rain lashed my face and stung my skin as I struggled to my car. By the time I got the door open and climbed inside, I was soaked through. I fired up the silent engine and slipped up his drive and out of his gate onto the road. There I paused a moment to think, and instead of turning south toward St. Francisville, to pick up Route 10 to the Full Moon, I turned left and crossed over onto Main Street.

The windshield wipers were going like they were in a frenzy, but the road was a river, a foot deep in water, and the rain was so dense visibility was no more than four or five yards ahead. I took a left at Chartres Avenue, crawled a block to Congress Street, and pulled up outside Hays' house. It was a small, green clapboard place with a gabled, slate roof and it looked like it was about to collapse under the weight of the water. I leaned on the horn until he opened the door with a heavy coat on and an umbrella in his hand. He slammed the door shut and ran for the car. It was only four strides, but by the time he got there, the umbrella was inside out and he was wiping water from his eyes so he could see what he was doing.

He clambered in and I moved off, back toward Chartres Avenue while he pulled the door closed.

"Tell you what," he said. "You Yanks go on about how we're always talkin' about the fuckin' weather. But you lot get a bit of rain, and you never stop fuckin' moanin'."

"A bit of rain..."

"Yeah. So where are we goin'?"

"We might have a breakthrough."

"Good to know."

I crawled around the corner and pulled up in front of the hotel.

"Try not to get washed away by the drizzle on your way to the door."

"Don't be such a fuckin' wuss. Sir."

We got out, leaned into the lashing wind and struggled to the entrance to the Soniat. We stepped through into the patio, wiping water from our faces and our hair. Above our heads, the awning thundered to the sound of the wind and the drumming downpour. Luis stood in reception looking at us and shaking his head.

I said, "Ask Mr. Hirschfield to come down, will you? And get us some towels."

Ten minutes later, Hirschfield found us in the bar, toweling our hair and drinking whiskey. We took the table behind the fern and I started to speak.

"I'll make this brief. I haven't got a lot of time. In about ten minutes, I'm going to go to the Full Moon club."

Hirschfield raised an eyebrow at me. "Have you gone completely crazy?"

"No, there is a logic to this. Listen…"

I related my meeting with Carmichael in detail and they listened in absolute silence. When I had finished, Bat said, "I don't like it. It stinks."

And Hirschfield made a face like sour cream and said, "Grumman? I know Grumman. This isn't Grumman's scene."

To Hirschfield, I said, "If he turns up, it's him." To Bat, I said, "I know, but it's the only shot we have and we have to take it. But we do it my way. Our way. I have an arsenal in the back of the car. You come with me. You take up a position in the forest with my assault rifle, while I place the bugs and prepare a few surprises."

He nodded. "OK. What you got, the HK?"

"Yeah, the 416 A5, eleven inch."

"OK, cool."

"The bugs will transmit to a cell, which I will leave with you. It will record any conversation that goes down in that room. I'm going to come back and collect Carmichael. My guess is the targets won't get there till after we arrive. If they do, you stay put and record."

"Will Carmichael know I'm there?"

"No. It's not that I don't trust him, but we operate on a need to know basis. We three know it, nobody else. We get the recording and then we go in and take them down. I want you watching my back every step."

"Got it."

Hirschfield coughed. "Are you making me a party to a murder conspiracy?"

"No. We are going to arrest them, not kill them."

"That is not what Carmichael thinks."

"I need him on board. When the time comes, I'll stop him. I'm trying to get Hays *off* a murder charge, remember?"

Hirschfield smiled, satisfied.

IT TOOK a full forty minutes to get to the Full Moon. We pulled off the road shortly before we got there and hid the car among the trees in the woodland. There, I popped the trunk and opened my kit bag. I handed Bat the Heckler & Koch and he helped himself to ammunition. Meanwhile, I collected the bits and pieces I was going to need.

Then, we picked our way silently through the forest until we came to the rear of the building. We selected a position among the trees and the ferns where Bat could keep the front of the club covered, and at the same time see the windows at the back, where Ivory had his private rooms.

When Bat was settled, I sprinted across the thirty feet of open ground that separated the trees from the building. On the left, there was a shed, and beyond that a door that I figured led to the kitchen and the storerooms. I didn't have time to waste, so I blew the lock and went inside.

It was a storeroom, stacked with crates of coke, gin, and whiskey. I moved quickly past them and came, as I had expected, to a small kitchen kitted out to make hamburgers and hot dogs. I moved on through and came out behind the bar. It was very still and silent. It was a silence that was oddly enhanced by the howl and whistle of the wind, and the lash and spatter of the rain.

I vaulted the bar and moved across, past the small stage, to the door marked private. This was a lock I didn't want to blow, but it took me only fifteen seconds to pick it and let myself in. The room was dark, but there was enough light coming through the window at the back to see what I was doing.

I set the bugs, one under the table, the other on the lamp fitment overhead, then I went to the window. I couldn't see Bat, but I knew he could make out my silhouette in the glass. I spoke in a normal voice.

"Testing, one, two, three. If you can hear me, oh Lord, give me a sign."

A hand rose up out of the ferns, waved once, and disappeared again. Then, I set about the second part of my plan, which took another five minutes or so, and I left the way I'd come.

Ninety seconds later, I scrambled in among the ferns and the undergrowth next to Bat. He grinned at me.

"All set? I haven't had this much fun since I shot me future mother-in-law."

"All set. So who was the woman you paid me to shoot?"

"Oh, that was my ex-mother-in-law."

We both laughed at the old routine, "OK, pal, I'm going to get Carmichael. I have no idea what is going to happen next, so stay alert."

"Gotcha."

I crouch-ran back through the trees till I came to the car. Then I pulled out the kit bag, buried it at the foot of a tree under a pile of leaves and branches, and took off back toward St. Francisville and Burgundy.

What I had told Bat was true. I had no damn idea what was going to happen next, except that all bloody hell was about to break loose. That much was for sure, and he knew it too.

That was why he was smiling when I left him.

TWENTY-ONE

The call came as I was arriving at the crossroads at St. Francisville. I didn't recognize the number. I set my cell on the jack and it put it on speakerphone.

"Yeah, Lacklan Walker. Who's this?"

There was a lot of hiss and crackle, but I recognized the voice. "Captain Walker, this is Katy Glendinning, from the lab."

I pulled over to the side of the road.

"The reception is really bad, we're in the middle of the storm here."

"You're *in* the storm?"

"It's a long story. I might lose the signal at any moment. What have you got?"

"OK, I'll cut to the chase. The blood samples were not a match. I repeat, *not* a match."

"OK, listen. Have you got access to Federal databases? Can you check the profiles?"

"Yes, of course, and I am running one of the samples through CODIS as we speak..."

"Why only one?"

She hesitated a moment. "Because the other one was pig's blood."

"*What?*"

"The one you asked me to label 'DA', belongs to an as yet unidentified person, but the one you asked me to label 'Walker' is pig's blood."

"Are you certain? Is there any possibility of a mistake?"

I heard her laugh through the crackle. "You must know yourself that that is absurd. Of course not. It's pig's blood."

"OK, thanks, Kate. I'll be in touch..."

"I'll email you my report as soon as I've finished the search on CODIS."

"Thanks."

The wind and the rain hammered the car. I sat for a full two minutes with my mind spinning, struggling to get to grips with the implications. I reached in my pocket, pulled out my cigarettes, and lit up, forcing myself to work methodically through the facts, forcing myself to see what they meant.

Finally, I put the Zombie in gear and turned north, toward Burgundy. The road was invisible under the flow of water, and my headlamps did nothing to penetrate the fog of windblown spray that battered and drenched everything in its path. I crawled, leaning over the steering wheel, squinting through the windshield, trying to make some sense of what I saw, trying to identify where I was. And all the while, my mind was screaming at me to go, to go faster, before it was too late. Because I had understood at last what the pig's blood meant, and I knew I had to get to Simone.

After what felt like hours, but was probably only minutes, I finally recognized the gas station and knew that I was leaving St. Francisville, and the next left would take me into Simone's drive. I pulled across the road and plunged in to the dark tunnel formed by the tossing, waving woodland that surrounded her driveway. The screaming and howling was deafening, even inside the car, but the trees shielded the path from some of the downpour and the visibility improved enough for me to accelerate, sliding and swerving in the mud.

As I came out of the trees, I saw light in her windows, and the front door was open. I skidded to a halt at the bottom of the stairs that rose to her porch and scrambled out of the car. The wind was slamming her door, over and over, like it was trapped in an eternal, childish tantrum of cosmic proportions. I ran up the steps, shouting her name. But the wind snatched my words and hurled them out and over the trees.

I stepped over the threshold, closed the door, and locked it, muffling but not extinguishing the fury of the tempest outside. The walls seemed to sigh and creak, and everywhere, there were the chaotic noises of random objects being tossed, hurled, and rolled across roads, paths, and lawns. I shouted her name again and moved into the broad, open space of her living room. The lights were on. The shutters had been closed to protect the glass in the windows. They rattled and creaked. On a coffee table, a tall glass held four cubes of melting ice, and a slice of lime. I raised my voice. "*Simone!*"

A bubble of impenetrable silence seemed to hold the

house, keeping the noise and the chaos on the outside. My voice was lost.

In the kitchen, a pot of cold rice stood on the cooker, and beside it a pan of meat in tomato sauce.

I ran up the stairs and went into the bedrooms one by one. They were empty and bare. In her room, the bed was still unmade and the familiar scent of her body invaded my mind for a moment, taking me back to the texture of her skin and the smell of her hair. On impulse, stupidly, I shouted her name again.

Her study was at the end of the landing, overlooking the front of the house. I pushed in and flipped on the light. The room wasn't big, not more than fifteen feet by twenty. The walls were lined with modern, blond-wood bookcases. Where Carmichael's books were all hardbacks, Simone's were mainly paperback textbooks, and looked well-used. Books by Freud and Jung knocked elbows with Juliet Mitchell, Karl Pribram and plastic-bound drafts of articles and reports. A coffee pot and a stained demitasse stood beside her computer on a substantial pine desk.

I bellowed her name again, knowing I was being absurd. She was not there and she could not hear me. Suddenly, I was wrenching open the drawers in her desk, pulling out papers, correspondence and documents, throwing them on the floor. What I was looking for was not there.

Two filing cabinets stood against the wall. I yanked open those drawers too, going through file after file. They were all patients and case studies. I searched for a safe, but there wasn't one. Then I saw the lever-arch files on the shelf above her desk. Bank statements, electricity bills, gas bills, tax.

And then I had it. Correspondence with her attorney. I

sat in her chair and opened the box. There, at the top, was Sarah Carmichael's last will and testament. It was a photocopy. The original would be with her attorney. It was dated 30th September, less than two months ago. It was not a long document, but I read it slowly, carefully. It stated categorically that this document revoked all prior wills and codicils, and that being of sound mind, and without coercion, she left everything that she owned, both realty and personality, to her stepsister, Simone D'Arcy.

There followed a comprehensive list of everything that she owned, and it began to dawn on me that Sarah Carmichael had been a very rich woman indeed. There was not only a substantial fortune in cash, stocks, and bonds, but her property holdings ran into several million dollars, including the land that Simone had talked about, that ran for over a mile on both sides of the Sara Bayou.

I put aside the will and started going through the correspondence with her attorney. It soon became apparent also that the dealings with Carmichael had not been as friendly as he had led me to believe. In fact, the letters and emails from Wilberforce were nothing if not openly aggressive, alleging coercion and manipulation, and threatening not just legal action, but prosecution to the full extent of the law.

Carmichael was threatening prison.

For a moment, it struck me that two people were going down for Sarah's death, both of them were black, and both, to some extent, had been Sarah's lovers. My head throbbed. It was like trying to read letter soup through spaghetti Bolognese.

Images flashed in my mind: the light streaming from the windows and the doors out onto the veranda, among the mist, rain, and the howling gale. The door, open, slamming over and over. The empty house, the empty glass with the melting ice and the lime.

I swore under my breath, snatched up the will, and ran, clattering down the stairs three at a time. I slipped and fell at the bottom, scrambled to my feet, and hurtled across the room, wrenched open the front door, and clambered into my car.

Again the agonizingly slow crawl north up Route 61, along a road made invisible by the deluge, the mist, and the spray. The beams from my headlamps danced on the flow, and reflected back at me off the billion shining needles that fell and danced, hurled this way and that, like gossamer drapes in the wind.

Finally, the gates to Carmichael's house loomed ahead on the left. They were open, and through them I could see lighted windows. I turned in, crunched to a halt in front of his gabled portico and sat staring.

Like a bizarre, resonant synchronicity, his door also was open, and creaked and banged in the wind to the slow, angry rhythm of a dirge. As though I were acting out a strange *déjà vu*, I climbed the steps, wiping rain from my eyes. The lock had been shot out. I stepped inside and wedged the door closed with a heavy umbrella stand. This stone house did not creak like Simone's, but the gale coiled and whipped around it, howling and moaning like a host of mourning banshees, peering and reaching through the keyholes and trying to crawl down the chimneys.

I stood on the checkerboard floor in the vaulted entrance hall and called his name. My voice echoed and died unanswered. My footsteps were startling and loud as I crossed the floor to his study and pushed through the tall, walnut door. The flames were still dancing and quivering in the grate. His glass of bourbon was still on his small table by the chesterfield. But he was not there.

I went across the echoing hall and into the drawing room. Here, too, there was a fire in the grate. It was the only light in the room, save the gray, dying luminescence of the day, dwindling under the heavy blanket of unforgiving cloud overhead. The double glazing of the windows and the French doors muffled Sarah's rage, but I could see the trees through the glass, twisting and writhing, and the lash of the rain against the glass.

The dull light was enough to see his body. There was not much blood, because he had died almost instantly. It had not been a slow, cruel death, like Sarah's, but a quick, efficient one. It had not been a murder of passion, but of expedience, appropriate to a man who had admired the army so much.

I approached and looked down at James' wide eyes, staring up at the ceiling, as though it was the last thing he had ever expected to see. His right hand was extended, half-open, cupped around the butt of a Colt revolver. The shot had been a good one, right through his forehead. There was no exit wound, only a snake of dark blood across his brow that had pooled on the floor and now reflected the flames from the fire. But it had no fire of its own.

For a moment, I could see Sergeant Bradley, grinning wolfishly by the light of a camp fire, high in the mountains in Afghanistan with the flames dancing in his eyes. "Nobody gets out of here alive, mate. Nobody. Best you can hope for is to die well."

He hadn't been talking about Afghanistan. He'd been

talking about life. I hoped James had died well. I had liked him.

I went upstairs and checked all the bedrooms. I noticed that the master bedroom had finally been cleaned. I checked the bathrooms, too. There was no sign of anybody, no sign of a struggle, no sign of anything at all.

I went back down to his study. The door to the gun cupboard was locked, so I blew the lock out with my Sig. The cabinets were intact and no guns were missing, either from them or from the drawers.

Where the hell was he? Him and Simone. It was not a coincidence.

I stepped back into the hall. There was a uniformed cop standing in the doorway looking at me with no expression on his face. Another cop standing outside the drawing room door glanced at me, then spoke through the door. A moment later, Jackson came out. His face was like stone, if stone could look mad.

"You killed James? Why the hell did you have to kill James?"

I didn't know where to begin my answer, but he didn't let me talk anyway.

Instead he asked me another question. "Where is Carmichael? What have you done with him?"

TWENTY-TWO

I STUDIED JACKSON A MOMENT BEFORE ANSWERING, wondering if his concern was an act, or genuine. I pulled my cigarettes from my pocket and looked at them. They were soaked. I sighed and put them back.

"What the hell are you doing here, Jackson?"

His face flushed and his eyes were bright with anger.

"You? You gonna ask *me* questions?"

"I don't know where Carmichael is. I just arrived. James was dead when I got here. You know, you don't have to fuck up every homicide that lands on your desk, Jackson. You have the option of investigating and thinking for yourself sometimes."

The cop by the door sniggered and hid it behind a cough. I glanced at him, then repeated to Jackson, "Why are you here?"

The muscle in his jaw kept bunching. "I don't have to answer your damned questions." He drew breath and I knew what he was going to say. He was going to tell the cop to cuff me. If he did, I was going to kill him and the two cops, and I didn't want to do that. I spoke before he did.

"Did you look at the bullet wound?"

He frowned at me. "What?"

I shouted, "*Goddamit Jackson! Did you examine the bullet wound? In James' head? Did you examine it?*"

The hall fell very silent. The wind groaned outside. He stared at me resentfully but he didn't answer.

I said, "It's a .22. The hole is small and neat. There is no exit wound. My weapon is a Sig Sauer p226 Tacops, 9mm. I use hollow tips, and the magazine is full. The gun has not been fired. If I had shot James, the entry wound would be bigger and the back of his head would be missing. Also..." I held up my hands. "There is no gunshot residue. Do yourself a favor. Get it right once."

"You better stop riding me, Lacklan."

"I'll do that, just as soon as you start doing your job." He had nothing to say, so I pushed on. "I'm here because I had an appointment with Carmichael. When I arrived, his door was open, the lock had been blown out, James was dead, as you found him, and Carmichael was missing. Even you must be able to see that it all adds up to an abduction. James was devoted to his boss. He tried to defend him and was shot in the head for his efforts. And that all brings me back, once again, Jackson, to my original question. What are you doing here?"

The two cops who had come with him were looking at him curiously. I played a bluff and it paid off. I raised an eyebrow and asked him, "Do I need to call Washington?"

He swallowed. "No. He called me about an hour ago. Said he wanted me to drop by."

"How'd he sound?"

He shrugged. "Normal."

"Did he say what it was about?"

He hesitated.

My mind started racing. "Did he say something about the Full Moon?"

He swallowed again, eyeing the uniforms sidelong. My mind was reaching, but it was reaching into the void. I had found a corner of the jigsaw, but I had found sky where there should be earth. I half-grinned. "Son of a gun. He wanted you to go with him to the Full Moon..."

"That's all he said. He had to go there. He wouldn't say why, but he wanted support... Is that where he is?"

I thought about it and shook my head. "I don't know, Jackson. I don't know where he is. But if he's there, why the hell would he shoot out his own lock and kill James?" I gestured back at his study. "And none of his weapons is missing..."

Jackson was looking worried. "He said something, it didn't make a lot of sense. He sounded upset. It was about a meeting between..." He looked at the floor, like he was trying to remember.

I said, "Grumman and..."

He nodded. "Yeah, Grumman and Ive?"

"Did he say anything else?"

He looked distressed. "He just said he was arranging some kind of meeting. Is that where he is? Do you think that's where he went?" He looked over at the door, then back at the drawing room. "Who the fuck did this? If you didn't do it, who the fuck did?"

There were only two possibilities, and I had only one option.

"Get a grip, Jackson. Either he killed James, shot out his own lock and went to the Full Moon voluntarily, or they came and took him. Either way, it looks like that's where he went. And if we don't go and get him, there is going to be another death tonight."

I stepped up close to him and looked him in the eye. "Listen to me, Jackson, if you fuck this up, people will die. These men are armed and very dangerous."

"Save your advice for your regimental rookies, Walker. I know what I'm doing."

"Then do your thing, but stay the hell out of my way."

"I should arrest you and throw you in a cell."

"Sure, and then you can all die out there tonight. You're incompetent, Jackson. If you want to commit suicide, that's fine by me. I won't mourn you. But don't kill your men in the process."

"I don't have time for this crap." He turned to his men. "Come on. Let's go."

I stepped out after him and watched them clamber into a Dodge RAM, holding onto their hats with their coats flapping around them. Then they drove out to the road with the silver rain swirling around their headlamps. I counted thirty and got into the Zombie. I left my headlamps off and followed after them.

I stayed on their red taillights, leaving forty or fifty feet between us. They were practically invisible to me in the fading light. I must have been completely invisible to them. It took us fifteen minutes to get to the St. Francisville crossroads. There, they turned onto Route 10 and I dropped back till their rear lights were nothing more than a dim, red glow in the thickening mist of spray. To the south, vast areas of what should have been green pastureland glowed a dull silver where the flood reflected what little light there was from the sky.

As we moved in among the woodlands, the road became littered with branches that had been torn from the trees and scattered across the blacktop. Here and there, oaks and pines were visible on the fringes of the forest that had been uprooted and dumped in the mire.

Eventually, I came to the spot where I had left my car earlier. I pulled off the road and concealed the Zombie among the bushes on some higher ground that had not yet become a swamp. I retrieved my kit bag, extracted the takedown bow and six of the aluminum broad heads, then ran silently through the trees. I knew Bat was aware of me and probably had a bead on me already. I also knew he had probably recognized me. When I was within eight feet of where I guessed he was hidden, I dropped to the ground and spoke to the foliage.

"Unless you hear the precise words, 'code red', do nothing but record. Have you had anything yet?"

The foliage spoke back to me. "Yup."

"Is Carmichael here?"

"Nope."

"Have we got targets on the outside?"

"One at the back, AK47, hunkered down out of the wind by the shed at the back door. You have a clear line of fire from thirteen yards to my left, by the large oak. Another in the Dodge truck at the side of the building. Fifteen yards to my right. Guard at the front is being fuckin' useless indoors, nobody on the far side."

It wasn't hard to be quiet with the wind whistling and screaming among the branches. I made the fifteen yards and took up my position by the old oak tree. The light was failing fast, but I could see his waterproof coat glistening by the side of the door, in the lee of the shed. I closed my eyes, slowed my breathing and counted to one hundred and twenty. When I opened them again, I could see him clearly. He was sitting on a couple of coke crates he'd pulled out and set against the shed.

I put the weapon together, strung it, and nocked an arrow. The hickory bow had a sixty-five pound draw weight, which was enough to skewer him to the wall of the building, and the broad, razor-sharp heads were designed to cause maximum bleeding and minimum pain. Death was fast and silent. The way I liked it.

The wind was coming from the front of the club, so the back was sheltered to some extent from the air turbulence. I drew back to my ear, adjusted for what wind there was, and loosed.

You do not fire a bow, because there is no gunpowder involved. You shoot a bow or you loose an arrow. I loosed the arrow and there was a soft scrape and a whisper. After a moment, I heard a grunt and a sigh, and I knew he was dead. I didn't even know who he was, but I knew I'd killed him.

His pal in the truck was going to be more complicated. The wind channeling down the side of the club would be gusting at fifty miles an hour. The bow was not an option. I ran back the way I had come, left the bow beside Bat, and moved on till I was five or six yards behind the truck. Then, I crawled to the rear wheel, pulled my knife from my boot, stood, and knocked on the glass with my left hand.

He pushed open the door and shouted, "*What?*"

The blade went in through his throat and severed his brain stem. He didn't even know he was dead. His nerves jumped and he quivered for a couple of seconds. I pushed him back in the truck and closed the door.

Then, I staggered to the front of the building and up the stairs to the entrance. I hammered for about thirty seconds and saw a light come on inside, which I knew was the private room at the back. A few moments later, the door opened and Jackson was peering out at me.

He said, "He's here. In the back."

I pushed in past him and the door slammed behind me. I said, "What happened to James?"

"He doesn't know. He says he was OK when he left."

"How come he didn't wait for me?"

"Ask him yourself."

He turned and walked across the darkened bar toward where a sliver of yellow light leaned out across the wooden floor. I followed him. We pushed through the door and he closed it behind me.

I was not surprised to see Ivory sitting at the table, smiling. There was no silver-haired businessman sitting with him, no Grumman, and that didn't surprise me either. There were half a dozen big, brawny gorillas sitting around the room, and on the floor, the two uniformed cops were lying with their eyes open and big, gaping holes in their chests. They'd had a bad feeling about their boss back at

Carmichael's house. I'd seen it in their eyes. It was a shame for them that they didn't act on it.

I glanced at them for a moment and then at Jackson. "What were their names? Did they have families? They didn't deserve to die."

There was nothing but contempt in his face. "Stop, you're breaking my heart. You want to know why they died? They died because you couldn't keep your damned nose out of our business. If you'd listened to me and got the hell out Burgundy, Joe and Phil would be going home to their wives and kids tonight. Satisfied?"

I smiled and shook my head. "So it's my fault you murdered two police officers? My fault because I wanted to save an innocent man from being framed for murder?"

Ivory started his high-pitched wheezing laugh. "What is this, a cheap B movie? Will somebody please tell me what the *hell* I am doing here tonight? Where is Carmichael?"

Jackson broke in, "More to the point, where is Hays? I went to pick him up and he wasn't at home and he wasn't at the hotel. What have you done with him?"

I shrugged. "He's probably in Canada by now. See, when I saw that this was a frame up, I got him out of here until I can get a federal investigation going."

Ivory was giggling.

Jackson said, "Bullshit. Bull-*shit!*"

Ivory said again, "Where is Carmichael?"

I studied his face a moment. His expression was hard to read. I said, "I thought you might know. He was scared you and Grumman were going to kill him."

His eyebrows shot up to his hairline. "Grumman?" He

grinned. "Carmichael thought *Grumman* was going to kill him, huh?"

"You and Grumman, Ivory. And I think he suspected Jackson here, too. You did kill Sarah, didn't you?"

He shook his head several times, then slammed his palm down on the tabletop. "*Man!*" He pointed at me and spoke to nobody in particular. "Take his weapons and check him for a wire."

I let them take my gun and my knife, watching Ivory all the while. When they had checked me for a wire, I said, "Why'd you kill her, Ivory? Were you jealous?"

He stared at me a long time. "I should kill you right now, you know that? Because you are a very dangerous man. But you know why I *ain't* killed you yet?" He didn't wait for an answer. He turned to Jackson. "You know why I ain't killed him yet, Mr. Pig?"

Jackson shook his head. "No, but I wish you would. This guy gives me the creeps. Kill him and dump him in the swamps."

"No..." He wagged his long finger in the negative. "No, *because* he is so dangerous and *because* he gives me the creeps. Why is he here? Why has he, with total disregard for his own safety, set up this phony meeting with Carmichael, and waltzed in here, with no wire, no back up, and just handed over his weapons? Why?" He pointed at me and craned his neck toward Jackson. "This son of a bitch came in here the other night, killed Eustace, Chave, Paul, and Miles, cut off their goddamn thumbs, and put them right here on the table in front of me!" He got up from his chair and came around the table. "Now you tell me, Jackson, why does a man like that come in here, in this way, knowing we could kill him at any moment?"

"I don't know and I don't care. We should finish him now."

Ivory nodded. "And that's what makes you stupid, Jackson, and me smart. Because information, my friend, is power. And I aim to find out why this son of a bitch arranged this meet, and why he is here."

While he had been rambling, my mind had been working. Now I frowned at him and said, "You say you don't know where Carmichael is, but that's kind of odd, isn't it?"

He narrowed his eyes. "Why? Should I?"

I shrugged. "You killed his wife..." I said it like one thing followed from the other.

He shrugged back at me and shook his head. "So I killed his wife. So what?"

I frowned and laughed at the same time, like I was surprised at how dense he was being. "You shot her with your .38, in her bedroom at Solitude..." I paused like I was waiting for the penny to drop.

He stared at me a long time. Eventually, he said, "What the *hell*...?"

"Maybe I'm missing something, Ivory, but it seems to me that if you shot her with the .38 at Solitude, in her bedroom, you have to know where Carmichael is now."

He was staring at me like I was crazy. Maybe he was right, cause the play I was making had one chance in a million of paying off. But it was the only chance I had right then. He stepped up close to me, with his face screwed up and his eyes like slits.

"What the fuck are you talking about, man?"

I sighed like he was being stupid. "You got Bat to handle the .38, right?"

He nodded, "Uh-huh..."

It was good enough for now. I said, "Stay with me, it isn't complicated. You were screwing his wife and you went to Solitude, where you used to meet, and you shot her in the bed, correct?"

"Yeah...so what?"

I shrugged and grinned. "So nothing, I just wanted you to confirm those couple of points."

His face twisted into an ugly mask.

"You mother fuckin'... You gonna play *me? I'm gonna fuckin' gut you, you piece of shit!*"

I spoke quietly. "Yeah, your man with the goatee thought he'd do the same. Why'd you kill her, Ive? Was it because she didn't want to fuck you anymore? You were boring her? She decided that in the end, her sixty-year-old white boy was a better lover than bad-ass Ivory? Is that why you killed her?"

His laugh was like a screaming parrot. "You so full of shit! You don't know *nothing!* Jackson was right, man. You got balls, but aside from balls, you got *jack!* I'm gonna gut you right now."

I saw the silver glint of the blade and smiled. "Your mistake, Ive, was to think that I was unarmed. I'm not unarmed, Ivory. This is code red, now."

Speed does not come from strength. It comes from technique. It comes from knowing which parts of your body to tense and move, and which ones to leave loose. It took a microsecond to shift my right foot, flick my hip and put all my strength into my abdominals. My fist traveled from my hip to his face in the split second it took to rotate my shoulder.

His nose exploded and he went reeling, staggering back across the table. The gorilla who had checked me for a wire and taken my weapons gaped, and at that instant, the glass in the window shattered and his head exploded. As his big body folded slowly to the floor, I lunged at him and snatched my Sig.

Then all hell broke loose.

TWENTY-THREE

There are some things you just can't prepare for.

Ivory crashed into the table, sending three chairs flying. The headless gorilla folded to the floor among a shower of sparkling glass as the gale howled in through the shattered window. That left four stunned apes shying away from the gaping hole and the flying shards as I seized my Sig.

I managed to get two rounds off. I double-tapped the guy nearest me, his legs did a funny little dance, and he leaned against the wall and slid down, whispering. "Oh, man..."

I had a bead on my next target when Bat's second shot came through the window. He got his man in the head, but the guy was moving, running for the door, and the slug glanced off his skull, ricocheted off the steel frame of the mirror, and embedded itself in my left shoulder. The pain was excruciating. My left arm went into spasm and I missed my shot.

Ivory was screaming over the noise of the gale, "*Get down! Get down! Get down!*" as he scrambled into the corner. Next moment, Jackson charged and head butted me in the gut, sending me crashing to the floor. Then he was sitting astride me, plunging his thumb into my wound and wrenching the Sig from my right hand.

I screamed out, "*Kill the bastards! Kill them!*"

But Jackson had realized the place was bugged. He shoved the gun in my face and bellowed over me, "*One more shot and I blow the son of a bitch's head off!*"

We all froze and waited. The wind whistled and groaned. Rain lashed over the shattered glass, drenching the headless corpse. Ivory cowered in the corner. I counted the dead: three. Three more live goons lay on the floor, staring at the gaping black hole in the wall, through which death might enter at any moment. I said, "Three down, five to go."

Jackson pistol-whipped me and my head felt like it had been split in half. A warm trickle of blood ran down my face.

Jackson got to his feet, took a fistful of my collar, and dragged me up after him.

"Where's the bug?"

"Under the table."

He turned to Ivory, who was still cowering, watching us. "Get up, you piece of shit! Get the bug." He turned to the three guys on the floor. "You! Get up! Tie this motherfucker's hands behind his back."

Ivory had found the bug. He got to his feet, staring at it in his hand. The three goons were up, too, and I got a good look at them. One of them, a huge hulk who looked like Godzilla only with less forehead, was removing his dead companion's shoelaces. He had the kind of still eyes you find in people who are absolutely obedient, and whose minds are completely untroubled by thought.

The other two had come to grab my arms. The one on my right was about six feet and had the build of a guy who spends a lot of time in the gym. He had a badly cut, shiny suit and insolent eyes. You could tell he thought he was smart. You could also tell he was wrong.

The one on my left was older than the others, maybe in his late forties. He looked like a family man, a tough guy who'd grown soft. Kids will do that to you.

Jackson reached out his hand to Ivory and said, "Give it to me." Ivory handed over the bug and Jackson smirked at me. "That you, Bartholomew? You better come in here out of the storm and lay down your weapons, 'cause your pal here is going to have a real rough time if you don't. And let me tell you this, friend. Every shot you fire is a bullet I am going to put in Walker's arms and legs."

Godzilla had come up behind me and was tying my wrists with his dead pal's laces. I said, "He won't come in. He's too smart, Jackson. He knows you'll kill him as soon as he steps through the door." I laughed. "And if I know Hays, he likes the odds. Five lightly armed morons like you, with handguns, against a guy like him. You don't stand a chance."

I expected another pistol-whipping for feeding Bat information about their number and weapons, but neither Jackson nor Ivory picked up on it. Their minds were on other things. Ivory had grabbed a chair and dragged it across the room where it was out of sight of the window. Jackson seemed to have read his mind, because he grabbed me and shoved me onto the chair, snarling, "Tie his ankles to the legs, and his hands to the back."

I frowned up at him, wondering where this was going.

"What are you hoping to achieve, Jackson? The game is up. The most you can do is kill me, but that won't stop the process. You're done. It's over."

The back-hander took me by surprise. It made my head ring and, with the pain in my shoulder, for a moment I was stunned and couldn't think.

He snarled, "Where's Carmichael?"

I blinked a couple of times and stared up at him. It was a good question. I had half-expected him to be at the Full Moon. But instead of telling Jackson that, I said, "Fuck you."

That earned me another back-hander. This one I expected and rode it as far as I could, but it still hurt and still left my head ringing.

Jackson raised his voice. "You listening to this, Hays? I am going to beat your pal to death unless one of you tells me where Carmichael is."

Before he hit me again, I asked him, "What's it to you where he is? Why do you want to know?"

His answer was another blow.

Then he started laying into me methodically, right, left, right, with his fists, adding the occasional jab at my shoulder. Eventually, he paused, out of breath. I could feel my left eye swelling up, and when I tried to spit the blood from my mouth, I realized my lip and cheek were swollen too. The pain in my head and shoulder were extreme. If Bat was planning to do something, he was going to have to do it soon.

Jackson raised his voice again. "How about it, Hays? Where is he? Where have you got Carmichael?"

I raised my own voice. "Do what he says, Bartholomew, we're in a lose-lose situation. Just *let him have it!*"

As I said it, I threw myself violently to one side. The strain of the movement made me feel like my left shoulder was being torn off, but it got me out of the path of Jackson's boot. He'd caught the double message, but just a second too late. The hail of lead exploded through the window, sending chairs spinning, ripping at the table, tearing wood from the walls. The mirror exploded, voices shrieked in panic and there was a stampede for the door.

Then Bat was through the window and crouching behind me, cutting at my bonds. As I sat up, he handed me my knife. "Still got that, hey? It was on the floor, over by the headless wonder. You're losin' your touch, sir, getting old."

I snarled at him, "You shot me, you son of a bitch!"

He frowned. "Really?"

"It's a ricochet, I'll live. Where'd they go?"

He jerked his head at the door. I counted the bodies on the floor. There were still three. "You didn't kill any of them?"

He looked embarrassed. "They all charged for the exit, didn't they? And I was tryin' to get Jackson off you. I wasn't exactly aiming."

Before I could answer, Jackson's voice bellowed from the barroom. "*Lacklan! You may as well give it up. You have nowhere to go and you're just about all out of ammunition. All we want is to know what you've done with Carmichael. Give us that, and you can go on your way. We all have a lot to lose here!*"

I stared at Bat's face a moment, thinking. "Give me a hand here. Kill the lights and help me pull that body over."

He doused the lights and we dragged one of the bodies to the door, like it was one of us taking up a defensive position. Meanwhile, I shouted, "*What's the big deal with Carmichael, Jackson?*"

To Bat, I whispered, "Out the window! Go! To the car!"

He vanished silently, like a ghost. I crouched down and yelled, "*If you want him so much, come and get him!*"

Then I let off four rounds and followed after Bat as a hail of bullets tore through the door. The wind almost lifted me off my feet as I staggered across the open ground and fell among the ferns and the trees. Bat was there waiting for me.

"I told you to go to the car."

"Yeah, well you ain't my captain anymore, are you, sir?"

I took my cell from my pocket and waited five more seconds till the lights came on and we could see the silhouettes moving across the open window as they stormed the room. Then I pressed # 9. The walls seemed to quiver and there was a smoky flash. Bugs hadn't been the only thing I'd hidden in the club room. It had only been a quarter of a cake of C4, behind the vinyl bar, but it was enough, and mirrors and bottles make great shrapnel.

"Come on, buddy, let's go."

We got to our feet and started moving through the swaying, moaning forest. He offered me his shoulder but I shook my head.

After a moment he asked, "Where are we going, then?"

"To retrieve my bow and my kit bag, and then to find Carmichael."

"What's the big deal with Carmichael?"

"I guess that's what we're going to find out."

Ten minutes later, we sat in the Zombie with the first aid

kit and, as I swallowed a handful of painkillers, Bat examined my wound.

"It's not very deep. You want me to dig it out?"

"How long will it take?"

He shrugged. "Thirty seconds at most. It'll hurt like fuck, but you're better off without it."

I nodded. "OK."

I handed him my Fairbairn & Sykes. He took it, doused it in alcohol, and took a wad of bandage from the box. He looked me in the face. "Ready?"

I nodded. My belly was on fire. He stuffed the bandage in my mouth and I sat on my left hand. He took a pair of scissors from the first aid kit and said, "Now don't move or you'll make a fuckin' mess of this, sir."

I nodded again. He didn't hesitate. He stuck the blade in, down the side of the slug. The pain was like nothing I had ever felt. I'd sworn to myself that I would not make a noise, but I heard myself screaming through the bandage, and my left arm quivered and jumped like it had a life of its own.

Bat ignored me and rammed the scissors firmly into the hole in my arm and levered with the knife. His face seemed to clench up, and next thing, he had the slug held between the blades of the scissors, and the extreme agony had subsided. I collapsed back into the seat, grunting and panting. I felt suddenly very cold and started to sweat.

He dressed the wound and gave me another couple of painkillers. "I drive," he said. I didn't argue.

He came around to the driver's side and I slid over to the passenger seat. The last thing I remember is him looking at the controls in disgust and saying, "What the fuck is this, anyway?"

Then I passed out for ten minutes.

When I came to, for a few moments I didn't know where I was. All around me there was darkness, and we were motionless. The sound of water drumming on the car and the high whistle of the wind filled my head and I couldn't think. Slowly, I became aware of Bat next to me, and I began to remember.

He spoke softly, and I saw that his eyes were on the rearview mirror.

"You back with the living, sir?"

"Don't call me sir. What are you doing?"

"I'm not sure. I thought maybe we'd picked up a tail. It's hard to tell in this weather. The trees are bouncin' around all over the place and you don't know if you're seein' the light from a house, or the headlamps of a car. So I thought I'd kill the lights and sit here for a bit by the side of the road. I think we're OK."

"Where are we?"

"Crossroads at St. Francisville." He frowned at me. "So where *is* Carmichael? I'm guessin' you have him safe somewhere. And why do these buggers want to get a hold of him so badly?"

I stared out at the blackness. The street lamps began to take shape, along with the trees across the road in front of the bank, and the shopping mall. It dawned on me that the lights were all out. The power had failed.

"I don't know, no, and I don't know."

"You don't know where he is, you haven't got him safe, and you don't know why they want him."

I nodded. "That's right, Bat. Bit of a mess, huh?"

"We've known worse. So what's the plan?"

The plan. All I could see was shadows moving in the dark, and all I could hear was a million banshees released from hell, screaming over the fields and the woodlands.

"I think I might know where Carmichael is, Bat. I think maybe I have been very stupid."

"Where?"

"I think he might be at Solitude, and I think we should go and ask him why Jackson and Ivory are so keen to find him."

He looked at me like I was crazy. "At *Solitude?* I didn't think he even knew it existed..."

I reached in the glove compartment, took a fresh, dry pack of Camels, and started to peel it. "Well, he knows now. Maybe I'm wrong. Let's go and see."

We stopped on the way at the Soniat. It was illuminated by hundreds of lamps and candles that wavered and danced in the drafts and breezes that crept in through the rattling doors and windows.

We deposited the recordings we'd made with Hirschfield. He insisted he didn't want to know how we'd got them, and we were happy not to tell him. We left him settling down to a candle-lit meal, alone in the somber dining room.

Again we crawled through the pitch black, almost feeling our way along the road, with the headlamps barely penetrating the sheets of rain and the dense mist of spray that rose up off the blacktop. We missed Tunica and ended up having to turn around and crawl back, with the window open, searching for the turn off. Eventually, we found it and plunged in among the tall trees, where the howl and whistle became more like the sigh of giant breakers against cliffs in a storm. We crossed the bridge and I saw that Sara Bayou had swollen to a bloated, roaring river, threatening to burst its banks.

At last, we came to Solitude Road and turned left, and after three hundred yards we made out the big, iron gates and pulled over.

In the lee of the trees I popped the trunk and took out my second Sig and gave it to Bat. We took spare ammo and I slipped the short-barreled S&W 500 in my waistband. I used it to blow off the padlock on the gate and we silently rolled through and down the drive toward the house. Carmichael's Jeep was parked out front, and there was the glimmer of lamplight in the windows. As Bat slowed, I pointed down the side of the house. I had a hunch.

"Leave it out of sight down there, Bat."

He nodded. He had the same feeling as me.

"What are we going to find in there, Captain?"

He swung around and reversed into the cover of some bushes at the back of the house, with the hood facing the drive, ready for a fast getaway if we needed one. He killed the engine and looked at me, waiting for an answer.

"I don't know. Whatever it is, it won't be nice. You've thought it through. You know what I know. It's bad."

He nodded and climbed out, shouldering the assault rifle and slipping the Sig into his belt.

"Front and back?"

I nodded. "You take the back. I'm going to knock on the door."

He slipped up the steps to the back veranda and I walked around the side to the front of the house. I peered through the glass in the door, but all I could see was a couple of lamps casting a dull glow on the sofa and the chairs. I could make out part of the dining table, and there was light coming out of the bedroom door. I hammered a few times with my fist and saw a shadow move inside. I hammered again and the shadow resolved itself into a silhouette, moving steadily toward me; a silhouette I knew very well.

Simone.

TWENTY-FOUR

She stood frowning at me. "Lacklan? Your face... What happened to you? What on Earth are you doing here?"

I raised my voice over the wind and the roar of the downpour. "I went to your house. You weren't there." We stood a moment staring at each other. "What are *you* doing here?"

She hesitated. Behind her, I saw the back door open and Bat slip in. She caught my glance and I raised my voice again. "You going to keep me out here all night in the storm? Can I come in?"

She looked distressed. "This is a really bad time..."

I laughed. "Really? *This* is a bad time? What? Are you with someone?"

She shook her head. "Why did you come here?"

"Let me in."

She turned and walked away. Bat had disappeared. I stepped in and pushed the door closed behind me, shutting out the roar of the gale and the rain.

"What's going on, Simone?"

"This doesn't concern you."

"*What?*"

She turned to face me again.

"Are you out of your mind? It doesn't *concern* me?"

She raised her hands and shut her eyes. Her face was tight, drawn with stress. "Shut up, Lacklan. Shut up. I know your friend is accused of Sarah's murder. And I am sorry about that. And I am sorry that you and I have become close. I didn't mean that to happen, but this, *this*, what is happening here, now, tonight. This has nothing to do with you, and you should go."

"What? What is going on here tonight, Simone?"

"Go away, Lacklan."

"I can't do that."

"You don't *understand!*"

"Then explain it to me."

She shook her head.

"Where is Carmichael?"

"Go *away!*"

"Where is he?"

She reached behind her back and suddenly, she had a .22 in her hand. It wasn't a surprise. I had expected it.

"You'll try to stop me. I won't let you stop me."

"Do you know how many people have died tonight, Simone?"

"Don't! I'm not interested. I don't care."

I stepped toward her and she backed up a step. "I don't believe you. You're a doctor, a healer of minds and souls. That's why Sarah loved you."

"Stop it!"

I shook my head. "Too many people have died already. It has to stop."

She took another step back and gripped the gun with both hands. She was trembling badly. I pressed on.

"James didn't deserve to die."

"He pulled a gun on me. He tried to stop me."

I took another step closer. "From doing what?"

"*Stop it!*" Her eyes were wild and I knew she was close to pulling the trigger. Another step and she might snap. We stood our ground.

I spoke softly. "You know I am never going to back down, Simone. We have a good thing. I am on your side. Just tell me what is going on, and where you have Carmichael."

She swallowed. I could see her jaw muscles bunching. "If you try to stop me, I swear I will kill you and him both. He has to pay, Lacklan. He *has* to pay."

I frowned. Over her shoulder, I could see Bat signaling to me and pointing at the bedroom. I took a deep breath and sighed.

"Simone, Bat is here with me."

She swung around, pointing the gun at him and at me, and backed toward the bedroom.

"Stay away from me."

Bat said, "All right, Simone?" Like he was greeting her at the pub on a Friday night.

I said, "I'll tell you what we are going to do. We're going to sit there at the table and have a drink. And you can explain to us what this is all about, and what it is that Carmichael has to pay for, OK?"

While I was speaking, I walked toward the dining table and pulled out a chair. Bat did the same, signaling me with his eyes to look at the bedroom. Simone was moving to the bedroom door, still holding the gun on us with both hands, saying, "No! *No!*"

But it was too late. I had seen him. Like a grotesque parody of Sarah's painting of Simone, Carmichael was on the bed, stretched out, with each ankle and each wrist bound tightly to a post, and a gag in his mouth. I narrowed my eyes and shook my head.

"What are you doing? This isn't you."

Her scream was shrill, a strange echo of the gale outside. "*He has to pay!*"

"For what?"

"For what he did to Sarah!"

"What did he do to Sarah, Simone? Tell me so that I can understand."

"Don't fucking patronize me! I do that for a living, remember?"

I ignored the outburst and repeated the question. "What did he do to Sarah?"

Her rage was turning to grief and tears were starting to spill from her eyes. "He killed her. He *killed* her..."

I shook my head. "No, he didn't."

The rage returned with a flash to her eyes. "He *killed her!*"

"That is not what happened that night." She stared at me, breathing heavily, but she didn't answer. I pressed her. "That's not what happened that night, Simone, is it?"

"You don't know."

"He was dining at the restaurant. He was seen by lots of people."

"He killed her."

"Why don't you tell me what happened?"

"It's none of your goddamn business."

"She was shot in that bed, wasn't she?"

"I didn't know..."

"Is that why you brought him here, so that he would die in the same place, in the same way that she did?"

"I didn't know."

"You didn't know that she had been killed here?" I stood and walked toward her.

She waved the gun at me. "Get back! Sit down!"

But the moment had passed. Her resolve was shaken. I shook my head. "I am not a threat to you, and you are not a killer."

I took hold of the gun and gently levered it out of her fingers. Her face crumpled. She stared at me with horror in her eyes. "No... *No, Lacklan!* He has to pay..."

I held her in my arms. Bat got up, came around, and took the .22 from my hand. She sobbed into my chest for a while. Then I maneuvered her to the table and sat her down. "Tell me what happened, Simone."

Her face was sodden and twisted with grief. "He killed her. He has to pay, Lacklan. You can't. You can't take this away from me."

"Quit saying that. You know it's not true."

"*It is!*"

The pain and the exhaustion overwhelmed me for a moment and I snapped. "*She was shot in that bed, Simone! He wasn't here!*"

She glared at me and half-screamed, "*And neither was I!*"

Her meaning became clear. I glanced at Bat and he read my mind. He went into the bedroom and Simone started to get to her feet. "What are you doing?" I stood and took hold of her. She struggled. "Don't you let him go! *Don't you let him go!*"

"I'm not! *I'm not!* Simone! Settle down, goddamit!"

We both stared into the bedroom as Bat approached the bed, leaned down, and removed the gag. It was like blowing a dam.

"*You stupid, fucking bitch! You'll pay for this. I swear you'll pay for this!*"

I got up and went to stand in the doorway, looking down at him, helpless on the bed. The windows rattled and rain lashed the glass.

"Lacklan, for God's sake, man, cut me loose! This woman is crazy! She was going to kill me!"

I nodded. "I know."

He stared at me, aghast. "You're not with her, Lacklan! For God's sake, tell me you're not with her!"

"I'm not with anyone, Carmichael. Right now, I am exhausted, in pain, and badly in need of a cigarette and a drink. You people are driving me crazy."

"*Lacklan!*"

"Don't worry, nobody is going to kill you, at least not yet." I turned to look at Simone. She was still at the table, with her head in her hands. I gestured to her to come, and as she approached, I pointed at the chair near the foot of the bed. "Sit. And if you move, I will shoot you in the leg. Believe me, I don't hesitate. I just do it."

She looked disgusted and went to sit down. I pulled my cigarettes from my pocket and lit up. I inhaled deeply and let the smoke out slow through my nose, watching Carmichael watching me from the bed.

"Cut me loose, Lacklan, for crying out loud."

I nodded. "But you see, there are things that confuse me. You were going to call Grumman and Ivory to be at the Full Moon, so we could record them and ambush them..."

He was suddenly shouting again, "*And I would have been there if this crazy bitch hadn't...*"

"Can it, Carmichael. We'll come to that. Just listen." I took another drag. "You called Grumman and Ivory, but only Ivory turns up, with seven of his men. Grumman never shows. Why was that?"

"I don't know! How should I know? Maybe he spoke to Ivory and Ivory said he'd take care of it."

I smiled. "Ivory thought you were crazy to suspect Grumman. And so did Hirschfield."

"What are you getting at?"

"Here's something else that surprised me. Grumman didn't show up, but Jackson did, at your house. He came along with two uniforms. Two uniforms he later murdered in cold blood."

"I don't know what you're driving at, Lacklan. Just cut me loose, will you?"

"What am I driving at? Why did you lie about Grumman being involved in a conspiracy to kill you? Why did Jackson, who *did* try to kill *me*, turn up at your house to pick you up? I keep asking myself, if Simone hadn't come and dragged you off for a special evening of bondage and murder at Chez Sarah, what would have happened to me, when you and Jackson and Ivory all got me alone at the Full Moon?"

"No, you're wrong. I had no idea about any of that! I am

victim here, Lacklan! My wife was murdered, and now this bitch wants to kill me, too!"

I smoked for a bit, watching him on the bed. None of it was conclusive. My brain was tired and I knew I was missing things, but the pain in my limbs, my shoulder, and my face kept threatening to overwhelm me.

"Here's something else that confuses me. The blood."

"What blood?"

"When I saw the bed, the bed where Sarah was supposed to have been killed..." I shook my head. "I have shot a lot of men, Carmichael, and I have seen a lot of men shot, but I have never seen as much blood as I saw on that bed that day, not from a bullet wound to the gut. I kept wondering about that. So I requested a sample of the blood to be handed over to my attorney. But to be on the safe side, I took a sample myself, personally. And I took them over to Houston to have them analyzed privately in a lab."

He had gone very still. So had Simone.

After a moment, he said, "Analyzed for what?"

"To see whose blood it was."

"It was hers, of course! Who else?"

I shook my head. "Here is the confusing thing, Carmichael. The sample that was sent to me by the DA, via Detective Jackson, was somebody's blood. But the blood I collected from the bed..." I watched his face carefully. I gave a small shrug. "Hazard a guess."

"You can't play games with this! This is my wife's murder you're talking about!"

"It was pig's blood, Carmichael. Pig's blood!"

Simone screamed. I turned to look at her. She had her

hands over her mouth and her eyes were wide. She was shaking her head and whispering, "No... Oh God... *Why?*"

Carmichael's face was screwed up and he had tears streaming down his cheeks. He was also shaking his head and sobbing, "This is grotesque. Please let me go. This is inhuman. Poor Sarah! Why? Why...?"

I watched him a while. Bat was frowning at me and I knew he didn't approve of what I was doing. I ignored him and went on. "Then I remembered something James had said to me. On the night that Sarah was killed, he heard a pig squealing like it was being murdered, those were his words, down by the corrals at the back of your house. 'Round about eleven o'clock."

I pointed at the bed where he was lying. "She was shot by Ivory right there, where you are lying, and that is where she bled out. Then he loaded her into a vehicle and took her to your house, where he placed her in your bed. Then, to make it seem she was murdered there, he went and slaughtered a pig, collected the blood in a bucket and soaked the bed with it. He knew the blood would never be tested, because the investigation would be in the hands of his friend, Detective Jackson, and the weapon would be found with Bartholomew Hays' prints all over it. It would be a slam dunk." I frowned and shook my head. "But what confuses me, is, why? Why would he do that? Why would he go to all that trouble, and risk getting caught at your house? How did he know you would be out? And, if he had gone to all the trouble of getting Bat's prints days before, why did he kill her here? Why didn't he just kill her at the house?"

Carmichael had started sobbing like a child and he

wouldn't stop, but Simone had gone very still and very quiet.

Carmichael opened his eyes. He was staring around the room like he was looking for a solution. "I don't know what you want from me. I loved Sarah more than anything in the world. I am heartbroken, and all you can do is torture me and humiliate me with these insane innuendos. What are you driving at? What are you insinuating?" He lifted his head to look at me. "Why don't you come out and say it?" His head flopped back. "Because you have nothing but theories, and your mind has been poisoned by this madwoman."

Simone spoke suddenly and her voice was like poison become sound. "You killed her, you filthy piece of shit. If you didn't do it with your own hands, you had that bastard Ivory do it."

He stared at her in despair. "*Why? Why would I do that? I loved her? Where would I find another woman like her?*"

"*Lies! She Told me! She told me herself that she was through with you and couldn't stand you anymore!*"

"*In your fantasies, you sick bitch!*"

"*She was fucking every man she could get her hands on!*"

"*No! No! No!*"

He turned to me and his face was desperate. "Lacklan, you have to believe me! We had our difficulties. I was older than her and we had different likes and tastes. It was normal. But we loved each other and we were determined to fix it. We were working together. She was coming back to me."

I sighed. "She had changed her will, Carmichael. She had left everything to Simone."

"That's a lie! Lacklan, this woman is poisonous! There is nothing she will not stoop to. She forged Sarah's signature!

She's an artist! Who do you think taught Sarah to paint? All to lure her away from me! Half of these painting on the walls are not Sarah's, but *hers!* Especially that disgusting nude! Sarah would never paint anything as base as that!"

I turned to Simone and raised an eyebrow at her. She glanced at me and said, "Bullshit!"

I sighed again and rubbed my face with my hands. "I am tired. We are not going to sort this out tonight. Bat, I say we cut Carmichael free. But we tie them both to their chairs so they can't kill each other. We have something to eat and sit out the storm. Four hour watches. What do you say?"

He nodded. "There's a lot of intel to process here, sir, and I'm shagged. I think we should have Hirschfield look it over an' all."

"Agreed."

Simone was looking at me with narrowed eyes. "You are going to tie *me* to a chair?"

"And if you resist, I will give you a damn good spanking and throw you in the bayou. Don't try me, sister, I am in no mood! Bat, we need some rope..."

He looked embarrassed for a moment, then went to the chest of drawers. He pulled open the top drawer and extracted two sets of handcuffs. He looked at me and shrugged.

We cuffed Carmichael and Simone each to a heavy, wicker chair, Bat went to cook some food, and I poured myself a large whiskey.

Then we all settled down to sit out the storm.

TWENTY-FIVE

I SLEPT FITFULLY, AND MY DREAMS WERE PLAGUED with the sounds of howling and screaming, which eventually descended into deep groans of pain. Every ten or fifteen minutes, the aches and throbs in my body would wake me. I would try to adjust to a more comfortable position, but it was impossible, because everything hurt. The battering of the wind was relentless and instead of dying down, if anything, it was getting worse. The timbers in the house were creaking like an old ship on the high seas.

In the end, I lay on the floor and watched the room, hoping that sooner or later exhaustion would win over pain. I noticed Carmichael, eyes closed, snoring softly in his chair, oblivious to the storm. I guessed maybe that was the story of his life. Bat Hays, solid and dependable as the Rock of Gibraltar, wide awake on the sofa with the HK416 across his legs. It was good to have him there.

And Simone, also awake, watching me as though she were in a trance, with no expression on her face at all, no clue to her thoughts or feelings. I looked at my watch. It was two AM. The wind gusted, rattling the doors and windows, lashing rain against the glass. The house creaked and groaned.

I saw Bat cock his head on one side, frown, and get to his feet. He put out the lights and stepped silently to the window. He hunkered down, moved the drapes half an inch, and peered out through the corner. I sat up and he said, "We have company, Captain. Now, who'd be out on a night like this?"

I slipped over to the other window and looked out. All you could see was the dark driveway, the thrashing trees, and sixty or seventy yards up the path, a black bulk that was darker than the darkness around it. I said, "A Dodge RAM."

"Probably, hard to tell from here."

"I'm guessing Jackson and Ivory sent the boys in ahead to make sure we were dead."

"Back at the Full Moon? Yeah, makes sense. I thought we'd picked up a tail. I wonder how long they've been here."

I shook my head. Then, something caught my eye and I sighed. "Look at the hood of Carmichael's Jeep. It's been opened. If we leave here, we leave on foot. What the hell do they want?"

"Carmichael."

"What for? What do they want him for?"

Simone's voice came like a drop of acid. "Their cut..."

I turned and looked at her.

She went on, "They want me, too, you know? But they want him alive."

"The original will is with your attorney?"

"Yes, and they know it's authentic."

"Your attorney is in Baton Rouge."

She nodded. Bat glanced at me and finished my thought. "They get rid of her, and raid the offices while the security services are stretched too thin to respond. Destroy the will and Carmichael has no challenger."

I grunted. There was still plenty that didn't make sense to me. I said, "That's going to have to wait. Here's the plan. You go out the back and circle 'round through the woods. I'm going to count to three hundred, then I'm going to draw their fire. Give me the rifle. You use the Sig. I need one of them alive, but incapacitated."

"That'll work. Any preference?"

I looked at Simone and noticed in passing that Carmichael was still asleep. I asked her, "Which one is most useful?"

She shrugged and looked disgusted. "They're both in it up to their necks."

I turned back to Bat. "Jackson might have more information. Kill Ivory, keep Jackson."

"OK. Start counting?"

I nodded and he made for the back door at a run. He wrenched it open and the sound of the gale and the torrential rain was suddenly deafening. Too loud. It was like being on the beach with giant breakers crashing at your feet. I watched him stagger back a few steps into the room, then grab the door and pull himself forward again. The house was creaking badly. Carmichael opened his eyes and looked around. Bat struggled out onto the veranda and I went after him. That was when I heard him shout over the wind, gripping the wooden banister.

"*Holy fuck!*" He turned to look at me, blinking in the wind. "*Holy fuck, sir! You have to see this!*"

I dragged myself out. The gale had increased in power and almost lifted me off my feet. I gripped the rail next to him and looked out. We might have been on a boat on the ocean. Sara Bayou had burst her banks and the water was lapping at the decking on the veranda, four feet above the lawn. The steps down were underwater and a powerful current, dragging the water down into the river, was making huge eddies around the house. Bat pointed and shouted, "*Look! Your weird motor!*"

I looked and saw the Zombie, half submerged, slowly twisting and inching toward the bayou. Bat tried to look at me, with the wind battering his face. "I'll never make it, sir! I'll be sucked away by the current!"

A creak and a groan of timbers, loud enough to be heard over the roar of the water and the screaming and whistling of the wind, confirmed what he was saying. Then the house shifted. It may have been a few inches, or a foot. But it was a clear, powerful shift of the entire structure. The soil was saturated, and the combined power of the wind and the sucking current was shifting the foundations of the building.

We had a problem.

I jabbed my finger at the door and shouted, "*Get inside!*"

We dragged ourselves in and slammed the door closed. We needed to make some decisions, and make them fast. I spoke without thinking.

"We can't go back, we can't go to the sides, we can't stay where we are. We haven't got time to make a plan. We have to go forward."

"Loaded down with two prisoners..."

"We can't leave them in the house. You got the keys?" I crossed the room toward where Carmichael and Simone were watching us. I kept talking to Bat as we went. "Cuff Carmichael to me. Let Simone go. Here's the plan..."

I spoke as Bat released Carmichael from his chair and cuffed him to me, then released Simone.

"The bayou has burst its banks. The house is about to get either washed away or blown away. We have a truck up the path which probably has Jackson and Ivory in it. We have one chance of survival. This is how we play it. Simone, you go left into the trees and circle through the woods up to the gate. Carmichael, you and me scramble to the tree cover here on the left of the door. Bat, I'll cover you with the rifle. You head into the trees on the right and circle behind their truck. Plan as before. Take out Ivory. Disable Jackson but don't kill him."

"What if there's more than one of them in the truck?"

He wasn't doubting or fearful, he just wanted a plan. I gave him one. "Kill them all. We'll have them trapped between two fields of fire."

Simone spoke with real venom. "This plays right into your hands, doesn't it, Charles? It eliminates your witnesses and gets you off the hook. Now you'll only have me to worry about."

He shook his head. "You're mad, Simone. You're out of your mind."

"We haven't got time for this. Everybody clear?" They all nodded. "Simone, wait for us at the gate. Within ten minutes, we should have a truck. We'll go back to the hotel."

I hunkered down and eased open the front door a few

feet. The wind was coming from the southeast, so at the front door, we were in the lee of the house and the gale was not so bad. I spoke to Simone as she prepared to slip out. "Crawl on your belly until you get to the trees. They will protect you from the wind and should keep you invisible at this distance."

She slithered out and crawled left along the veranda. After a few moments, she had disappeared from sight.

"OK, Bat, now you. When you get to the end of the decking, we'll go. Ready?"

He nodded and slipped out, and within seconds he'd vanished.

"OK, Carmichael, let's go. You do anything stupid and I'll kill you."

We couldn't crawl with our wrists cuffed, so we stepped out and crouch-ran to the left. Then, we scrambled down the steps, ran a few yards to the trees, and took cover behind a large oak.

I took aim at the large, black bulk, where I estimated the windshield to be. My spare ammo was at that moment drifting gently toward Sara Bayou, so I kept my fire to a short burst of three rounds. I let off three bursts and paused a second. It was hard to tell for sure, but I thought I could hear shouting. Then, there were flashes of flame from the shadow, and reports like firecrackers, which were whipped away by the wind.

I hissed, "*Move!*" and dragged Carmichael forward six paces, belly-flopped and let off three more bursts. I saw four flashes from among the trees beyond the Dodge, scrambled to my feet, and ran another six paces. I was about to drop and fire again when a noise, like the Earth ripping open, tore the night in half.

A powerful gust of wind knocked me to my knees, dragging Carmichael with me. There was a screech and a grinding of timbers and the house seemed to fold in on itself, slide to the left and collapsed in a massive heap. As it did so, the clapboards on the walls came loose. The wind gathered them up and hurled them into the air like spray, followed by the slates from the roof.

Then things went really bad. The headlamps on the Dodge came on and the wheels ground on the wet gravel, kicking up stones and mud. I opened up at the engine and the windshield, spraying them with bullets, and from the trees, Bat did the same. But the Dodge was moving, the wind was insane and we were unstable on our feet. If any of the rounds found their mark, they didn't kill the driver, whoever he was. The truck spun on a dime and hurtled up the hill.

I screamed at Bat, "*Simone! Simone!*" and we took off after the truck. But Carmichael was a lead weight on my arm, and it was a good five hundred yards from the house to the gate. In that gale, the mud and the rain, it was an impossible task. My only hope was that she had not got there yet, that they would get there before her.

We sought the cover of the trees on the left of the drive, and half-ran, half-marched. Even at that pace, it took us a good five or six minutes to get to the gates. They stood gaping, wet, iron stencils against a wild, inky sky. There was no sign of Simone. I went in among the trees, screaming her name above the whistle and howl of the wind and the deafening sigh of the branches, but there was no trace of her, no sign of her anywhere.

Finally, Bat and Carmichael grabbed me and pulled me toward the gates, shouting that the only chance to get her back was to get to town, to the Soniat. They hadn't killed her. That meant they wanted to use her, to trade her in exchange for Carmichael.

We tried to keep the forest between us and the wind, but even so it was not easy. The gale was strong, gusting at times to hurricane force, I was sure. It tore branches from the trees and hurled them across the road. It set up powerful eddies and twisters that lashed rain with such force, you felt it would tear your skin from your face. It took us almost twenty minutes to walk the four hundred yards from the gate to the bridge that spanned Sara Bayou on Tunica Road. When we finally got there, what we found was no more than what we had expected, but still, my heart sank at the sight.

The bridge, made of solid, riveted iron, had been completely overwhelmed by the swollen river. The good news was that there was no way that Jackson and Ivory had driven across that bridge. They would have been forced to turn back and head north, to cross further upstream, giving us more time. The bad news was that we ourselves had maybe one chance in a thousand of making it across alive. If the water didn't get us, the wind would for sure.

I gathered Bat and Carmichael close in a huddle and shouted in their ears. "*Our belts!*" I pointed at the rail that ran along the bridge. "*All three of them! We loop our arms through and give each other support! We stay on the near side! The bridge protects us from the wind, and the water pushes us against the frame!*"

They nodded that they understood. We removed our belts and looped them around the rail so that together they formed a strong anchor to the bridge. We stayed on the windward side, so that the frame of the bridge gave us some protection from the gale; and at the same time, the current of the engorged river, rather than dragging us away, crushed us against the iron parapet.

The bridge was one hundred and seventy-eight yards long, and crossing it, even with the provisions we had made, was one of the most exhausting and painful things I have ever done. The pressure of the water against our legs was enormous, and it hammered our bodies, painfully and relentlessly, against the hard iron of the bridge's frame. The three of us had to take each step huddled together, so we could all keep a grip on the three belts, the only thing that stood between us and almost certain death. Each step had to be coordinated against the wind and the current, and taken together, with the lashing rain in our faces and the gale screaming through the iron arches of the structure.

It took us a full fifteen minutes to cover one hundred and seventy-eight yards, and when we finally got to the far side, we had lost the protection of the forest and the furious wind lashed and whipped us with steel needles of rain. Clinging to each other for support and added weight against the gale, we struggled to the nearest hedgerow and collapsed in its shelter.

From there, by stages, we made it at last to Dauphin Street and the shelter of the stone buildings. The street lights were out and the roads were rivers, a foot deep in water. There was nobody to be seen but us. Only a mad person would be out on a night like this.

Finally, at four AM, we arrived at the hotel and collapsed through the door, drenched, bruised, and exhausted. I hammered on the bell at the reception desk and yelled for Luis. Then I turned to Bat. "Organize some coffee and toast. Don't let this son of a bitch out of your sight. I'll be down in five minutes. Then you two can get dried."

I dragged my aching body up the stairs, toweled myself dry, and changed my clothes. Every part of me was screaming out for rest and sleep, but I was not done yet, not by a long way. For what I was going to do, I needed the cover of the storm, and I needed to do it before Jackson and Ivory got back.

When I got down, I found Luis in his dressing gown, fussing over Carmichael and Bat. There was a large pot of coffee on the table and a stack of hot rolls.

"What happened? What happened to you?"

I snarled, "We fell in the bayou. We are going to need more coffee and more rolls. Go!"

He scurried away back to the kitchen. I turned to Bat and Carmichael.

"Go get dried. Carmichael, I may be wrong about you, and if I am, I apologize in advance for what I am going to do. But it has to be done. You are under arrest, you understand? I am putting you in the care of Bat Hays and David Hirschfield. If you try to escape, Bat will kill you without hesitation." I turned to Bat. "Do not let him out of your sight, not to sleep, not to go to the can. He is under lock and key at all times until I get back."

Carmichael was shaking his head. "Lacklan, do not listen to that woman! She is *evil!*"

Bat interrupted him, talking to me like I was insane. "Where the hell are you going?"

"Baton Rouge, into the storm."

TWENTY-SIX

It's a matter of principle with me. If my life is on the line and somebody asks me where I am going, I lie. It makes good economic sense.

I borrowed a large rain-mac from Hirschfield and went back into the gale. I'd seen what I wanted earlier, as we were approaching the hotel. It was one block away in the parking lot outside the mall. It was a big Dodge RAM weighing in around eight metric tons with an engine that could scale mount Everest. I hammered the small blade of my Swiss Army knife into the lock, fiddled around with it, and after ten seconds I was inside. I twisted the fat red to the thin red and gently stroked the green, and we were in business.

I had told Bat and Carmichael I was going to Baton Rouge, but I had no intention of doing that. I was pretty sure that, even if the documents I was looking for were at Wilberforce's offices, it would be almost impossible to lay hands on them in the time I had available. There was a much easier, more direct route to what I wanted. Wilberforce himself, and I was pretty sure I knew where he was.

I took the longer route, via the Full Moon and Jackson, because the shorter way, through St. Francisville, was going to take me deep into the storm, and in the end it would take longer—if I made it at all.

The truck had a range of spotlights on the roof and powerful headlamps, it was heavy, and it gripped the road like it had talons, even in the torrential downpour. I hit fifty going south on Route 61, though I slowed after the crossroads because I had the wind on my right and it kept threatening to blow me off the road whenever I got over forty miles per hour. Even so, I made it to Wilberforce's stack of cuboids within the hour.

I turned in at his drive and it didn't surprise me to see light coming from his windows. He was the kind of man who would have his own generator. I pulled up outside his entrance—you couldn't really call it a door. It was more like an elaborate construction of boulders and mossy banks under an arched, organic portico with a massive, oak doorway set in the middle.

When I climbed out of the cab, I could see him silhouetted in one of his vast, plate glass windows, holding a glass and watching me. I staggered to the shelter of the porch, then rang the bell and hammered on the door with my fist.

It was eventually opened by a guy in a white jacket, with white gloves on. He frowned at me like I was crazy. Before he could say anything, I told him, "I need to see Mr. Wilberforce right now. It is very urgent. I know he's here."

He looked at me like I was everything that was wrong

with the world and said, "Please wait. I'll see if he is in. What is your name?"

I put my hand on the door and smiled a smile that was designed to freeze his blood. "I will not wait outside, pal. Take a look at the weather. Come to that, I won't wait inside. I'm not in the mood to wait. He's in. I told you he's in. And my name is, The Guy Who's Going to Break All Your Bones If You Don't Take Me to Wilberforce *Now!*"

He stepped back.

I stepped in and slammed the door behind me. "Where?"

He swallowed hard, turned, and led the way up a broad flight of wooden stairs encased in a glass tower, onto an expansive landing and through a vast set of highly polished blond wood doors into a broad room with parquet floors, a large copper fireplace in the middle of the floor, and an entire wall of glass, looking out onto the madness of the tempest that was Sarah.

Wilberforce was standing, watching me, with one hand in his pocket and the other holding a drink. He said, "Stephan, who is this man?"

Stephan began to babble an apology. I smacked him in the back of the head with the butt of my Sig, and as he went down I pointed the business end at Wilberforce. He didn't look fazed.

"Who are you?"

"That isn't important. I haven't much time, and you should know that I have killed at least five men tonight, and I have lost count of how many I have killed in my life. Right now, you are part of the solution. That's good for you. The moment you become part of the problem, I will kill you. But what is really bad for you, is if you are both. Because then, I will do very bad things to you. Do you understand me?"

I have to hand it to him. He was cool. When he spoke, his voice was steady and even.

"Of course I understand you. It is perfectly simple. What do you want?"

"Papers. I want all the documents relating to the sale and/or development of Charles and Sarah Carmichael's properties."

He lifted his chin and stared at me. "Ah..." He strolled away from the window, toward the fire. "You represent Simone D'Arcy." He looked down at his shoes, chewing his lip.

I was mad, tired, and exhausted, and I was ready to grab his head and stick it in the fire just to motivate him. But something—some kind of instinct—told me to hear him out.

"This is a foolish move. She doesn't need to go to these extremes."

"Really?" I loaded the question with heavy irony.

He gave a small shrug. "All we want is to negotiate, for her to stop being quite so intransigent. After all, the man has a moral claim on his wife's estate."

I nodded. "And then there are all the deals he's done, on the strength of the property he was due to inherit, right?"

"I couldn't comment on that, Mr..."

I shook my head. "Wrong, you *can* comment, but you don't want to. And you know how it is, Wilberforce, sometimes in life, you just make a bad choice. This is one of those times."

I stepped up and back-handed him across the face. He

dropped his glass, staggered back and fell on a bearskin rug. I kept the Sig trained on him all the way.

"I told you, Wilberforce, as long as you are part of the solution, we're OK. But as soon as you become part of the problem, then things start to turn sour. Now, I am going to ask you again, was Carmichael making business deals on the strength of the property he would inherit from Sarah?"

He wiped the blood from his lip and levered himself up into a sitting position.

"That was unnecessary. No, not exactly. They were very close as a couple. I advised them on all their legal matters. They were a unit. They were both the sole beneficiaries of each other's wills. She was aware of all his property deals, and gave them her blessing."

"What about the property along the Sara Bayou?"

He got to his feet. "What about it?"

"Did she agree to develop that land?"

"Of course."

"When? And how?"

"Early in the summer. We had dinner here. We all discussed it."

"I want to see the documents—agreements, contracts, negotiations, emails, letters—everything!"

"They are not here. They are at my office in Baton Rouge..."

"Left or right?"

He frowned. "What are you talking about?"

"Which kneecap do you want to lose first, the left one or the right one?"

"Don't be ridiculous!"

I rammed him in the solar plexus with the muzzle of the

Sig and winded him badly. I back-handed him again and he went down on his back. I knelt on his left arm, grabbed his hand, forced out his baby finger and rammed the muzzle of the Sig on it. He was screaming hysterically for me to stop. I shouted him down, "*What do I have to do, Wilberforce, for you to take me seriously? You complacent fuck? People are dying and you tell me not to be ridiculous?*"

I pulled the trigger, there was a loud, flat bang, and his finger skipped across the floor. His scream was shrill and hysterical. I stood and grabbed him by the scruff of his neck, dragged him to his feet and hauled him toward the fire. He was kicking and slapping at my arms, sobbing like a child.

"*No! No! No!*"

I stopped and shoved my face into his. "*Have you understood me?*"

"*Yes! Yes! Yes!*"

"Now! Get me the documents or I will blow your left kneecap off."

"OK, OK, OK..."

He could barely walk, and his trousers were soaked from where he had pissed himself. I didn't like doing what I had done, but he was too cool and too complacent and we would have wasted hours, and in that time Simone, Hirschfield, and Bat could have been killed—even Carmichael, if my reading of the situation was wrong. He needed to know I was committed. Now he knew.

He led me across the parquet floor to a door at the back of the room. His hands were trembling so bad he couldn't open it. I opened it for him and shoved him through. I stepped in after him and switched on the lights. Like the rest of the house, it was spacious, with a strange mix of clinical, minimalist lines and pockets of organic shape where the outside seemed to come inside.

He had a black, glass desk and a large, black leather chair. There were low, blond wood bookcases and modern paintings on the walls. He walked unsteadily to the painting behind his chair and lifted it down.

He couldn't look at me. "I... I can't remember..."

"You're something, Wilberforce. Let me tell you how this works. If I have to go back to my car and get some C4, I will cripple you and leave you in the room while it detonates. How far do we have to go before you get with the program?"

"I'm in shock..."

"Open it. It will come to you. I guarantee it."

He reached up, hesitated a moment, then turned the knobs and the door clicked and swung open. I pushed him gently aside. There was a stack of files inside the safe. I pulled them out and went through them. One of them was labeled 'Carmichael'.

I looked Wilberforce in the face. "Is there anything else I need so I can get a complete picture of Carmichael's deals?"

He shook his head. "No, everything you need is there." He dropped into his black leather chair and frowned at me, shaking his head. His skin was pasty. He was shivering and sweating with the shock. "You have to understand, you can't get away with this..."

"If I am right, you have been party to a conspiracy to murder, to framing a man for that murder, and the wholesale theft of land. You better start praying that Hurricane Sarah blows all of this away by morning, pal."

It was approaching dawn as I made my way back along the devastated roads, among the flooded fields and shredded woodlands, toward Burgundy, but you would not have guessed it. The sky was black with churning clouds that you could almost reach up and touch. No light seeped through that dense nebula. It was the low ceiling of a prison in which the only sentence was hell.

I left the Dodge back in the parking lot, with a C note on the seat to pay for the damage I'd done, and staggered my way back to the hotel.

In reception, Luis told me that Carmichael and Bat were asleep upstairs. I looked at my watch. It was six AM. I reached across the counter, picked up the receiver of his phone and punched in Hirschfield's room number. After a few rings, his angry, sleepy voice said, "Who the hell is this at six in the morning?"

"It's Lacklan. Get your ass down here, I have something to show you before I drop dead."

"Promises, promises..."

He let the ambiguity stand and hung up. I looked at Luis. "Coffee, Luis, lots of coffee."

I met Hirschfield in the dining room. He looked disgruntled, but toned it down when he saw the state I was in. I buttered a hot roll and poured myself a third cup of strong, black brew. I could see my hand shaking with exhaustion. So could he. He sat and said, "What the hell have you been doing?"

I nodded. "I need you to listen with great care, Hirschfield, because I might keel over at any moment. Somewhere, in the great fiasco that I am about to describe for you, is the answer to exactly what happened, but I am too tired to see it. So I am going to tell you everything that happened, and I am going to give you these documents..."

I lifted them off the chair and placed them in front of him.

"Then I am going to go and sleep for four hours. By the time I wake up, I hope you will have solved the whole mystery, and I can be on my way."

He poured himself a cup and picked up a roll. "I am listening."

I told him everything. Occasionally, he would stop me, squinting as though either he or I were insane, and say, "You did *what?*" And I would repeat what I had told him, and carry on. Finally, at about seven, I rose, and he watched me leave the dining room with an expression that you might have described as dismay on his face.

I reached my bed and passed out.

TWENTY-SEVEN

I SLEPT FOUR HOURS, THEN SHOWERED AND dressed. I didn't feel rested and everything still ached, but I didn't feel like I was about to drop dead anymore, and my mind was working just fine.

I met Hirschfield down in the bar. He was sitting in his corner behind the fern with what looked like a ream of papers spread out all over the tabletop. He glanced at me as I came in, but he didn't say anything. I ordered a pot of coffee, two cups, and a bottle of J&B Scotch whiskey at the bar. Then I brought them over to the table.

"Do not," he said sententiously, "utter the phrase, 'good morning', there is nothing good about it, and that it is *ante meridium* is a fact with which we are both already acquainted. *This!*" He flicked the backs of his fingers on the papers. "This is a *nightmare!*"

I sat, poured us both a cup, and laced them generously with Scotch. I sipped, watching him, and asked, "What's nightmarish about it?"

"What isn't?" he snapped.

I waited. He sipped and read.

Finally, I said, "OK, we got that sorted. Now you want to answer my question?"

He sighed heavily through his large, pock-marked nose.

"Charles Carmichael entered into a number of extremely lucrative deals involving land development around Louisiana. From what I can see, many of them—*most* of them—involved land belonging to his wife. It would seem that either he was not developing his own land, or using his own money, *or*, more likely, there was very little to use. What was happening here, by and large, was that he was *de facto* acting as his wife's agent..." He paused and then added savagely, "*Prima facie!*"

"Why *prima facie*, and why do you sound mad about it?"

Another big sigh. His eyes flicked over the papers on the table. He looked like he was mad at them for not fitting into the patterns prescribed by the law. "Because, there is a body of correspondence, within these documents, that could be construed by a skillful attorney, such as Wilberforce, as a *de facto* sharing of property."

"What does that mean?"

"It means that though the title..." He glanced at me as though he wasn't sure I knew what 'title' meant. "The *legal ownership* of the properties involved, the name that appears on the deeds—though that was Sarah Carmichael's—the rights to development and exploitation were, implicitly, transferred to Charles."

I frowned and scratched my head. "Jesus, you'd have to be a lawyer to get to a place like that..."

"Indeed, and he has a very good one."

"So you're telling me that even though she owned most of this property, because of a bunch of letters and emails that she wrote, it could be interpreted that she had given Charles the right to sell and develop her land as he saw fit?"

He looked at me as though I had just painted a moustache on the Mona Lisa. "Very much in layman's terms. It is not just her emails, but a large number of emails exchanged between her, Carmichael, and Wilberforce. An exchange of correspondence can be a contract. Any exchange of words and promises, in whatever form, can be a contract. If I say to you, 'will you sell me your horse for three hundred dollars,' and you nod, that is a contract. And more to the point, it is legally binding."

I shook my head. "How could you prove it?"

"That, my boy, is an evidential problem, *not* a legal one. Just because I can't prove it, does not mean it isn't a contract. However, in this case..." He waved a wad of papers at me. "We have ample evidence, in the form of her emails, to prove that she did intend him to act as her agent, and more to the point, she intended him, as her husband, to *own property rights in her land!* So though he did not own the title, and his name was not on the deeds, she handed over to him most or all of the *rights* to use the property *as though it were his own*."

"Shit. But they are emails, there is no signature. Surely they have no value..."

"This is the twenty-first century, Lacklan! What do you think would happen to international trade if emails were not considered by the courts to be binding? The presumption in a court of law is that an email was sent by the owner of the account, and that he intended to say what it says. Anyone alleging the contrary must prove it. So if you want me to go before a judge and claim that these emails are not from Sarah, or that she did not mean to say what is written in them, you must prove it."

"What do you think? Do you think they are genuine?"

He shrugged, spread his hands, and raised his large eyebrows all the way up. "They cover over five years of marriage, and in all that time, she never once sued him or objected to his business activities involving her land. They both made a lot of money and there is *no evidence* to suggest she was not entirely happy with what he was doing. On the contrary, she seemed to be very happy—according to everybody except Simone, who has a vested interest in proving the contrary."

"What about the revised will?"

"That would cancel his claim to the rights in the property, but where is the original?"

"Simone's attorney has it."

He picked up his cup in his huge, hairy hand and sipped from it. His signet ring was almost the size of the cup.

"Wilberforce—Carmichael—they are contesting the validity of the signature. They allege that Simone forged it. They also allege that if she did not forge it, she was exercising undue influence over Sarah." Again he raised his eyebrows and waved the papers at me. "And they have a good case! I have to tell you, Lacklan, if I were the judge, or on the jury in this case, so far, I would be persuaded."

I sank back in my seat. "Why don't I believe it?"

He looked at me. "Perhaps because you are fucking Simone, and she is one of the most sexually alluring women on the planet." He sighed. "I envy you, you *hound!* But, Lacklan, here is a man who has devoted his entire married life to making his wife a rich, happy woman. There is not a soul in this town, in this entire parish, who would not vouch for the happiness of their marriage. He has, in every meaningful interpretation of the expression, been a good husband. There is no record anywhere of his having attempted to screw her, except in the idiomatic sense to which he was entitled at law by his status as her husband. He had..." He formed a circle with his thumb and middle finger and punctuated every word as he enunciated it, "*No-reason-to-want-his-wife-dead!*" He shook his head. "You have *not* provided me with a motive." He drew breath and sighed again. "And as to means, Lacklan, your theory so far of his employing Detective Jackson and Ivory as hit men is nothing but fanciful amphigory."

"...Amphigory."

"Yes."

"What about Jackson and Ivory's behavior last night?"

"There could be a million and one explanations, many of them brought on by your own, wildly excessive, violent, and menacing behavior. And at the end of the day, if you were a Louisiana jury, who would you believe? A detective with fifteen years experience on the force, or a couple of soldiers of fortune from an English regiment, one of whose fingerprints are *still* all over the murder weapon?" He flapped his hand at me. "The average IQ is one hundred, Lacklan. That means that in every eight or nine juries, you might get one juror who is actually smart. The chances of Hays' jury looking beyond the fact that his prints are on the gun that killed Sarah Carmichael are *minimal!* That-is-the-*reality!*"

I sighed. "So we are where we started when I first arrived."

He leaned forward and poured more coffee. He took his time unscrewing the cap on the bottle and laced the two cups. Then he sat back and held out one of his huge, hairy hands.

"Give me one of your Camel cigarettes, will you?"

I took one myself and handed him the pack. I flipped the Zippo and we lit up. He inhaled deeply, held the smoke a moment and let it out slow, like he was smoking a joint. I figured he was in his sixties and wondered for a moment where he was and what he was doing in the summers of '68 and '69.

"No." He said it emphatically and shook his head. "You now have a working theory. If—*if*—it is correct, and not just the product of your lust and your devotion to your friend and colleague, then the proof is out there." He lifted the papers again. "What this proves is that Sarah owned a lot of land, and Charles did not. It proves that he made deals that purported to be on her behalf. But it shows nothing more."

I nodded. "OK. A question, what does it say about the land she had running on either side of Sara Bayou for a mile to the south of the bridge on Tunica Road?"

He frowned. "That's the Sara Bayou Park project."

"Were the state and the university involved? Was this the Louisiana Regeneration Project?"

He laughed. "Hardly! The license they were seeking was for a theme park." He found one of the documents and leafed through it till he found the page he was looking for. "...To create an artificial rapids, to remove poisonous snakes, to keep the existing alligators in captivity, to set up rides, cafeterias, a hotel... You get the idea."

I nodded. "I get the idea." I thought for a while. "Simone told me that Sarah's dream was to convert that land into a nature reserve, to be used for research by the state and by the university, for the regeneration of the natural environment of Louisiana."

He thrust out his bottom lip. "If that is true, you have a conflict between Charles and Sarah involving hundreds of millions of dollars. *That* is a motive for murder."

I nodded. "Yes, but surely it would be in Simone's interest to highlight that conflict."

"Didn't she?"

I shook my head. "No. She told me he was on board, and loved the idea."

He stared around the room, like he had suddenly noticed the décor and thought it was very stupid décor indeed. "That doesn't make any sense, *at all*."

"No, it doesn't."

He squinted at me. His face and his voice were incredulous. "Carmichael and Simone...?"

"She was going to kill him last night."

"Why didn't she?"

I thought about it. "I don't know."

"Find out."

I nodded. "I plan to."About twenty minutes later, Bat and Carmichael came down. Bat looked like he'd spent the morning relaxing on the beach, Carmichael looked like he hadn't slept for a week. Bat put Carmichael's phone on the table and said, "Jackson phoned ten minutes ago. He wants to meet." He jerked his head at his prisoner and said, "He spoke to his nibs here."

Without waiting for an answer, he went to the bar to order more coffee. Carmichael pulled up a chair and sat.

I said, "What's the deal?"

"They hand Simone over to you, you hand me over to them."

"Why do they want you so bad?"

He studied me. His expression was resentful and scared.

"I employed you to find Sarah's killer, and all you've done is betray me and seek to further Simone's interests. Why do they want me so bad? Probably because Simone is paying them to kill me off!"

Bat returned to the table and sat. We stared at each other a moment. It was a semi telepathy that we had developed over the years. I turned back to Carmichael.

"What are you telling me, that you think Simone was responsible for Sarah's death?"

He looked frustrated. "Well, isn't it beginning to look that way? With me out of the way and no challenge to her fabricated will, she gets everything! Everything that Sarah and I worked for all these years!"

I thought for a moment. "Speaking of which, tell me about the Sara Bayou Park project."

He looked surprised. "What about it?"

I pointed at the papers on the table. "According to this, it's a theme park. I thought you and Sarah were on the same page about regenerating the natural environment around here. There is no mention of the involvement of the university, the state, or the CPRA in this project. It sounds more like Disneyland."

He nodded. "Yes, that is perfectly true, and Sarah was not happy about it. Neither was I. But there were lots of interests involved and we were both aware that there had to be give and take."

I shook my head. "What does that mean, Carmichael?"

"It means this was a deal that was worth hundreds—*hundreds*—of millions of dollars. Dollars that we could invest into the Sara Bayou Park project, tax exempt, and at the same time create the Sara Bayou Institute for Research into Environmental Regeneration. But it meant postponing the project a few years."

"Where would this park be, if not on the land along the bayou?"

"That was still under negotiation. Personally, I favored land closer to the coast." He shrugged. "It would have been more relevant to the cause, and more attractive to the State of Louisiana, and the university. We might have attracted investors from Texas and Florida too."

Bat said, "And how did Sarah feel about this delay?"

"She didn't like it, naturally. Neither did I. But in business, as in life, things don't always work out the way you want."

I grunted. "But this wasn't business, was it? This was her life's dream, being postponed indefinitely, for *your* business priorities. The fact is, she had everything she needed to be able to go ahead, but you wanted to postpone it so *you* could make more money."

He sighed. "You can put whatever spin you want on it, Lacklan. The fact is that we discussed it and she agreed. And Wilberforce is a witness to that."

Bat's voice was surprisingly bitter. "Would you have noticed if she hadn't agreed?"

Carmichael flushed and half rose to his feet.

"That is damned impertinent! How dare you?"

Hirschfield snorted what might have been a laugh. "I think it is very pertinent, Carmichael, and it is also a damned good question. However, it is a question that cannot be satisfactorily answered here and now. As things stand, if I may draw everybody's attention back to the central fact of this case, the *only* compelling evidence we have is the *fact* of Mr. Hays' fingerprints on the murder weapon. All of your theories, Lacklan, Carmichael, are so much hooey. There is not a single, compelling fact. It is, if you will excuse me, verbiage. Nothing more."

I nodded. "Agreed. We need a plan. Where do they want this exchange to take place?"

"At my house." He glanced at me without humor. "Please, no explosives! This afternoon. They will insist that you and Mr. Hays are visible and visibly unarmed. You hand me over to them, and they hand Simone over to you."

I frowned. "What makes them think we care what happens to Simone?"

He looked a little embarrassed, like I had said something vaguely inappropriate in polite company.

"Gossip travels fast in a town like this, Lacklan. She has been observed leaving your room, and you leaving her house in the early morning. Besides..." He shrugged. "If I am right, she has told them that you care for her."

"Fair enough. Call him. Set it up. We'll be there."

He frowned and gave a small laugh. "That's it? You're going to hand me over? They will probably kill me!"

I studied his face a moment. "No. We will be unarmed. They will frisk us and find nothing. Then, as the exchange goes ahead, we'll kill them both. We have all the evidence we need to clear Bat, even if we can't close the case. That's not my job."

Hirschfield and Bat both frowned. Hirschfield drew breath to speak. I cut him dead.

"Who pays the bills around here, Hirschfield?"

He raised a withering eyebrow at me. I held his eye. He closed his mouth and sighed.

I said, "That's the way we'll do it." I turned to Carmichael. "Are you happy with that?"

He nodded. "Yes, it will be a relief to have the whole thing settled and poor Sarah avenged." He hesitated, frowning. "But, what about Simone?"

I held his eye for a long moment. "We'll discuss that privately."

He frowned, hesitated.

I said, heavily, "Later."

He nodded. "Fair enough."

TWENTY-EIGHT

THE DOOR WAS STILL BANGING A SLOW, DIRGE rhythm. The storm was showing no signs of letting up. A million voices screamed through the low, bellying clouds, tearing at the trees and hurling roof tiles, shards of ripped up fence, and clapboard like shrapnel through the gray, apocalyptic afternoon. And through it all, Carmichael's door hammered out a rhythm of death.

We went in and I wedged it closed, and the three of us stood looking at each other in the echoing, checkerboard entrance hall, under the great, domed ceiling.

I said, "We have half an hour. Bat, will you set things up? I need a moment alone with Carmichael."

He nodded. "No worries. I'll get some chairs."

He made off toward the dining room and I took Carmichael into his study and closed the door. Outside the double-glazed windows, the trees seemed to be doing some kind of crazy, silent, ritual dance. I pulled my cigarettes from my pocket, shook two out and handed one to him. His hand was steady as he took it. I flipped the Zippo and we lit up. As I blew out smoke, I said, "I think I owe you an apology."

He looked surprised. "How's that?"

"I'd made up my mind you had killed Sarah. My first priority was to clear Bat. If that meant taking you down, that was what I was going to do. But I misjudged you and I owe you an apology."

He nodded. "I won't deny you had me scared there for a while. But that's a handsome apology and I accept." He hesitated a moment and then added, "That's the kind of man I had you down as, and you proved me right." He smiled. "I hope I never get on the wrong side of you again!"

I returned the smile. "It's not a good place to be." I reached behind my back and pulled out one of my two Sigs. The other was under my arm. I handed it to him.

"It's loaded and chambered. The safety is on. She killed your wife, Charles, just like she was going to kill you. I know what it means to lose the woman you love."

He considered my face a moment, then took the gun.

I went on, "I'm not telling you to kill her, but I think you have the right to choose. If you do, use my weapon, not one of yours."

He didn't say anything, but after a moment, he slipped it into his waistband, behind his back. I went and sat on the windowsill.

"When they come in, we'll all show our weapons, but not you. I'll demand we lay them down before we talk and make the exchange. When she is half way across the room, that's when you make your move. If you decide to kill her, Bat and I will deal with the consequences. If you decide to let her live, then we'll take it from there."

He stared hard at the carpet. After a long while, he said, "Thank you, Lacklan. Not many men would understand that."

"Like I said, I'm not a good man to be on the wrong side of."

We had a drink of whiskey in silence, then stepped out into the entrance hall again. It looked bizarre, like a scene from a modern, expressionist play off Broadway. Bat had brought four chairs from the dining room. They looked like genuine 18th century antiques in red and gold. He had put them near the center of the floor, each pair about fifteen feet from the other, and seven or eight feet apart, forming an oblong. If nothing else, the setting would unsettle them.

Carmichael blanched when he saw the chairs. He looked at me anxiously. "They won't get damaged, will they? Each one of those chairs is worth a small fortune."

I shook my head. "No reason why they should." I looked at Bat. "All set?"

He nodded. "What if they try to hit Mr. Carmichael after the exchange?"

I shook my head a second time. "It's taken care of. Besides, we are all going to frisk each other. We'll all be unarmed." I smiled. "And if it comes to unarmed combat, I think we can hold our own."

He grinned. "I think so, sir."

Outside, barely audible over the howl of the gale and the roar of the downpour, we heard the grinding of a large truck. We took up our positions in front of our chairs, Bat armed with the HK416 and I with the 9mm Sig Sauer. Carmichael was behind us, apparently unarmed. In Jackson and Ivory's mind, he was our prisoner. It would make perfect sense that he was unarmed.

The door was shoved open and they half staggered in. The noise of the storm was suddenly magnified and echoed around the great, domed entrance hall. Jackson had Simone with a rope tied around her neck, like a leash on a dog, and her hands bound behind her back. She was barefoot and drenched from the rain. It was clear from her face that she had been weeping, but she was fighting hard to hide the fact. I ignored her and looked from Jackson to Ivory, who was forcing the door closed and wedging it shut.

Jackson had a 9 mm Glock in his right hand, and Ivory had a Colt .45 Desert Eagle. It was the kind of gun he would use. He turned from the door and they all stood staring at the weird set up that Bat had arranged for us. Before they could say anything, I spoke out.

"This is how this is going to work. If you don't like it, you can turn around and get the fuck out of here, and hope you make the gates before we close them and blow you and your truck to hell. I want to be clear about this. You are outgunned and outclassed. You're alive because I want this settled in the easiest, quickest way. Are we clear so far?"

Jackson curled his lip and started to speak, "Quit waving your dick around, Walker..."

"Ivory, you and Bat will lay down your weapons. You will meet in the middle of the floor. You will each frisk the other to make sure you are unarmed. You will then return to your seat and sit down. Then, Jackson, you and I will do the same, return to our seats and sit down. We will discuss terms and conditions, and when we are done, we will exchange hostages. You will then leave with Carmichael. Understood?"

Ivory flapped his hands at us. "Yeah, whatever, man."

He and Bat carefully placed their weapons on the floor and walked to the center of the hall. Bat raised his hands and Ivory frisked him thoroughly. He found nothing, because there was nothing to find. Ivory then raised his hands and Bat frisked him. He found a switchblade in his pocket, placed it on the floor, and kicked it out of reach.

Ivory grinned. "Take it easy, man. That has sentimental value for me. My ex-wife gave it to me ten minutes before she died."

He walked back to his chair, wheezing a laugh like a smoker's cough and walking like a dancing chicken.

Then Jackson and I repeated the performance. We laid down our pistols out of reach, then walked to the center of the floor. He told me with his face that he wanted to kill me right there and then. I told him with mine that I was going to kill him, a little later on.

He frisked me and found nothing. I frisked him and found the same. I said, "Go and sit down, Jackson."

We returned to our chairs and sat. Carmichael was standing behind us. Ivory had Simone on her leash, standing by his side. Jackson was the first to speak, like a spoiled child demanding an ice cream.

"OK, hand over Carmichael."

I smiled. "Why are you so keen to get your hands on Charles Carmichael, Jackson?"

I caught the quick glance. Then, "That's none of your goddamn business."

"I disagree. He employed me to find his wife's killer. I am

responsible for whatever happens to him if I hand him over to you."

"Quit stalling, Walker. If you don't hand over Carmichael, we don't hand over Simone. Stalemate."

I shrugged. "All I'm asking for is information, Jackson. I don't see why that's a problem."

Again the glance. "OK, I am the detective in this town. A lot of stuff has gone down in the last couple of days. Me and Ivory had an arrangement. Everything was cool and everybody was happy. Then you had to show up and everything went to pieces. All I want is assurances, guarantees, that when you get the hell out of here, things will go back to normal."

"What about the case against Bat?"

"We'll drop the charges. We'll produce a confession from one of the guys you killed."

I stared at Jackson a long time. Then, I said, "OK, Jackson, you have the .38 with Bat's prints on it. I have the recording of your discussion at the Full Moon last night, of your admission that you killed Sarah, and of you torturing me." I shook my head. "If you decide to play hardball, we could all go down."

I saw him and Ivory frown. They were both trying to remember what they had said that night, what they had admitted. I smiled.

"We both have insurance. It's a stand off. Now I need to know that you will not hurt Carmichael when we hand him over to you."

They both smiled and exchanged a glance. Then, Jackson shook his head. "No, we won't hurt him." He shrugged. "We need him alive and well, right, Ive?"

"Yes, sir. That we do."

"OK, we both release our hostages at the same time. They cross at the center of the floor and you leave. Then we leave. Once the storm eases, Bat and I get out of town. You'll never see us again."

Jackson was frowning. He was confused, but he was keen to get the deal done, so he didn't question the arrangement. All he wanted, all they both wanted, was to get their hands on Carmichael. He nodded. "OK, deal."

Charles Carmichael came around and stood in front of us, staring at Simone. Ivory let go of Simone's leash. Both hostages started to walk toward the center of the floor. After four steps, they were level with each other. One more step and they were almost back to back, six feet apart. Carmichael didn't hesitate for a second. Jackson and Ivory watched him, surprised but not yet alarmed, as he turned toward her and pulled my Sig Sauer from his waist band. He took aim at her retreating form, practically point blank. At that moment, Bat leaned forward and reached under his chair. I did the same.

Carmichael pulled the trigger.

It was a very small sound in a very large, echoing hall. It should have been drowned by the wild, raging noises of the storm, but instead it echoed loudly around the cold, tiled space. The repeated, empty click of a weapon with no firing pin.

Bat's aim was surgical. He double-tapped because that was his training, but both rounds smacked square in the middle of Ivory's forehead. Then he was on his feet, striding toward Jackson, and I moved over to Carmichael, who was gaping, uncomprehending, at me and at his gun. I levered it out of his hand with my left and smashed my right fist into the side of his jaw. He staggered three steps sideways and fell to the floor.

Simone was staring at me, at the gun, at Carmichael sprawled on the floor. I looked her hard in the eye. "Not now. Keep it together."

I went and stood over Jackson. Bat put his weapon in his waistband and walked away. He dragged Carmichael to his feet and led him and Simone toward the study. Jackson was staring at me. There was real terror in his eyes.

"You're a lucky man, Jackson. I'm going to give you a choice. You can spend the rest of your life as a black cop in prison, or you can die now, fighting for your life." I jerked my head toward his weapon on the floor and laid my own down at my feet. I said, "Go ahead."

He stood, cautiously, and moved over to his gun. He was slow and out of shape. He lunged, stooped, scrabbled with his fingers. By the time he had a hold of the weapon and was upright again, I was standing in front of him. I didn't bother to collect my weapon. I didn't need it.

I took a hold of the barrel with my left and twisted, and slammed hard against his inside wrist with my right hand. The Glock came out easily. From that position, it was also easy to slam my right elbow into his jaw. I did it automatically, without thinking. As he staggered and sank to the floor, I followed him down and knelt on his chest. I put the Glock back in his hand, held the muzzle against his temple, and did what he should have done a long time ago.

It was the best thing for him, the best thing for his family, the best thing for everybody.

The Buddhists say that your dying thought conditions

how you will be reborn. I figured Jackson would come back as a vaguely confused rat.

I went to the study.

Carmichael was in his chesterfield with his head in his hands and a glass of bourbon by his side. Bat was in front of the cold fireplace, stacking logs over screwed-up paper and firelighters. Simone was on the sofa holding a glass of whiskey in both hands, staring at Bat. She looked a wreck, but she was still the most beautiful woman I had ever seen.

I walked to the tray with the decanters and poured myself a large measure of Irish. "You got a drink, Bat?"

"Not yet, sir."

I poured him a thirty-year-old Scotch single malt. I figured he deserved it. There was the scratch of a match and the slow, gentle roar of flames taking hold of dry wood.

I went and handed my old friend his drink.

He took it and went to the window. "I think the worst might be over, sir."

"You might be right, Bat. I think you might be right."

He sat on the windowsill and I eased my aching, exhausted body into the other chesterfield in front of the fire. Carmichael looked at me with the flames dancing in his resentful eyes. Simone just looked curious, and very tired. Oddly, it was Bat who articulated the question they were both wanting to ask.

"So, can you explain now what the hell is going on, sir?"

I looked at him and smiled.

"I'll try, Bat, but it's kind of complicated."

TWENTY-NINE

I POKED A CAMEL IN MY MOUTH AND LIT UP, TOOK a deep drag, and exhaled smoke at the fire. Then, I took a generous slug of old, Irish whiskey and allowed it to spread its warmth through me while I gazed at the fire and gathered my thoughts. Behind me, the door opened and closed quietly. Carmichael and Simone looked and frowned.

Carmichael said, "Hirschfield? What the hell are you doing here?"

"Hello, Charles. May I help myself to a drink? I was in the dining room. While you and Lacklan had your little chat, Mr. Hays taped the guns from your cabinet under the chairs, and I set up a little arrangement with a web cam and a microphone. We managed to record..." He paused and glanced at me with disapproval. "...*most* of what transpired." He poured himself a drink and sat next to Simone on the sofa. "Don't let me interrupt you. I am keen to hear exactly how this whole thing plays out."

I took another drag and started to speak.

"I have to admit that I was pretty confused myself until this morning. Then I remembered something, and everything else fell into place.

"Hirschfield, you said not so long ago, that the motive for murder is always either money or love..."

"Actually, I said sex."

"Let's be generous and say love. This murder was all about money and love. Am I right, Carmichael?"

He shrugged and shook his head, not in denial, but refusing to answer.

"When Charles Carmichael and Sarah D'Arcy met, they fell in love. She was, by all accounts, a beautiful woman, not only in appearance, but inside. She was kind and charming and, what is most rare, honorable. She genuinely cared about the world and the people around her. And back when they met, I believe you were like that yourself, Charles, only maybe not quite as wholeheartedly as Sarah. Because there was another great love in your life, wasn't there? The love of wealth; not just money, but wealth in its deepest sense. Land, houses, and above all, beautiful things of incalculable value. I am guessing that this is something that was handed down to you through your father, and his father before him.

"Like them, your great weakness was the need to surround yourself with beautiful and valuable things. And I suspect that, as you grew older, that need grew stronger, and at some point Sarah, by now your wife, had stopped being a person of great beauty, and had become one more priceless item in your collection. The problem was, she was a person, not a thing. And as a person, her feelings were liable to change."

Carmichael was still engrossed in the flames, but Simone was watching me like a hawk. I paused and took a sip.

"There were two great loves in Sarah's life. She had lost her mother at an early age, and I'm prepared to bet that family was important to her. She loved her stepsister, who was also her best and closest friend, and she loved her husband, though with time, that love began to change. She began to see you not so much as a husband and a lover, as father figure, a guide and a protector. And that was a position that you began to abuse. I don't think you ever consciously admitted to yourself that that was what you were doing, but it's what ended up happening.

"She was much richer than you were, and that is something that you never told me. She brought to the marriage a real fortune in property. At first, because of your skill and know-how, you both agreed that you, Carmichael, would administer your joint estate. And you did it well, and you *both* became very rich.

"But where you could never quite satisfy your need for wealth, there came a point, a few months ago, where she wanted something more. She wanted to put something back. Where your instinct was to hoard, hers was to share, to love and care for those around her."

Simone had stopped staring at me and was looking at the floor, nodding. Carmichael's face twisted with sudden rage.

"It was this *bitch* who changed her. She started filling her head with crazy ideas about 'fulfillment' and 'integrity' and being 'one with her environment'. *Bullshit!* All she ever wanted was to get her hands on *our wealth!* She twisted her mind! She twisted her *soul!*"

Simone looked at him with dead eyes. "You mean I helped her to break free from your paralyzing prison."

He turned on her savagely, "*I should have killed you when I had the chance!*"

I spoke quietly. "Take it easy, Carmichael. Let's not make things worse than they are. The fact is that Sarah began to gravitate back to Simone because you and she were drifting apart. She didn't feel that you were both on the same page anymore. Your focus was on amassing an even bigger fortune, hers was on the thing that had become her great passion, the Sara Bayou Park. I don't know for sure, but by piecing together what I have learned, I am pretty sure that this is what happened.

"She kept trying to talk to you. She kept trying to tell you that what she wanted was the park. But you, in your growing blindness, steamrolled her. You didn't listen. Instead, you and Wilberforce told her how it was going to be. And day by day, she watched her dream slip away from her, knowing that it would never become a reality. I can imagine that she felt completely powerless before you and that ass Wilberforce. The only option you left her, the only person she could turn to for support, was her sister."

Now it was Hirschfield who was nodding. "Hence," he said, "all the correspondence granting Carmichael the license to act as though the property was his starts to peter out about four months ago."

I nodded. "That is when things started to get complicated. Because, as Sarah and Simone were thrust together by circumstance, and by loneliness, so old feelings long repressed in both women began to reawaken.

"We will never know, but I imagine that Sarah was probably never fully conscious of her feelings. Or if she was, she buried them. But Simone, with your freer background and your interest in psychology, you became aware of your feelings many years ago, probably in your teens."

She smiled. It was a sad expression. "On my sixteenth birthday. When she hugged me and kissed me, and gave me my birthday present. In that moment, I knew I loved her."

Carmichael spat the words at her, "You fucking, twisted *pervert!*"

"You have to wonder," I said to Simone, "at the kind of mentality that considers sex a perversion, and murder an acceptable expedient."

He glared at me like I was the one who didn't get it.

I pushed on. "Whatever the ethics or morals of the case, the simple fact was that Simone's love for Sarah flowered. She helped Sarah to become more assertive, she began to teach her to paint, encouraged her to use the house on Solitude Road as her studio, to place some distance between herself and her husband, to go out and listen to jazz without him. Each small step toward her own independence, could have, and should have, alerted you, Carmichael, to rescue your marriage. Instead, it became a nail in the coffin of your relationship."

I sighed and took another sip. My cigarette had burned down. I stubbed it out in the ashtray and lit another.

"Even at this stage, I think it might have been possible to avoid total catastrophe. But something happened then that pushed everything beyond the point of no return. Originally, Simone, you had encouraged Sarah to go out alone. She was known and respected in this town, and James could always deliver her and pick her up. She was not at risk. But eventually, you started going out with her. She would pick you up and deliver you home afterward. That wasn't smart. In your mind, in your feelings, it was almost like you were dating, like you were a couple. And after a few drinks, with the good feeling of companionship, of conspirators *contra mundum*, you both began to enjoy it.

"And then one night, it became too much to control. You made a pass at her. If she had not shared your feelings, that is probably where it would have ended. She would probably have sunk into depression, and back into her husband's control, and your relationship would have dwindled, become a cool, distant friendship.

"But that wasn't the case. She did love you, but had lied to herself for years about the nature of her feelings. Your pass..."

She interrupted me suddenly. "It was more than a pass. We kissed. Then she panicked and ran. We were several days without speaking to each other. Then she telephoned me. She said she was going crazy and needed my help. As a psychologist."

I nodded. "This isn't my field. I am just a soldier, but from what you told me, and from what I can put together, she went on a kind of sexual rampage, trying to prove to herself that she was not a lesbian. She slept with one man after another, never more than one or two nights, and then she moved on to the next man. She didn't care who they were, they just needed two characteristics—they must be aggressively male, and they must be black."

Simone had covered her mouth with her hands and tears were running down over her fingers. "I was too close. I didn't realize what it meant at first, but then it dawned on me. She wanted to prove that she was hungry for men, but in choosing only black men, she was sublimating. In her unconscious, she was sleeping with me."

Carmichael snarled, "Psychobabble bullshit!"

I drew on my cigarette. "It didn't take long for the rumors to get back to Carmichael. Who told you? Was it Jackson? Or was it Ivory at one of your poker games, where you and the local WASPs got together to feel like real men, with whiskey and whores at the Full Moon?"

"They both told me."

"But the crazy outburst was short-lived, wasn't it, Simone? Less than a month, probably. Because she was beginning to admit her feelings to herself, and to you. And as she realized how she felt, and what she had to do, she changed her will. Perhaps she had an intuition of what was going to happen, or perhaps it was symbolic. Whatever the case, she wrote a new will and filed it with her attorney, making Simone her sole heir. Did she tell you, Carmichael? Or did she just tell you she was planning to do it?"

"She threatened me. The ungrateful whore threatened me. If I didn't halt the theme park project, she would alter her will and leave everything to this unnatural slut."

He jerked his thumb at Simone. I nodded.

"So you spoke to Ivory. You needed the situation taken care of, and you sentenced your wife to death. He knew about her spree of sleeping with black guys and so he started frequenting the Blue Lagoon. It wasn't hard for him to hook up with her. He was dangerous and exciting, and exactly what she was fantasizing about. Now two things happened. The very thing that excited her about Ivory was also what brought her to her senses. He was too much, too dangerous, and ultimately *not* what she was looking for. I suspect that was when she finally admitted to herself that she was in love with Simone. And that was when she finally altered her will."

Simone said, "She told me she had done it. She was going to file for divorce so that we could move in together."

Carmichael spat something about twisted bitches. I ignored him and continued.

"At the same time, Ivory had decided he needed a fall guy. He'd heard from Harry about the English jazz player who'd been in special ops back in the UK. He had been one of the guys chosen by Sarah, and both of those facts together made him the ideal candidate. So he set up the elaborate visit that night, in which Bat was tricked into putting his prints on the gun. It was a win-win situation. If he accepted the contract, they had a professional hit man for Sarah. If he didn't, they had his prints on the weapon, and the investigating detective as a co-conspirator. It was, as I was told repeatedly, a slam dunk.

"But here was where it got complicated." I shook my head. "Here was where things just stopped making sense."

Hirschfield stirred. He stood and made his way to the decanters. "Can I refill anybody?"

Bat stood from where he was sitting on the windowsill. "I wouldn't say no. Simone?"

She nodded and smiled and handed him her glass. Carmichael stared sullenly into the fire. As he poured, Hirschfield said, "The blood?"

I shook my head. "That was part of it. There was too much of it, which suggested very strongly to me that, A, she hadn't really been killed there, and B, logically, it was not her blood. That raised questions which were crazy to say the least: why would you kill somebody and then go to all the trouble of taking them home and dousing their bed with somebody else's blood? But there were other things.

"The grouping of the shots in the murder was good, whoever shot her was a good marksman, yet the shots downstairs were wild. You have a Marine gunnery sergeant and a good marksman shooting it out in the living room, with the lights on, at twenty feet from each other, and the shots are going all over the place." I smiled. "And this was when my suspicions were first aroused against you, Carmichael, with all that wild shooting going on, every shot managed to miss all those priceless works of art. The most valuable thing damaged in that room, packed with treasures, was your stucco. It was very far from conclusive, but it was a red flag.

"And then there was what I found at Solitude. Either somebody else had been killed there, or Sarah had been killed there and moved to the house. But again the crazy question, why dump the mattress, all the bedding, and the mat from under the bed into Sara Bayou at the foot of the garden, but take the body all the way back to the house? Especially knowing, as everybody did by then, that Hurricane Sarah was coming, and whatever was in the bayou was going to end up in the Gulf of Mexico within a few days.

"And then there were the blood samples. Jackson was just a little too keen to keep me off the case, and too determined not to listen to what I had to say about Bat. It was clever to employ me, and seem to be at odds with Jackson. I almost bought that. But the amount of blood on that bed was nagging at me, so I got Hirschfield to request a sample from the DA so that we could run our own tests, and to be on the safe side, I got a sample of my own when I had a look at the room.

"When I had them tested, the result blew my mind. It turned out that either the DA, or some intermediary, had switched the sample, and the official one showed up as Sarah's blood—or at least human blood. But the real sample, the one I had collected myself, that proved to be pig's blood.

"And I remembered what James had told me, that on the night of the murder, at around eleven o'clock, he had heard a pig screaming in the corrals at the back of the house. So it was clear what had happened. Sarah had been murdered at Solitude, her body had been brought home and dumped in her bed. Her killer had then gone and slaughtered a pig, collected the blood, and doused the bed and the body with it, so that if the sheriff, uniforms, or the press got a look at the scene, they would see that the murder had taken place right there, in her bed.

"He had then gone downstairs and fired some carefully placed shots and left by the back door. All this time—or practically all of this time—Carmichael was conspicuously at a restaurant in town. He got home only in time to disturb the killer and get shot at."

Bat was frowning. "It don't make a lot of sense."

I shook my head. "No, it didn't. It gave me a real headache. Not only did it make no sense that he would bring the body to the house and go to so much trouble to make it seem she was murdered here. It also made no sense that, having been so careful and methodical in his planning as to get your prints on the murder weapon, he is then so ham-fisted as to murder her somewhere where he has to take the considerable risk of moving the body. Why not simply kill her at home? Surely that would not be a difficult thing to do.

"And then something happened that changed my whole thinking."

I stood and went to refill my glass. Then, I went and stood by the window beside Bat. It was hard to be sure, but it seemed the crazy dance of the trees was perhaps a little less wild, and the rain clogging the earth perhaps a little less dense.

I turned to face them. "It was something you said right at the beginning, Carmichael. Remember that, until this morning, I was still unsure whether you had conspired in your wife's murder or not. But then it dawned on me. You had said that the reason you did not pursue the intruder was that you ran upstairs to check on your wife, and you found her dead." I smiled and shook my head. "It was so simple, yet I had not seen it. You went to the wrong room. Simone had told me, and you had confirmed it, that you and Sarah were sleeping in separate rooms. So why did you go to the master bedroom?"

I shrugged. "Of course, you didn't. Because you already knew she was there, dead, but your *story* was that you ran to the room you *shared* and found her there, murdered. In your arrogance and your stupidity, you ignored the fact that gossip was rife that you and Sarah were no longer sharing a room. You needed the world to believe that you still owned her—your treasure.

"And there it was, the reason why her body could not be found at Solitude, the reason it had to be brought back at so much risk, because of the damage it would do to your reputation if she had been murdered at her love nest. Because the myth must be preserved that you were both deeply in love. Not just for your ego, but also to support your challenge against the new will."

Hirschfield heaved a heavy sigh.

"That is very satisfactory, and well supported by all the evidence you have gathered. My compliments, Lacklan."

I shook my head. "Not quite, Hirschfield. There is one other point."

THIRTY

Simone stood up abruptly and went to stand at the window with her arms crossed.

"Do we have to do this? You have your killer. Can't you just leave it at that?"

I shook my head. "No. You know we can't."

Bat was frowning from me to Simone and back again. "What's this?"

Carmichael snarled. "Yeah, go on, Walker, tell the whole damned story! Tell it how it really was!"

Hirschfield sank back into the sofa. "Are you sure about this, Lacklan?"

I nodded. "It has to be told. If these people are to move on, there can be no skeletons left in the closet."

Simone sighed. "Fine, go ahead."

"It was the one thing that I just couldn't get to fit. If Ivory had planned the murder in advance, and meticulously enough to entrap Bat into putting his prints on the gun—and gone to the extreme of taking latex copies of those prints to leave in the bedroom, as he clearly had—the big question remained: why did he not simply kill her at home, in her bed? Why did he not do it the way he made it *seem* he'd done it?"

Hirschfield was frowning. "And?"

"That night, Sarah was due to go out to hear Bat play at the Blue Lagoon. It was Bat's night off, but he was going to go in anyhow because..." I smiled at him. It was not a happy smile. "Because you had a big soft spot for Sarah, didn't you?"

He nodded and smiled at Simone. "It was hard not to."

"But things were reaching a crisis point between Sarah, her lovers, Carmichael, and above all Simone. She went to Simone's to pick her up, but they got talking. I imagine, Simone, that she had recently confessed to you how she felt..."

She spoke to the window, as though we were not there, and she were reciting the words for the storm outside. "I begged her not to go to the club, not to pick up any more men. She agreed. She said she was tired of the whole charade. I asked her to spend the night with me. She said she couldn't, that before she took that step, she had to end it with Charles. It made me crazy that she could *fuck* these men, night after night, without it meaning anything, without it troubling her conscience, but she could not be with me, with the woman she truly loved. And all because of her *respect* for this piece of human excrement, who had been abusing her and exploiting her for years!"

"So you decided to confront him."

"Yes."

"You persuaded her to come with you. It was still early at

this stage, probably no more than eight or eight-thirty in the evening, at the latest."

Carmichael went crimson suddenly and screamed at me, "*These bitches threatened to kill me! Me! After everything I had done for her! After all the love and care I had given her! I adored that woman! I loved her! And they threatened to kill me! Me!*"

He folded over and buried his face in his hands. He looked suddenly very old and tragic, convulsing in his chair, making ugly noises in his throat.

"You pulled your .22 on him, didn't you?"

She nodded. "I told him it was over, to stay away from her. She begged me to stop. She believed that we could solve the whole thing by talking, by being nice to each other, that we could all end up being friends." She snorted with contempt. "After all the years she had been married to this monster, she still didn't realize what kind of a man he was. I knew that he would never let go of her, that he would never leave us in peace, unless he was in fear for his life. I told him to leave us alone, or face the consequences."

"But you miscalculated, didn't you, Simone? You misjudged him, you misjudged his influence in this town, and you misjudged her, too. He went for you. He pulled a gun on you—on both of you—and you had to run for your lives. You believed still that he didn't know about Solitude, because you didn't know that Ivory was in his employ. So you went home, to wait for Carmichael. You hoped he would turn up to confront you, and you would have the opportunity to kill him and claim self-defense. And Sarah made the last of a long string of fatal mistakes. She needed to get away from you all, and she went to spend the night at Solitude.

"But Carmichael, out of his mind with rage, called Ivory and told him to do it then, that night. To find Sarah and kill her. Ivory called her on her cell and asked where she was. Who knows if she told him to come over and keep her company or not. People behave in strange ways when they are afraid. The way it looked in the house, they had sex that night. Then he killed her, with the gun he had prepared with Bat's prints, loaded the body into his truck, and brought it here. Once in the bed, he shot her again, through the quilt. And that explained another thing that mystified me, why the bullets had gone right through *and* penetrated the mattress. Of course, her belly had already been perforated with the first shots." I shrugged. "The rest we know already.

"Carmichael pretended to find the body, reported it to his friend Jackson, and a few days later, Bat was arrested and placed in the frame." I paused a moment. "One of the things that confused me for a long time was the way that, even though you hated Carmichael, Simone, you were careful at first not to incriminate him. Then I realized why. Because if you incriminated him, you also incriminated yourself."

Hirschfield nodded. "Very nearly a perfect murder."

"Yes, but unfortunately for you, Carmichael, and Jackson and Ivory, I happened to be on my way to New Orleans, and I happened to pick up a copy of *The Advocate*."

"And am I glad you did, sir!"

Simone was still staring at the storm outside. "So where does all this leave me?"

I shrugged. "For my part, I think you have paid a very high price for your stupidity. Your behavior was reprehensible and adolescent, but love doth make fools of us all. I just hope you learned your lesson." I turned to Hirschfield. "I am pretty sure that the DA will be grateful for a swift, uncomplicated prosecution of this case. What do you think?"

"That's very likely. He has two officers murdered by a Burgundy PD Detective. It's an ugly mess and the brooms will be out." He glanced at Simone's back. "If you are prepared to act as a witness for the prosecution, there's a good chance they won't press charges against you."

She nodded.

Carmichael made a noise of disgust. "How cozy, how convenient."

I studied his face a moment. "A lot of people are dead because of your greed, your avarice, and your vanity, Carmichael. Frankly, you're lucky to be alive. I suggest you just exercise your right to silence, while Hirschfield calls the sheriff."

He glowered at me sullenly, but said no more after that.

EPILOGUE

Over the next forty-eight hours, Hurricane Sarah, the biggest and most violent in recorded history, steadily blew herself out. The flooding was unprecedented and the cost of the destruction was off the chart. As Bat and I watched the last blustery gusts drag the debris of planks and slates and refuse containers across the old, cobbled streets of Burgundy, and as the last shreds of tattered cloud drifted across a sky that was slowly turning to blue again, I wondered what Ben and the elite of Omega had made of it all back in Washington.

I was pretty sure that to them it was a series of statistics, of notable facts, a marker on their road toward their clinical, mindless utopia. What it was not, was a good woman murdered because a damaged, twisted man could not bear to lose her, or her property. It was not about a broken heart, a lonely woman aching for a lover she could never have, it was not about a solitary soldier of fortune who had glimpsed for a moment a fleeting vision, a dream of love and home. For them, it was not about three human beings, imprisoned by their dreams and their needs, trying to hold on to the things they loved, or break free from the things they had grown to hate.

For Omega, Hurricane Sarah was the first loud alarm announcing that the old order was dying, and the new order, their new age of power, was coming.

But their new order was not here yet.

Fortunately, my car, the deadly and silent Zombie, was not dragged into the bayou. I was able to recover it, and once it had dried out, the damage proved to be superficial, and, a week after the storm had finally subsided, Bat and I shook hands outside the Soniat, because British guys like Bat don't embrace other guys, and said our farewells.

"You know my address now, you have my phone number, stay in touch. And if you ever get arrested again, don't even dream about calling me, you son of a bitch!"

He laughed noisily. "Don't worry. Once is enough for me. I'll keep my nose clean."

As I headed down Route 61, I slowed and almost stopped at Simone's house. I'd heard from Hirschfield that the DA was not going to press charges against her. Carmichael had pleaded guilty to all charges, and had given up his challenge against the new will, so she had been granted probate. She was now a very rich woman.

I thought for a second or two that it would be good to see her, and say goodbye, but for some reason I kept going. Some things you can't go back to. They have their moment, and it's best simply to remember them as they were at that time, and not try to hold on. In the end, all you can do in life is keep going, keep moving forward, searching for something you may never find, and make the most of whatever comes your way, while it lasts.

I cruised down through the flooded wastelands that flanked Route 61, and then through Baton Rouge, like the Zombie knew where it wanted to go. I didn't mind, I was happy to follow. As we crossed the Horace Wilkinson Bridge, I even began to smile. I poked a Camel in my mouth, flipped the Zippo, and lit up. Then, I switched on the radio. They were playing the Eagles, Desperado, a classic.

I had no idea where Marni was, or where my search for her would lead me, or even if she ever wanted to see me again. But right then, as I cruised along the I-10 toward Houston, Texas, listening to the Eagles, I didn't mind letting her do the searching for a while, if she felt so inclined. Personally, I had a promise to keep with Dr. Katy Glendinning, regarding the next time I was in town. And it was a promise I was pretty keen to honor.

Don't miss THE HAND OF WAR. The riveting sequel in the Omega Thriller series.

Scan the QR code below to purchase THE HAND OF WAR.

Or go to: righthouse.com/the-hand-of-war

NOTE: flip to the very end to read an exclusive sneak peek...

DON'T MISS ANYTHING!

If you want to stay up to date on all new releases in this series, with this author, or with any of our new deals, you can do so by joining our newsletters below.

In addition, you will immediately gain access to our entire *Right House VIP Library,* which includes many riveting Mystery and Thriller novels for your enjoyment!

righthouse.com/email

(Easy to unsubscribe. No spam. Ever.)

ALSO BY BLAKE BANNER

Up to date books can be found at:
www.righthouse.com/blake-banner

ROGUE THRILLERS

Gates of Hell (Book 1)
Hell's Fury (Book 2)
Ice Burn (Book 3)
Judgement by Fire (Book 4)

ALEX MASON THRILLERS

Odin (Book 1)
Ice Cold Spy (Book 2)
Mason's Law (Book 3)
Assets and Liabilities (Book 4)
Russian Roulette (Book 5)
Executive Order (Book 6)
Dead Man Talking (Book 7)
All The King's Men (Book 8)
Flashpoint (Book 9)
Brotherhood of the Goat (Book 10)
Dead Hot (Book 11)
Blood on Megiddo (Book 12)
Son of Hell (Book 13)
Merchant of Death (Book 14)
Extinction C-14 (Book 15)

HARRY BAUER THRILLER SERIES

Dead of Night (Book 1)
Dying Breath (Book 2)
The Einstaat Brief (Book 3)
Quantum Kill (Book 4)
Immortal Hate (Book 5)
The Silent Blade (Book 6)
LA: Wild Justice (Book 7)
Breath of Hell (Book 8)
Invisible Evil (Book 9)
The Shadow of Ukupacha (Book 10)
Sweet Razor Cut (Book 11)
Blood of the Innocent (Book 12)
Blood on Balthazar (Book 13)
Simple Kill (Book 14)
Riding The Devil (Book 15)
The Unavenged (Book 16)
The Devil's Vengeance (Book 17)
Bloody Retribution (Book 18)
Rogue Kill (Book 19)
Blood for Blood (Book 20)
The Cell (Book 21)
Time to Die (Book 22)
The Reaper of Zion (Book 23)

DEAD COLD MYSTERY SERIES

An Ace and a Pair (Book 1)
Two Bare Arms (Book 2)
Garden of the Damned (Book 3)
Let Us Prey (Book 4)
The Sins of the Father (Book 5)
Strange and Sinister Path (Book 6)

The Heart to Kill (Book 7)
Unnatural Murder (Book 8)
Fire from Heaven (Book 9)
To Kill Upon A Kiss (Book 10)
Murder Most Scottish (Book 11)
The Butcher of Whitechapel (Book 12)
Little Dead Riding Hood (Book 13)
Trick or Treat (Book 14)
Blood Into Wine (Book 15)
Jack In The Box (Book 16)
The Fall Moon (Book 17)
Blood In Babylon (Book 18)
Death In Dexter (Book 19)
Mustang Sally (Book 20)
A Christmas Killing (Book 21)
Mommy's Little Killer (Book 22)
Bleed Out (Book 23)
Dead and Buried (Book 24)
In Hot Blood (Book 25)
Fallen Angels (Book 26)
Knife Edge (Book 27)
Along Came A Spider (Book 28)
Cold Blood (Book 29)
Curtain Call (Book 30)

THE OMEGA SERIES

Dawn of the Hunter (Book 1)
Double Edged Blade (Book 2)
The Storm (Book 3)
The Hand of War (Book 4)
A Harvest of Blood (Book 5)

To Rule in Hell (Book 6)
Kill: One (Book 7)
Powder Burn (Book 8)
Kill: Two (Book 9)
Unleashed (Book 10)
The Omicron Kill (Book 11)
9mm Justice (Book 12)
Kill: Four (Book 13)
Death In Freedom (Book 14)
Endgame (Book 15)

ABOUT US

Right House is an independent publisher created by authors for readers. We specialize in Action, Thriller, Mystery, and Crime novels.

If you enjoyed this novel, then there is a good chance you will like what else we have to offer! Please stay up to date by using any of the links below.

Join our mailing lists to stay up to date --> righthouse.com/email
Visit our website --> righthouse.com
Contact us --> contact@righthouse.com

facebook.com/righthousebooks

x.com/righthousebooks

instagram.com/righthousebooks

EXCLUSIVE SNEAK PEEK OF...

THE HAND OF WAR

CHAPTER 1

His face was deceptively flabby. You'd be forgiven for thinking he was a weak man. But there was steel in his eyes. He watched me without emotion, observing me from his large, black leather chair. Through the plate glass window behind him I could see the morning sun, molten copper on the East River, and the Four Freedoms Park on Roosevelt Island. I had told him my story—my edited version of the story, minus the murder and the conspiracies—about how Marni was like a sister to me, we had lost touch over the last few years, and now I was trying to get in contact with her again.

He raised an unruly eyebrow and heaved a big sigh.

"Mr. Walker, I don't really see how I can help you. I am not at liberty to release Dr. Gilbert's contact details."

"I don't expect you to, Mr. Staines. But if Marni's address to the conference is on Friday 18th, she will be here for at least a week. What I was hoping was that you could get a message to her for me, and then perhaps she could contact me."

He spread his hands and made an unhappy face. "Mr. Walker, this is the United Nations, not a hotel switchboard. I have an international conference to organize..."

I interrupted, fighting down the pellet of anger in my belly. "Mr. Staines, I hear you. You are not interested in the personal problems of the speakers at your conference. That's fine. But it so happens that her father was killed and my father stepped in as her surrogate dad. We grew up together like brother and sister. All I am asking is, will you see her before the conference?"

He sighed again, noisily. "Yes."

"Would it interfere an awful lot with your busy schedule to hand her a piece of paper with my name and telephone number on it, and say, 'Please call him'?"

He was good at sighing. I guess he got a lot of practice because he sighed at every opportunity. That's how you get good at things in life. Now he sighed again and held out his hand. I put my card in it and stood up. "Thanks."

When I got to the door, he said, "Mr. Walker."

I turned.

"I'll tell her you were persistent and would very much like to hear from her."

Something like a smile moved his jowls and just for a moment he looked like a kindly St. Bernard.

I nodded once. "Thanks again."

I stepped out of his office and into what looked like a vast set for a *Star Trek* movie. The words 'sterile environment' seemed to be encoded into the architecture and the décor, along with an obscure, subliminal message about the destiny of mankind. It appeared to promise a future in which everybody would smile and all behavior would be 'appropriate', all genders and all races would be not so much equal as the same, though displayed in an appropriate rainbow of aesthetically pleasing variations on a theme. And that theme was to be inoffensive. Inoffensive to whom was not clear—a great abstract United Nations ideal, where nobody would ever disagree because nobody ever asked difficult questions. Because difficult questions could be offensive. And therefore inappropriate.

Especially if they were questions about the United Nations Ideal.

I stepped out into the early May sunshine and as I walked through the ugly, iron gates onto First Avenue, I hesitated and looked both ways, as though I were not sure where I wanted to go. It gave me a chance to spot the Omega men who were waiting for me. They were in the garden at the bottom of the steps that lead up to 43rd Street. I acted like I hadn't seen them, crossed over the road to make it easier for them to follow me, and started walking toward the parking garage on West 40th, where I'd left my car.

I knew they'd parked up the road at a meter, where they could keep watch and follow me when I came out. So I stepped into the entrance to the garage and stood with my back against the near wall, where they wouldn't see me, staring at the screen of my cell phone. A minute later they walked past. There were two of them. They had that unmistakable look of men who were clones of each other, who spent too many hours in the gym, having fantasies about living the 3D shooter dream, and not enough time looking into the eyes of dying men, or men who wanted to kill them.

I moved after them and matched my stride to theirs. They were dressed in off the peg Armani, because that was the uniform, and they drove a dark blue Audi, because that was what you drove if you were a black ops bad boy. They were the living embodiment of the UN promise. As they came up to their car I called out in my most pleasant voice, "Oh, excuse me!" and ran two steps to catch up.

They both turned. The nearest one was six-two and built like a brick shithouse. He looked at me with expressionless eyes in a pale, unfeeling face. That changed when I broke his knee with a short, sharp kick to the side of the joint. I didn't waste time following up. I'd heard it snap and I knew he was out.

His pal was a bit taller and more athletic. He was gaping at his fallen comrade and at me. It is estimated that a person takes a full four seconds to react to an unexpected attack. It may be three in the case of a highly trained operative. If you count out three seconds, it isn't hard to imagine how much damage you can do in that time.

I stepped in close and rammed the heel of my right hand up into his jaw. He said, "Oh..." like he'd suddenly gone dizzy, and his legs went wobbly. As he exhaled, I rammed my fist hard into his solar plexus and, as he doubled up, I took hold of his collar and the seat of his pants and rammed his head against the side of his dark blue Audi bad boy car. In all it took about as long as he would have needed to react to my breaking his friend's leg.

I knelt down beside that broken friend now and looked deep into his pale eyes. His skin was the color and texture of butter. He was sweating and trembling. I reached inside his jacket and pulled out his Glock. I released the magazine and put it in my pocket. I checked to see if he had any other weapons. He'd started to whimper, clutching at his knee. A couple of people passed and frowned at us, but when they saw the Glock they kept moving.

He was clean so I pulled his cell from his jacket and handed it to him. He took hold of it but I didn't let go. I forced him to look into my face.

"Tell Ben to back off. The next pair of primates he sends to follow me I'll kill. Get a job you're qualified for, will you?"

I left him sobbing and dialing and went up to my car.

Ben was Omega's mouthpiece. My father had been a big shot in the organization before he'd died; before Marni had killed him. And Ben had been his right hand man. When I'd buried my father at the family graveyard in Weston, outside Boston, Ben had tried to persuade me to join Omega, to step into my father's shoes. But I knew by then that my father had grown to hate Omega and everything it stood for. Since that time I had been searching for Marni, not to exact revenge, but because on his deathbed, my father had made me promise to take care of her and keep her safe. She had not made it easy[1].

Marni was important to them because her research, and most of all her father's research, if exposed, could bring Omega down. So Omega wanted Marni either on side or dead. Ben and I had finally reached an uneasy truce at their office in the Pentagon. At least I had allowed them to think we had. I would find Marni, they would give me any help I

---

1. See *Dawn of the Hunter*

asked for, and in exchange I would try to persuade Marni to talk to them[2].

But Marni had stopped communicating with me. She had vanished without a trace—until a week ago, when I had seen in the *New York Times* that she and Professor Philip Gibbons of Green College, Oxford, would be speaking at the United Nations International Conference on Climate Change and Overpopulation. I had been in Houston at the time, but I had dropped what I was doing, climbed in my Zombie 222, and headed east. I knew that this might be my last chance to talk to her. Omega would be weighing up the situation, figuring that if they had Marni at the UN, they didn't need me. With both of us dead, they'd be in the clear.

So I had to get to Marni before they got to her, and before they got to me.

The Zombie 222 is an electric car produced by a couple of crazy geniuses in Texas. It has the body of a 1968 Mustang Fastback, but its twin engines deliver eight hundred bhp, one thousand eight hundred foot-pounds of torque, straight to the back wheels. She'll go 0-60 in just over one and a half seconds, and she is totally silent.

As I slipped out of the parking garage, I saw the Tragic Two still on the sidewalk. The guy with the broken leg seemed to have passed out. The other one was on his knees, holding his head. I didn't feel bad for them. They were lucky to be alive.

Among the things I had inherited from my father, apart from a manor house in Weston and a butler to go with it, there was a penthouse apartment on Riverside Drive, in

---

2. See *Double Edged Blade*

Bloomingdale. That wasn't my style, and I kept telling myself that when this was all over I would return to my small house in Wyoming, where I had briefly been happy, fixing cars.

But that had been in another life. And besides, who said this would ever be over?

I took First Avenue as far as 79th Street and then crossed the park to the Upper West Side. I rode the elevator to the tenth floor and let myself in. It was a family-sized apartment. My father had bought it when I was a young kid—when my brother and I had been young kids. My mother, accustomed to the high life in London, had complained that Weston was going to drive her crazy. The bohemian, arty set had suited her better, but in the end it turned out it was not Weston that was driving her crazy, it was my father. My father was driving us all crazy.

Now that the apartment was empty, it seemed to swell to three times its size, and to be three times as empty. A family home without a family is like a body without a soul. It's unsettling to look at. Physically it has not changed, yet it becomes pitiable, and uncomfortable to be with.

I went to the kitchen, cracked a beer, and stepped onto the terrace. Across the canopy of trees, the Hudson lay heavy and massive, almost black in the late morning sun. It seemed to foreshadow something, like a black tide spreading imperceptibly over the city.

I took a pull of the cold beer and told myself that's what happens when you start thinking; you start getting ideas. My cell rang. I forced myself to let it ring three times before I answered.

"Yeah, Lacklan Walker."

The line was silent so long I was about to repeat it. Then I heard an intake of breath, and Marni's voice. It had been a year since I'd heard it, but it was as fresh as though it had been that morning.

"Lacklan, it's me, Marni."

"Hi, you're a hard woman to get hold of since you hang out with university professors."

"Lacklan, let's not make this any harder than it is. You need to stop pursuing me..."

"*Pursuing* you?"

"Lacklan, listen to me..."

"No. I'm not going to listen to that shit. Do you know how many times I risked my life for you in Turret? *You* asked me to follow you! You *asked* me to follow you to Tucson! You were mad at me that I *didn't* follow you to Washington! And now you tell me to stop *pursuing* you?"

"Lacklan, I know this is hard to understand..."

"It's not hard. It's impossible!"

"Do you want me to hang up?"

"No!"

"Then stop storming at me every time I open my mouth."

I drew a deep breath and let it out slow. "I'm sorry."

"This is not your fight anymore, Lacklan. You need to give it up."

"Can I answer without you hanging up?"

A small sigh. "... Yes, of course."

"First of all, what makes you say that? And second, what makes you think you get to decide whose fight this is?"

"Lacklan, I can't get into this discussion with you. But you need to understand... You *have* to back off!"

"Why?"

"What you did in Arizona. It was insane. You are so violent, *so* destructive!"

"Do you know what they were doing at Biosphere 3?"

"... Not exactly, no. But..."

"I do. Do you know who was investing money in that research?"

"Lacklan, listen to me!"

"Do you?"

"No!"

"I do! And among others it was the Sinaloa drugs cartel. And every one of the programs they were funding involved some form of mind control. Those insane, violent things I did drew media attention to them, and the programs were shut down."

"You were not meant to do that."

"Meant? Meant by who?"

"You were supposed to follow to Washington."

"Supposed by who, Marni?"

"You are not dependable. You are not reliable, Lacklan. You go off half cock and start killing people."

"Now you listen to me, Marni. If you'd talked to me, instead of trying to use me like a pawn, maybe I would have followed to Washington. And maybe you, and whoever is doing all this 'meaning' and 'supposing', would have seen the need to put an end to the Biosphere 3 project. But let's be clear about one thing, anytime you try to use me as a pawn, it is not going to work, because I am nobody's pawn, Marni!"

She sighed loudly. "You see? This is exactly why..."

"You think? Maybe it's you who hasn't understood.

Because from where I am standing, this whole damned business is about not letting people become drones. Let me ask you something, Marni."

"What?"

"When was the last time that you, or one of your pals who do so much 'meaning' and 'supposing'..."

"Please, stop saying that."

"When was the last time you shut down an Omega program?" I waited. There was no reply. "When was the last time you were inside their office in the Pentagon?"

This time she said, "You were at their office?"

"Yeah. From where I am standing, the one thing you *have* managed to do, aside from getting Professor Engels tortured and killed in Tucson, is to kill my father, the one high-ranking ally we had inside Omega."

"*What?*"

"Oh, now you want me to talk?"

"He killed *my* father, Lacklan!"

"I know. Are you forgetting that I hated that man all my life? He lived several hours after you shot him, Marni, and he told me everything. He made me promise, before he died, that I would look after you and keep you safe."

"I can't believe it."

"Well you'd better believe it. You and your pals may know a lot about climate and social geography, but you don't know shit about warfare. And so far you are screwing up at every step of the way. You need me, Marni. You don't understand your enemy. We *need* to talk."

"Lacklan, I called you to tell you to back off and desist."

I shook my head, even though she couldn't see me. "That's not what you want."

"Philip doesn't trust you."

"Who the hell is Philip?"

"Professor Gibbons."

"What the hell would he know?"

"Will you *please* stop being so aggressive!"

I breathed and counted five, backwards. "You know me, you turned to me when you left Weston, I was there for you. I destroyed the sun beetle farm, I destroyed the Biosphere 3 Project. What more do you need, Marni?"

"He thinks..."

"*Fuck* what he thinks!"

"No! Lacklan! Can't you see? It is precisely this bullying, aggressive attitude that makes it *impossible* to work with you! If there was one thing your father was right about, it was this!"

"OK, OK, OK! With the greatest respect for Professor Gibbons, you are better qualified to know whether I can be trusted or not than he is." A long silence. "And you know I can be."

"Yes, I do."

It was my turn to sigh. "Let's talk, in person. Then take me to meet Gibbons. There is a lot I can tell you about Omega." I hesitated, then said with heavy meaning, "We need each other, Marni. You know we do."

She was silent for a long moment. Then, "It's a shame you didn't realize that five years ago in London."

"Yes. I made a mistake. But this is not the time to discuss that."

"OK, Lacklan. I'll talk to Philip."

"You leaving the decision up to him?"

"No. We'll meet, but I need to discuss it with him. I'll get back to you."

"When?"

"Soon, Lacklan! Stop pushing so hard. In the next day or so."

I thought for a second. "They are hunting for you, you know that. The longer we delay, the greater the danger to you. Don't spend a week agonizing over this, Marni. You made a decision—the right decision—now we need to act."

"I know. *Stop pushing!* I'll get back to you."

And then the line was dead.

I finished my beer, went inside, dropped my phone on the bookcase, and threw myself on the sofa. After a while, to numb the ache of the silence, I switched on the TV. I scrolled through the channels, not seeing the images or listening to the voices, just searching for something I didn't know and couldn't find. Finally I got up and went to the kitchen to make some early lunch. I'd left the TV on a news channel, and as I cracked eggs into a bowl and started beating them, the litany droned in the background. I put the toast in the toaster, and went to lean on the doorjamb.

"...in a surprise development, former President Dick Hennessy is to address the United Nations Conference on Climate Change and Overpopulation next week, replacing former Vice President Al Gore. Alia Fadel interviewed him for the Right Now Program this morning..."

The screen was filled suddenly with the image of Alia Fadel sitting in a comfortable chair, gazing at Dick Hennessy. He was starting to look old, but he still had the eyes and the smile of a letch. She was nodding while he was talking.

"I'm real glad, Alia, that the United Nations has organized this conference, especially in view of the fact that we have pulled out of the Paris Accord. World leaders really need to get around the table and talk these issues through. As you know, Al has had a deep interest in climate change for a long time, and I know he was real excited about addressing the delegates, so when he asked me to stand in for him, I was real honored to accept..."

The shot cut back to the studio and the anchorman. "And you can catch the whole interview later this evening at a quarter after six..."

I went back to the kitchen and poured the beaten eggs into hot butter. As I watched it congeal I wondered to myself if there had ever been a time in human history when mankind had not been divided into parasites and hosts; the few, spreading fear—terror—and the many, pliantly believing what they were told, and offering up their lifeblood in exchange for... For what? The promise of guidance and leadership toward a promised land that was always just beyond the horizon, but never reached.

Because once you reach the promised land, the one thing you no longer need, is a leader.

CHAPTER 2

THE CALL CAME AT SEVEN AM THE NEXT DAY, AS I was stepping out of the shower after my morning run. I dried my hands and my hair and wrapped the towel around me before answering. The screen displayed a cell number I didn't recognize.

"Yeah, Walker."

The voice that answered was English and cultured, and had that unmistakable Oxford resonance to it. "Good morn ing, Mr. Walker. This is Professor Gibbons. Forgive me for calling so carly, Marni said you would be up."

I knew what he was going to say, but I asked anyway. "What can I do for you, Professor Gibbons?"

"I wonder if we could meet and talk."

"I'm sorry. I have to keep my schedule free."

There was a barely perceptible sigh. "May I ask what for, Mr. Walker?"

I could feel the anger building in my belly and tried to control it. "I am expecting to meet Marni."

"That is what I want to talk to you about..."

"No. That is what I am going to talk to Marni about, because, Professor Gibbons, my meeting with her is none of your business."

"That is where you are mistaken, Mr. Walker. It is very much my business."

"How's that?"

"I can't discuss it with you on the telephone. Please, meet me at the Bethesda Fountain at nine o'clock this morning. I assure you, you won't miss your meeting with Marni. And, Mr. Walker...?"

"Yeah?"

"Try not to confirm all the preconceptions I have about you. I would actually like to be proved wrong."

"Screw you, Professor Gibbons. I'll see you at nine."

I had scrambled eggs on rye and a pot of strong, black coffee. Then I walked the two miles to Bethesda Terrace through the morning sunshine, watching the joggers, the skaters, the people on bicycles and those walking quickly in business suits, some carrying attaché cases, others wearing stupid mini rucksacks on their backs. But if I saw five hundred people that morning, of all types, shapes and sizes, five hundred of them were connected in some way to a device. They were either staring at a screen or they had something plugged into their ears; at least half had both. I wondered how long it was since any of them had noticed a bird sing. But then I realized, there was probably an app for that.

You could go to Central Park, plug in, and listen to birds singing on your iPhone.

Gibbons arrived early. I'd found a place to sit in the

shade of a large hickory, and I was watching who arrived, who left, and who stayed. At that time of the morning, very few people stayed more than a couple of minutes. So it looked as though he was going to arrive alone.

At ten to nine I saw him approach through the trees, from the direction of 5th Avenue. He was about five-ten, with receding white hair and a paunch. He stopped by the side of the fountain and scanned the area. He made no attempt to be discreet or to hide the fact that he was looking for somebody. You had to wonder at these clowns, thinking that I was a liability. I stood and walked over to him, approaching from behind. When I was six inches away, I said, "Bang, bang, you're dead. Why don't you hold up a big sign saying, 'I'm looking for Lacklan Walker'?"

He turned to face me. His eyes were not friendly. "Not everybody is out to kill everybody, Mr. Walker."

"But it's the ones who are that you need to worry about. Can we go somewhere less visible? Walk and talk, we'll cross the bridge." I started walking toward Bow Bridge and he followed. I said, "So what do you want to talk to me about?"

"I want you to stop trying to contact Marni."

"That's not going to happen." I looked at him. "Why?"

He thought for a moment before answering. "I know about Omega, Marni has told me all about them, and about your father. Frankly, I don't think she is at risk from them. I think they are more interested in negotiating with her than harming her."

"And this conclusion is based on what?"

He took a deep breath, as though he was sifting through his thoughts, deciding which ones he wanted to share with me. "I have been a consultant to many governments over the years, not least the U.S. and the U.K. A long time ago, I realized that presidents and prime ministers come and go, but they serve higher masters, and I have gained some idea of who some of those masters are."

"So?"

"Like all conspirators, the men and women who run Omega fear public exposure. Conspiracy prospers in the dark, Mr. Walker. That being the case, they try to keep their assassinations to a minimum, because every high profile murder risks investigation and exposure. Add to that the fact that we have her father's research..."

I stopped. "You have it?"

He looked me over a couple of times, making no secret of the fact that he was suspicious. "That's important to you?"

"It's important to everybody, Gibbons. Omega will do anything to get their hands on that research."

He shook his head and started walking again. "No, they will do anything to suppress, and preferably destroy, that research. They will do anything to stop it coming into the public domain. And as long as they believe that Marni's death will provoke just that, they will take care not to harm her."

"That is a very dangerous game."

We had reached the bridge and he stopped to lean his elbows on the edge and look down at the water.

"Well, that's just it. I don't think it is. What I think is dangerous is this warmongering, confrontational approach you have." He frowned and shook his head, as though I had said something absurd and he was having trouble believing I'd said it. "You can never beat them, Walker. There is no way to beat them. All we can ever hope to do is influence them."

"How do you know?"

"What?" He looked at me like I was insane.

"How do you know that we can never beat them?"

"They are far too powerful! They control governments. They have entire armies at their disposal..."

"And yet they are scared stiff of Marni Gilbert, who murdered one of their senior members. And after all the damage I have caused them, here I am. You know why they are not coming after me?"

He turned back to look at the lake. "I can hazard a shrewd guess."

"They hope that they can get to Marni through me. And they want Marni, as you pointed out, because they are scared of what she can do with her father's research."

He didn't say anything, but he nodded.

I pressed the point. "That kind of fear does not come from being invincible. They can be beaten! You should not be afraid of them."

"I am not afraid. I am pragmatic. I am a realist."

"So was Neville Chamberlain."

His face constricted with irritation. "Don't be absurd. There is no comparison!"

"I disagree. These people are ruthless. They're beyond ruthless. I know. My father was one of them. Did she tell you that they had my father kill hers?"

"She told me, yes."

"Did she tell you why they chose him for the job?"

He eyed me a moment and told me no with his face.

I told him why. "They chose my father because Frank Gilbert, Marni's father, was his best friend."

He turned away. "I find that hard to believe."

"That's your choice. He told me the whole story when he asked me to find Marni after she disappeared. The price for refusing to kill him would have been the death of his own family, as well as Marni and her parents." I paused a moment, then asked him, "Are you able, fully, to see what they did to him?"

He frowned. "What do you mean?"

"They offered him a choice, but it wasn't really a choice, because only one of the two options was even conceivable. And the conceivable option meant the destruction of his own soul. It meant murdering his best friend, doing something so horrific that he would detest himself for the rest of his life."

I reached in my pocket and pulled out a pack of Camels. I lit up with my battered old brass Zippo and blew smoke across the morning air. Then I went on.

"Having forced him to make that choice, to kill his best friend, they then rewarded him. They elevated him to a position of inconceivable wealth and power. Can you begin to imagine what that did to his mind? They showed him two things. One, that there was no depth they would not sink to to achieve their ends; and two, that they owned him completely." I gave him a moment to assimilate the full horror of what I had told him. "You are like Chamberlain, Gibbons, wanting to negotiate peace in our time with people who have no conscience and no inhibitions. There is no limit to what they will do to another human being, or eight billion human beings, in order to consolidate their power. If you believe you can reach a compromise with these people, you are already dead."

His face flushed and he turned on me. "*And your solution is to kill them all?*"

I held his eye for a slow count of three. "Yes."

He threw his hands in the air. "You see! This is why it's impossible! Have you *any*..." He screwed up his face like he had brain constipation and put his fingertips to his forehead. "Have you *any* conception of the *enormity* of what you are suggesting? The *logistics*...!"

"I don't know, I spent ten years in the SAS, what do you think?"

"This is the real world, Walker! This isn't a bunch of overgrown schoolboys running around the desert shooting at each other! We are talking about people's *lives!*"

For a moment I considered picking him up and throwing him over the bridge into the lake. Instead, I snarled, "What the hell are you talking about?"

He sighed, "I'm sorry, Walker, but you and your chums in Hereford live in your own rarified world where things are solved by shooting people. That might work in Afghanistan, but in London, New York, and Beijing, things are done differently. It is a very delicate balancing of power and you simply *cannot* go in just shooting people and blowing them up!"

I sucked on my cigarette and inhaled deeply, then let out the smoke slow. "Gibbons, my father was a lawyer. He got his degree from Harvard. He was a very intelligent man, and if anybody understood power, he did. He used to say, 'Murder is the most serious of all crimes, not because it is the most heinous offence against the person, but because the

State reserves to itself the authority to inflict violence and take life. This is because the ability to inflict violence and take life is the root of all power.'"

He closed his eyes and groaned loudly. "Heaven preserve us! A philosophizing thug!"

I studied the burning tip of my cigarette for a moment. "OK, Gibbons, I've been patient, but I have had about enough of your arrogance and your insults. I'm not going to try to convince you that you're wrong. You're stupid and you can't help it. I figure soon enough Omega will convince you of that. Now, I want to see Marni, and I am not going to take no for an answer."

He looked at me as though my poodle had just shat on his doorstep. "Fortunately it is not up to me. She does not want to see you, Walker. She asked me to come here and convince you to leave us alone."

"I don't believe you."

"That's your choice. But she believes, as I do, that you are a loose cannon. You are a danger to everybody. You are out of control. You have no discipline..."

I shook my head. "Discipline is not about obeying orders, Gibbons, it's about staying cool and taking the right steps to achieve your ends. Believe me, I have discipline. Now you are going to listen to me, and you are going to listen with care."

His eyes were resentful, but there was a hint of fear there, too. "Don't try to bully me, Walker."

"Shut up and listen. You are right about one thing, I am dangerous, and I am all that stands between you and torture and death at the hands of Omega. The moment they realize that Marni won't come to me, they will destroy you, or worse. Now tell me, is she going to present her father's research at her talk?"

He nodded. "Yes."

"Is it as explosive as Omega fear?"

"Yes, it is."

I sighed and flicked my cigarette butt into the water. "As soon as she presents it, you'll have played your hand and you will have no defense against them."

"No, then they will have to talk to us…!"

"Don't be stupid, Gibbons! Once she exposes their research they will have nothing to lose. They'll kill you both and create the biggest cover up since Kennedy. Think about it! If they did that to Marni's father and mine, what the hell do you think they'll do to you?"

His skin had acquired the color and texture of porridge.

"You have to convince Marni to talk to me, Gibbons."

I reached out and took hold of his tie. I pulled his face close to mine. His eyes were wide and I let him see death in mine. "She is committing suicide, Gibbons. She knows it, but she figures your life and hers are a fair price to pay for bringing down Omega. But her death will be in vain. She'll hurt them, but she won't destroy them. Talk to her. Make her talk to me."

I let him go when I saw in his eyes that I had got through to him. Then I watched him hurry away toward Bethesda and 5th Avenue. It was odd, I told myself, how a man could be brilliant and brave, like Gibbons, and at the same time be so stupid and cowardly.

I smoked another cigarette, watching the dark water beneath me and wondering what to do next. I didn't have much time. Omega knew that Marni and I were both in the same city. Despite my stunt the morning before, they would be watching me. They'd be watching us both like hawks. And it wouldn't take long for them to realize that Marni didn't want to see me. When that happened, when they realized that I was no use to them in getting to her, two got you twenty they would kill us both. They were rats, and Marni and Gibbons, in their emotional stupidity, had put them in a corner. A rat in a corner is not a good thing.

I started walking back through the park, taking my time, and wondering if my time had come; if everything, my unhappy years in prep school; the fights, the girls, and the drinking in high school; the endless battles with my father; loving my cool, distant, unreachable mother at a distance; and then the ten years of relentless killing and surviving, living always with Death at my shoulder, if all of that now resolved itself into a single, breathless, shocking moment, when I too died.

For a moment I wanted to take it all in, every car, every tree, every pretty girl, every bird, every birdsong, every note on the blue summer air. I wanted to take it in and hold it and live it for eternity.

But that's not how it works. You live each moment as it comes. And then you die.

He was waiting for me at the 97th Street exit, leaning against the 'Do Not Enter' sign, watching me. He looked lean, healthy, and cruel. I wasn't surprised to see him. I had half-expected it.

"Hello, Ben."

"Hello, Lacklan."

I went and stood at the crossing, waiting for the lights to

change. He stood beside me. "Have you got anything to report?"

"I don't report to you, Ben. I keep telling you, but you don't hear."

He ignored me. "Why was it Gibbons and not Marni?"

I looked into his face. "Mind your own business."

The lights changed and we started to walk. "I've been patient, Lacklan. I need a result and I need it now, or I can't keep protecting you."

"I don't need your protection. You need mine and you know it."

He eyed my face as we walked, trying to read my expression. "Is she going to reveal her father's research at the conference?"

I shrugged. "I haven't spoken to her."

"What did Gibbons tell you?"

"He said he wants to negotiate with Omega. He believes he can influence you and reach some kind of agreement."

We reached the far side of the road and I stopped. He faced me. "What did you tell him?"

"I told him he was stupid. I told him the only solution was to kill you all." He frowned at me. I didn't smile. "I told him the truth, that the only thing standing between him and Marni and death was me, and that I needed to talk to Marni."

His eyes made little darting movements over my features, like he was trying to read them. Finally, he said, "What did he say?"

"He said he'd try to persuade her."

"Where is she?"

I smiled, then gave a single, humorless laugh. "I don't

know, Ben. And if you try and torture it out of him I guarantee she won't be there by the time he talks." I sighed. "He wants guarantees, Ben. He believes, and so does she, that there is common ground between you and them, and some kind of compromise can be reached."

He nodded. "I am sure they are right. I keep telling you that, Lacklan. Isn't it time you started listening?" He jerked his head in a northerly direction and said, "Have a drink with me."

He led me to Columbus Avenue by way of 105th Street, to a bar with bare red brick walls and rough wooden tables. He ordered two martinis and we sat. Neither of us drank. He leaned back in his chair to study me for a moment.

"Lacklan, we are at a stalemate. You and Marni, and Professor Gibbons, can do Omega a lot of harm if she publishes her father's research. You know that, we know that. You also know that we have the power to hurt all of you very badly. You know that we won't flinch, and you know that we can and will kill you, without hesitation. Right there is the stalemate."

"What's your point?"

"That if we play chicken, if we keep on this course toward a head-on collision, you will die—all of you. We will be very badly hurt, but we will survive. And in time we will recover."

It was, in so many words, what I had told Gibbons. I sipped my martini. "I'd rather die fighting you, Ben, than live serving you. I know what that did to my father, remember?"

He nodded. "Maybe there's a third alternative."

I told him with my smile that I didn't believe him, but I said, "Go ahead, I'm listening."

"We, the members of Omega, Lacklan, are just people. We are not evil aliens from a parallel dimension, and we are not clones of each other. We are just people, and not everybody agrees with the way things are done. I am not going to stick my neck out and put myself at risk, but I will tell you that there are people, among the twenty-seven leaders, who would be willing to listen. For God's sake, Lacklan, your own father was Gamma, and it was no secret that he had his doubts. We have one objective, and only one. That is to preserve the little of good that humanity has created, when the end comes. But how we achieve this end, we are open to new ideas about that. And I genuinely believe that the Twenty-Seven would listen to you and Marni, and Gibbons."

I sighed, letting him know that I was bored. "Words."

"OK. Let's go one step at a time. Tonight, there is a cocktail party at the residence of Prince Mohamed bin Awad, in honor of the delegates and speakers at the UN conference."

I frowned. "Why?"

"Because he is the New York consul for the Awadi Arabian Kingdom, and his family have a vested interest in the outcome of the conference. The Middle East stands to lose a lot if the planet keeps getting hotter." He shrugged. "Everybody south of parallel forty-five does, but let's face it, nobody stands to lose more than a bunch of billionaires living in a desert and making money from oil. Climate change is not good news for them, right?"

"OK, I see that."

"So they have an interest in this conference, at the very

least as observers, but more likely as attempting to influence the speakers and the delegates."

I shrugged. "So why are you telling me this?"

"Because Marni will be at the party, and I can get you on the guest list. I want you to go. Ambush her. Make her talk to you. Let us at least have a dialogue. We all have things to lose, and we all have things to gain."

He reached into his inside pocket and pulled out an invitation which he slid across the table to me. I stared at it and felt a hot pellet of excitement in my gut. I was going to see her, talk to her, and touch her, after all this time. I was going to see her that night.

CHAPTER 3

There are not a huge number of houses in the immediate vicinity of Central Park. This one was a neo-gothic monstrosity on East 79th Street that looked as though it had once belonged to Dr. Frankenstein. It had too many arches and gabled roofs, and Central Park as a back yard. I'd bought an expensive evening suit that afternoon, with satin lapels and a bowtie, and decided to arrive fashionably late, at twenty minutes to nine. But when I got there, there were still gleaming limos arriving out front and disgorging glittering people onto the sidewalk and the broad, stone steps that led up to the grotesque pseudo-Tudor arch over the doorway.

There was a man at the door dressed up like Jeeves. He regarded me with a special kind of contempt he reserved for people who were not famous or billionaires. I showed him my invitation and he looked at it without touching it, like he might catch vulgarity from it. He gestured me toward the door with something that should have been courtesy but wasn't, and I stepped inside.

The inside was carpeted in red and paneled in oak, and populated by more of the same glittering people I had seen outside. I took a glass of champagne from a passing tray and moved through a set of double oak doors, half expecting a portcullis to drop on me from above. I figured there were at least a hundred people there, possibly twice that many. Most were in their fifties or sixties and many had the look of senior academics, or those strange creatures that hover in the gray area between academia, politics, and the military-industrial complex. They stood in small groups, smiling urbanely at each other, preening themselves, discussing exhibitions, concerts, and plays, accidentally dropping names, letting slip connections, like peacocks with important friends stuck up their asses, instead of tail feathers.

Somewhere I could hear a chamber orchestra playing Mozart, and I headed in that direction. Nobody seemed to notice me, which suited me fine. I crossed one large room and entered another. By the size of it, and the checkerboard floor, I figured it was a ballroom. A small stage at one end held a string quartet with a clarinet and an oboe, all in traditional eighteenth century clothes. They were busily playing a selection of Mozart and Handel which made you want to grab the nearest woman and break into a crazy minuet. The crowd was more dense here, and I stood on the periphery a while, watching. But I couldn't see any sign of Gibbons or Marni.

I spotted a waiter approaching with another tray of champagne and signaled him over.

"Is there a bar where I can get a real drink?"

He smiled. "Sure, other end of the ballroom, they got all the beer and spirits you want."

I put my glass down by a palm and negotiated my way through the throng to a long table covered in a white linen cloth, silver buckets of ice, white wine, and champagne. There was also a reassuringly large range of spirits. The guy in the white dinner jacket behind the table smiled. I said, "Give me a Bushmills, straight up."

While he poured it, I looked around. That was when I saw her. She was in a mauve satin evening dress and had her dark hair lifted into a knot at the back of her neck. She had a glass of champagne in her hand and was listening to Gibbons talk. There was a small group around them. A couple of the men looked Middle Eastern.

I felt a jolt of cold anger inside. I ignored it and strolled over to join the group. Marni was the first to see me. She went pale and her eyes stared. I smiled down at her.

"Hello, Marni. It's been a long time. How are you keeping?"

Her voice was barely a whisper. "Lacklan..."

I was aware of Gibbons staring at me. The group had gone silent, smiling pleasantly, expectantly. I smiled back. "Professor Gibbons, how are you? Please don't let me interrupt. Do carry on."

He stammered. "Yes, I...Walker. I didn't expect to see you here."

"And yet, here I am!"

The groomed and polished guy standing next to me held out his hand. "Salman bin Awad, how do you do?"

I shook his hand. "Lacklan Walker."

"Professor Gibbons was giving us a most fascinating talk on political philosophy."

I smiled with my mouth while my eyes did something else. "He's very good at that. He gets a lot of practice, don't you, Philip?" He scowled at me and I took Marni's elbow. "Please, carry on, I am just going to borrow Marni for a second. I promise to return her in one piece."

Gibbons flashed a look at her and she sighed. "I'll be right back."

We stepped over to the wall and she glared at me. "What the hell do you think you're playing at, Lacklan? What are you doing here?"

I raised an eyebrow. "It's nice to see you, too. What am I playing at? Well, you know what? I've been wanting to ask you a question. You see, there was this cabin outside Turret, where you kissed me, and where you were so worried that I had been hurt after I destroyed the sun beetle farm. Then I blinked, and next moment you disappeared and showed up negotiating for a seat at the Omega high table. I blinked again and, after I'd helped you escape, you killed my father. Now, however boring and inconvenient it might be for you and your academic colleagues, I think at the very least you owe me an explanation."

She closed her eyes and took a deep breath. When she opened them again, the anger had gone out of her face. I noticed absently that the deep blue of her eyes looked deeper because of the color of her dress. She looked beautiful and for a moment, I was overwhelmed by a feeling of loss.

"I'm sorry, Lacklan. The part of your story that you omitted was where you told me that your father had murdered mine. You hated your father, but I loved Daddy.

He was my idol. And when I discovered that your father, whom I had trusted all my life, who had always been there for me and Mom, when I discovered that he had not only killed my father, but that he was a member of Omega..." She shook her head. "You can't imagine what that did to me."

"I think I can, Marni."

She looked away. "I'm sorry, that was a stupid thing to say. Of course you can."

"I am no stranger to betrayal."

She raised her eyes to meet mine.

"I have been betrayed by just about everybody I have loved."

"Don't say that, Lacklan."

"Why are you cutting me out?"

She stepped close and placed her hand on my chest. "Please believe me, you are too dangerous."

"What does that mean?"

"You don't realize the power our enemies wield."

"I think I do. I think I know them a damn sight better than you do. How do you think I got into this party?"

She frowned. "What are you saying?"

"I'm saying that we need to talk. *You* don't understand the danger you're in, or what will happen if you release your father's research at the conference. They will kill you, Marni, and they will kill Gibbons and they will kill me. We need to join forces. You have to stop running from me."

She was still frowning. "How did you get into the party?"

"You remember Ben, my father's personal assistant?"

She nodded.

"He is with Omega. I don't know what his position is, but he carries weight."

Her frown had deepened. "But why did they want you to come... To talk to me? They wanted you to talk to me?"

There was something like panic in her eyes. I gave her a moment, then said, "Look at me, Marni. Look at me." Her eyes met mine. "As long as they think that I am looking for you, as long as they think we have a bond, your life is safe. The minute they decide that I cannot reach you, we are both dead. Do you understand that? You need to assimilate that fact. Because it's the only thing keeping us both alive."

She nodded. "Yes, I see."

"They want you on board, but above all, what they really want is your father's research." I shook my head and narrowed my eyes at her. "What the hell did he discover, Marni? Why is his research so important to them?"

She didn't answer for a moment, examining my face. "You don't know?" She sighed and shook her head. "I can't tell you."

"How would I know? Why can't you tell me?"

"Not here. Lacklan, have you gone over to them?"

She must have seen the anger in my face because she closed her eyes and raised a hand. "All right, I'm sorry!"

"Marni, you're accusing me of being a loose cannon, but you are panicking and you are out of control. You need to get a grip, realize who you can trust. And we need to start making a plan together, coordinating our efforts."

She nodded again. "Yes, you're right. I have been so scared. I've missed you, but Lacklan, you scare me sometimes."

"Come home with me tonight."

"I..." She glanced at Gibbons. "I don't know..."

"Marni?" She looked back at me. "Come home with me tonight."

She hesitated, then nodded. "Yes, all right."

"We'll join them, chat for a while, then we'll walk out together."

"What if they are waiting for us?"

"They won't be."

"How do you know?"

"Because they know I would kill them."

"Jesus!"

"And that would attract too much publicity. They want to do this subtle and quiet. We'll play on that."

She was staring at me with horrified eyes. "What happened to you in England?"

"It wasn't in England. It was in Afghanistan, in Iraq, in a hundred other places. If you stop running away from me, maybe one day I'll tell you about it."

"What about Gibbons?"

"He can come along if he wants to."

She hesitated. "OK..."

"Come on, let's go and be sociable for a while. And Marni?"

"Yes?"

"Be nice to me, OK?"

She nodded. "I know, so we don't draw attention."

"No, because I'm tired of being brushed off by you, and I like it when you're nice."

She sighed and repressed a smile. We made our way back to the group. Gibbons was taking a break from lecturing, and Salman was speaking with an earnest look on his slim, handsome face.

"With the greatest respect, Professor, despite everything that has been said about politics, the many volumes that have been written on the subject—it has been defined as both an art and a science—in reality what it boils down to in the end is that it is a simple practice. And the practice is no more than the acquisition and retention of power. That is *all* politics is—'how can I acquire more power, and how can I retain the power I have?' And for both of these ends we need two conditions..." He paused and held up two long, delicate brown fingers. "One, the people over whom we exercise power must be divided, and two, they must fear some outside threat. It may be the Jews, or the Muslims, it may be the Communists or the decadent west, it may be the aliens..." He paused, holding his audience suspended from his arched left eyebrow. "...or it may be the *environment!* But as long as people live in fear of an outside threat, they will give their political leaders a good deal of latitude in how they are governed." He smiled. "In how they are *controlled!*"

A large man in a brocade waistcoat and a deep purple dinner jacket had moved up to us like a Spanish galleon in full sail, parting the sea of people as he went. He had a huge, leonine head, silver hair brushed back and a complacent smile on his face.

"What you say is absolutely true, Salman. But it is merely the circus part of bread and circus. The virtue of the circus is to keep people's attention focused on something other than the fact that their leaders are making free with their possessions and their liberties. There is no special virtue in a terrified populace. All you really need is a distracted one." He turned his complacent smile on Gibbons and then Marni. "Professor Gibbons, Dr. Gilbert. Speaking of circuses and distractions, I believe you have some entertainment in store for us."

I felt Marni stiffen and gave her arm a gentle squeeze. Gibbons curled his lip. "Your Excellency, what a pleasant surprise to see you at a conference of this type. The rate at which your country's rainforests are being depleted, one would be forgiven for thinking your government had no interest in climate change at all."

His Excellency chuckled the way a mountain might chuckle. "Climate change! Reds under the bed. We have other things to frighten our people with. But I'll tell you what I *am* interested in..." He looked around at us one after another. "Screens!" He announced it as though he expected us to gasp. "Screens," he said again. "You know, in 1955, the Generalissimo Francisco Franco, the last great fascist, was being conducted around the brand new studios of Television Española, due to be inaugurated the following year. Franco had been the supreme, authoritarian leader of Spain for some sixteen years by then. The fascist regimes of Italy and Germany had collapsed, the Allies had won the war, and there was a new mood of hope and liberalism in the world. So Franco was under a lot of pressure from his so-called technocrats to liberalize his regime. They wanted reforms, but Franco had been holding out, resisting their pressure.

"But on this day, he was shown around the brand new television studios at Prado del Rey, in Madrid, and it was explained to him how every village would have a television in the church hall, and with time, every home in Spain would own a television. And naturally, the government, and ultimately Franco himself, would control the content of the programs." His Excellency laughed out loud. "At the end of his tour, as they were leaving the studios, he turned to the leading advocate for reform in his government and said to him, 'You can have your reforms, *I* have Television Española!'"

There was much laughter around the group, except that Gibbons did not laugh. He looked sour. "The man was a swine, but he was prophetic. Today, practically every brain in the western world is controlled by a screen. Not even Orwell foresaw that we would willingly carry the damned things around with us."

Salman was nodding as he finished laughing. "As I say, politics is merely the practice of acquiring and retaining power, by whatever means. Franco was a past master at it, and he understood well the power of the screen in controlling people's minds. And let's be honest, ultimate power is the power to control people's thinking."

Gibbons scowled at him. "More than that, Salman, much more than that. The power of information technology, delivered via ubiquitous screens, is to mesh, by means of an information matrix, all minds into one single mind, controlled from one single source."

Salman and His Excellency smiled at the floor. Salman muttered, "A little extreme, science fiction, surely, Professor Gibbons."

Gibbons grunted ill-humoredly and I thought this was probably a good time to go. So I spoke up.

"Well, gentlemen, I think we'll be pushing off."

Gibbon's head snapped around.

I smiled blandly and went on. "It has been fascinating.

We must do it again." I turned to the professor. "Gibbons, are you coming or are you going to stay?"

He opened his mouth, looked at Marni, and said, "I...um..."

Marni turned to me. "Just give me a moment to fix my hair, will you?"

I searched her eyes behind a smile. "Sure." I grinned. "I think I'll fix mine too." I looked at the group. "Gentlemen, it's been a pleasure."

We moved across the ballroom toward the exit. The entrance hall was empty, save for the doorman, who had now moved inside and watched us with incurious eyes. Marni glanced at me. "The restrooms are upstairs." I followed her up a broad, mahogany staircase to the next floor, and then down a passage. She smiled, but there was an edge to her voice. "You going to come in with me?"

"No, but don't do a disappearing act on me again, Marni."

She stopped outside a door with a brass plaque that bore the legend *Ladies* on it in French script. She looked up into my eyes. "I won't. Just wait for me a moment."

I nodded and she pushed through the door. I strolled back to the landing and stood leaning on the banister, looking down into the entrance hall. After a moment, a man in a dinner jacket came into view and stopped to talk quietly to the doorman. I went cold inside. I knew him, but it couldn't be.

I watched him pull out a silver case, extract a cigarette, and put it in his mouth. He lit it with a gold lighter, made a comment, laughed, and went to step outside. Then Gibbons came strutting into view and asked the doorman something.

The doorman answered and jerked his head at the stairs. The guy with the cigarette turned to look at Gibbons and when he did, I saw his face. Hot rage welled up in my gut. It was him. It was Abdul Abbassi, nicknamed by his pals the Butcher of Helmand. It had been five years, but I would never forget that face as long as I lived. But the question that was burning inside me right then was, what the hell was he doing at this party?

I stepped back and watched Gibbons come stomping up the stairs. I moved down the passage and he followed after me with anger burning in his cheeks and his eyes. As he drew breath to give me one of his lectures I stepped close to him and drove my fist, not too hard—just enough to shut him up —into his solar plexus. He gasped and wheezed and I pulled him down the corridor toward the cans. There I slammed him against the wall and thrust my face close to his.

"Now you listen to me, Gibbons, and you listen carefully. There is a man at this party called Abdul Abbassi. His nickname is the Butcher. I have watched him murder an entire village and kill women and children with his own hands, just to make an example of them. If he is at this party, it is for one reason and one reason only, and that is to kill Marni.

"Marni is coming to my place, *now*, where I can protect her. You can come along if you want. But get in my way and I swear, Gibbons, I will gut you like a fish and I will not hesitate. Do you understand me?"

There was rage and contempt in his face, but no fear. He was too damned stupid to be afraid. "You damned fool!" he said. "*You are going to ruin everything!*"

I reached behind my back and slipped my Fairbairn &

Sykes commando knife from my waistband. I held it to his throat.

"Your call, Professor."

The door to the ladies' room opened. Marni stood staring at me, a mixture of horror and disbelief on her face.

"What in the name of God...?"

I snapped. "I can't explain now. Just trust me!"

"*Trust* you?"

I snarled, "Gibbons...?"

He spat the words at me, "*You're insane!*" Then he turned his head toward Marni. "*Get out of here! Go!*"

And she was running along the passage toward the stairs. I shouted, "*Marni! No! Don't!*" and made to go after her, but Gibbons was clinging to me, dragging me back, shouting after her, "*Run! Run!*"

I turned and gave him a savage back-hander with my left fist. His eyes rolled and his legs went to jell-O. He dropped to the floor and I slid the knife back into my belt as I ran after her. As I reached the top of the stairs she was running out onto the street. I took the steps three at a time and went to go out after her, but the doorman stepped in front of me, his left hand on my chest.

I didn't think. I didn't look at him. I took his wrist in my left hand and twisted. His arm locked. I jabbed my right savagely into his exposed floating ribs and stepped over him as he went down, wheezing. I wrenched open the door and ran into the night. She was there. Ten paces away, climbing into a yellow cab. I shouted, "*Marni! Wait!*" But the door slammed and she was away, moving down 79th Street and left onto Madison Avenue.

There was a dangerous rage inside me. I turned to go

back, get Gibbons, and beat him until he told me where she had gone, but the doorman was staggering out with a purple face, pointing at me, gasping. "I call the cops! They are coming for you! You in *big* trouble!" Next to him, watching us, was Abbassi, with one hand in his pocket and the other holding a cigarette. I swore violently under my breath and ran across the road to the parking garage to get my car.

Two minutes later, I was struggling to stay within the speed limit as I cruised down Park Avenue toward Union Square and Broadway. As I drove, I dialed the number for the FBI.

"Federal Bureau of Investigation. How may I direct your call?"

"I need to talk to somebody in the Counter Terrorism Division."

Printed in Dunstable, United Kingdom

68537430R00201